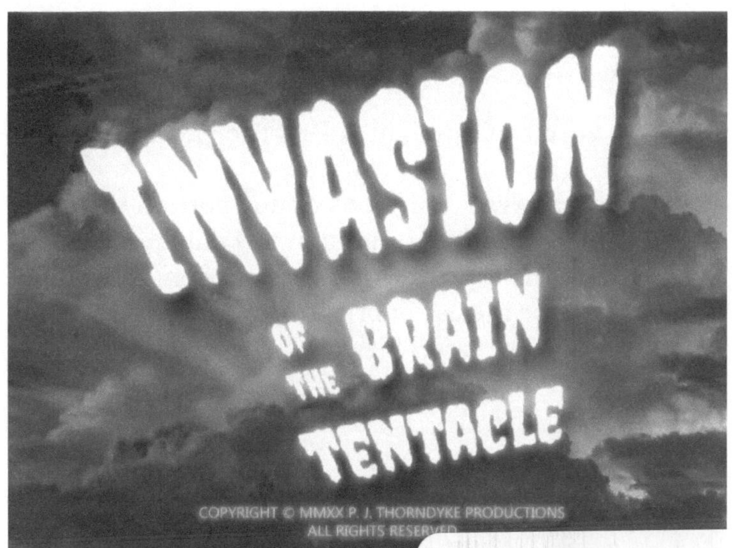

INVASION
OF THE BRAIN TENTACLE
COPYRIGHT © MMXX P. J. THORNDYKE PRODUCTIONS
ALL RIGHTS RESERVED

AF363318

Invasion of the Brain Tentacle
By P. J. Thorndyke

2020 by Copyright © P. J. Thorndyke

https://pjthorndyke.wordpress.com/

CHAPTER 1

As the arrow-straight road drew close to the snaking curl of the Tuolumne River, it abandoned its rigid beeline and began to imitate the river itself, twisting and turning as the ground rose into the foothills of the Sierra Nevada. Here the reservoirs overlooked fruit and vegetable country that stretched for as far as the eye could see. The endless patchwork of fields and orchards with their crops of beans and beets was sliced diagonally by wide irrigation canals that led from the reservoirs, their waters still as knives of silver under the beating sun.

"We're not going to be the first there, I hope you realize that, Fred," said Claire behind the wheel of the '55 Mercury Monterey. "There'll be folks from the Lick Observatory, the JPL, not to mention any locals who saw the breakup in the sky last night. It would have been quite a show."

"So what if we aren't the first ones there?" Fred replied as he loaded a roll of film into his camera. "They can't stop us from taking a look."

Claire bit her thumbnail in distraction. "We'll be lucky if the place isn't crawling with news broadcasters and journalists," she mused. "There hasn't been an observed fall in California before. It'll be big news."

She silently cursed the length of the journey. In the time it had taken them to drive from the Ames Laboratory in San Jose, through the Diablo Range and up to the network of reservoirs and dams on the other side of the San Joaquin valley, they would turn up as rubberneckers, desperate for a glance over the shoulders of others when they should have been first in line. If she had stayed home today instead of heading off to work completely oblivious as to what had happened during the night, then she *would* have been first in line.

But she knew she was being foolish, spoilt even. In the grand scheme of things, the meteorite was as good as on her doorstep. An observed fall, not only in California, but not fifty miles east from the town she had moved to when she took the job at the Ames lab was uncommonly fortuitous. *Damn near a miracle*, she thought.

Claire Weldon had studied meteorites her entire adult life. At Berkeley she had studied under John H. Reynolds, the physicist who had revolutionized the radiometric dating of meteorite samples. Offered a job as a researcher at the National Advisory Committee for Aeronautics laboratory in Virginia, she had worked diligently for several years while she dated a rather handsome schoolteacher called Ray and then, rather suddenly, married him.

Their eldest child – Judy – had been an accident and had necessitated some hasty wedding plans. Tommy had quickly followed, and he had very much been planned, if a little hot on the heels of their first. Then, after several distressing misfires, their desire for a nice round score of three had resulted in the delightful Rose who was now three years old.

They had been happy in Virginia, but Claire found that she missed sunny California. She had no wish to move back to Pasadena but the small valley towns of Northern California with their geometric streets and single-story businesses spread out like sandwiches on a picnic blanket appealed to her. It was the cleanliness, the sense of order and quiet decency that she found so very attractive. Then, in late 1956, a job opportunity came that called her home like a siren.

The NACA had decided to pursue space flight research. The Soviets were building warheads and Congress was keen that the U.S. kept up. Research was almost immediately stumped by the 're-entry problem'. When a warhead re-entered the atmosphere, aerodynamic heating caused it to vaporize. If the heat was not deflected somehow, dreams of a manned space flight were out of the question.

The director of the NACA's lab in Santa Clara County was Harry Julian Allen whose research into reducing aerodynamic heating led to the construction of the Ames supersonic free-flight wind tunnel. Allen was convinced that heat could be more evenly distributed if they looked to the blunt shape of meteors in favor of the traditional aerodynamic shape of rockets. He started hiring meteoriticists for his high-speed research division and, although Claire felt guilty to uproot Ray and the kids, she just couldn't turn the opportunity of a lifetime down. So, in the summer of 1956, the Weldon family upped sticks and moved west.

"Turn left here," Fred said, indicating a dirt track that wound up into the hills, circling the Ralston Reservoir.

Claire rolled the car off the state highway and they began their steady climb into reservoir country. The still water of the Ralston reservoir could barely be seen through dips in the yellowed hills, its flat surface almost hiding from the road. Distant clusters of trees that shaded boat landings were the only hint of its existence. As they climbed the foothills they were afforded a better view but Claire's attention was occupied by the gleaming white news van that was parked a little way off the dirt track. Its tires had gouged tracks into the edge of somebody's field.

Further up, the sheriff's car and a cluster of people could be made out. They were standing around a semi-circular crater in the side of one of the higher hills. The air shimmered above the crater with more than the usual Californian heat.

Claire parked behind the news van and, as they got out, she could smell the scorched land. "My God, it must be big," she said as Fred popped the trunk and began rooting about for their equipment.

A few heads turned to gaze at them as they climbed the hill. The heat made Claire's face prickle and she knew why the crowd was keeping to the edge of the crater. She edged her way around to get a glimpse of what lay embedded in the hillside.

It was the size of a small car, coal-black except for lines of deep red showing through its cracked surface. It hissed as it cooled.

"Who might you be, Ma'am?" asked the sheriff as he approached, identifiable by his gold star and gray Stetson. Another cop hung around in the background, making a token attempt at crowd control.

"I'm Dr. Claire Weldon, Sheriff. I work for the National Advisory Committee for Aeronautics at the Ames laboratory in Santa Clara County. This is my assistant Fred Stevens."

"A doctor, huh?" the sheriff replied as he looked her up and down while absent-mindedly taking Fred's offered hand. "You don't say. I'm Sheriff Benson."

"Did you say you were Claire Weldon from the Ames lab?" asked a stocky, bull-necked man in a green sleeveless cardigan and red tie.

"I did."

The man strode over to them, his hand outstretched. "I'm Charley Neal from the JPL. Good to know you. I knew your father."

Claire felt herself tense at the mention of both her father and the Jet Propulsion Lab. She caught the flicker of a smirk on Charley Neal's face. He had tried to suppress it out of politeness, but it was there all the same.

"How do you know who my father is?" she asked him a little coldly. "Weldon is my husband's name."

"Oh, we heard that John MacReady's little girl got herself hitched and took a job with the NACA. Your father would have been proud, I'm sure."

Claire ignored the intended compliment. It was an attempt to butter her up after the smirk. She had no doubt who the 'we' Charley referred to was. The old JPL boys. Men who had worked with her father, who had laughed at him, gossiped about him like old women and then ran him out like a town drunk. She bet they got a real kick out of the idea that his daughter had followed somewhat in his footsteps. Well, she wasn't going to let them ridicule her as they had ridiculed her father.

"What do you think of the space rock?" Charley asked her.

"I don't know what to think until I get a sample back to the lab. It sure is a big one, I'll say that."

"You've seen the other piece?"

"Other piece?"

Charley jabbed his thumb over his shoulder in the direction of the reservoir. Claire peered down the hill. Where it sloped down into the water, a second, slightly smaller piece lay half submerged, steam curling off it.

"Folks say the light show was quite something last night," Charley said. "Must be bits and pieces all over the area."

"But two such sizable pieces ...," said Claire. "That's unusual."

"Well, if a separate particle didn't land in the reservoir, then it's clear that a chunk must have broken off on impact and rolled into the water."

"Rolled uphill?" Claire asked.

Charley narrowed his eyes at her. "What do you mean 'uphill'? It's a steep slope from the crater all the way down to the water."

"What I mean is, the rock would have had to have rolled *out* of the crater first."

"Yeah, she's right," said Fred. "You can see over there, the trail of the rock."

They followed his pointed finger as it traced the streak of flattened ground up to the crest of the crater where a visible portion had been crumbled away by the passage of something large.

"Now what would have made it do that?" Charley asked.

"The force of impact most likely sent the loose particle hurtling up and over the edge," said Fred.

Claire said nothing. All she knew about high-speed impacts spoke against Fred's theory, yet she could think of no other explanation why a hunk of the meteorite would roll out of the crater when all its driving force would have been intent on pushing it deeper into the hillside. It could only have broken off after it had landed, so how then did it end up rolling *away* from the larger rock?

"Have any of you ever heard about the moving rocks phenomenon?" Charley asked.

They turned to look at him.

"I read about it happening in Death Valley. It's a geological phenomenon that causes rocks to move across the desert leaving great long trails without any human or animal intervention. So far, there has been no credible explanation. There's been talk of high-speed winds moving them about, the rocks themselves acting as a sort of sail but that doesn't explain the bigger ones being moved, the ones the size of people."

Claire repressed a shudder at the thought of man-sized stones moving about the desert of their own free will.

"When you're done here, Doc, do you want to go take a looksee at the other one?" Sheriff Benson asked.

"Yes," Claire said. "I can't take a sample from this one yet, it's too hot, but the water may have cooled the one down in the reservoir enough for me to chip a bit off."

They left the crater and wandered down the hill towards the water's edge. Before they even got close, Claire could tell that the meteorite fragment had split. The side of it that faced the water had fallen away at a sharp forty-five-degree angle.

"Must have cracked upon cooling," she said.

The thing still radiated heat and they kept a safe distance. Claire kicked off her shoes and tested the water with her stockinged toe. It was warm, but bearable. She ignored the eyes of the men on her calves as she hitched up her skirt and waded her way around the half-submerged rock.

The piece that had fallen away lay on the sandy bottom a few inches below the surface leaving the newly exposed side of the rock hanging over the water. She bent down, trying not to get the hem of her skirt wet and peered beneath the overhang.

What she saw drew a sharp gasp from her lips. There was a hollow chamber within the rock that was patterned with a bubbled texture. It wasn't so much honeycombed but marked by many concave depressions, smooth and regular. She had never seen anything like this before. The circular depressions were about two inches across, at a regular depth as if gouged out by an ice-cream scoop. The surface of the chamber resembled a large egg poacher pan.

"What have you got, Claire?" Fred asked, wading out to join her.

"I honestly don't know," she told him.

CHAPTER 2

The alarm clock did its little dance on the nightstand and Ray sleepily swiped it, fumbling with the switch to cease its shrill and unwelcome announcement that another day required his attention. He groaned and rolled over. Claire was facing him, fast asleep, her slumber uninterrupted.

She had come home late last night. Real late. After the kids had been in bed in fact. He had waited up for her as he always did. He never planned to but he could also never bring himself to turn in knowing that she might be driving through the night, the darkness of the mountain roads surrounding her on all sides. She thought he was silly, and she was probably right, but he just couldn't sleep until she was home and safe.

It was the meteorite business that had kept her at the lab. They had slept through it when the sky was lit up with explosions the previous night, but it had been the talk of the town all day. As for Claire, Ray could tell that she couldn't wait to get her mitts on a sample. It was stroke of stupendous luck that a meteorite should fall in California merely months after they moved to Ralston and Ray was happy for her.

When she got home, they had sat out in the yard and had a nightcap while she told him all about it. Most of it went over his head for Claire had a knack of forgetting that not everybody was a meteoriticist.

"You wouldn't believe it, Ray," she had said. "It's brittle enough but has no reaction at all to heat. We tried the oxyhydrogen torch on it, but it shows no volatility at any temperature. It also produced a negative on the borax bead test. Solvents could not attack it; we tried ammonia, caustic soda, nauseous carbon disulfide, nothing! All we know is that it's a metal, and magnetic too, but what metal, we haven't the faintest idea.

He let her ramble on. He was pleased for her. First the job at the Ames lab and now, the find of a lifetime. Things were certainly looking up.

He kissed her on the forehead as she slept, and her brow wrinkled in protest but she didn't awake. He got up softly, dressed in silence and crept downstairs to start breakfast. He had the coffee in the percolator and the eggs in the pan by the time Rose woke in her crib. He dashed upstairs to get her before she woke Claire.

"How you sleep through Dadda's alarm clock is a mystery," he said softly in her ear as he hoisted her up and hustled her into the bathroom for a diaper change. Then, remembering the coffee and eggs, he hurried her downstairs to catch them before they burned.

With breakfast ready and Rose in her highchair, Ray went back upstairs to rouse the other two kids. He was halfway done with their lunches while taking sips from his coffee by the time Tommy came down, yawning and running his fingers through his tufty hair.

"Judy's in the bathroom," he complained. "She's taking ages."

"Girls do," Ray sympathized as he placed a glass of orange juice in front of him. "Your eggs might be a little cold. I need more hustle out of you in the mornings, Kiddo."

"What about Judy? I came down first."

"Actually, of my beloved brood, *Rose* came down first."

Rose took the compliment and beamed one of her killer smiles at Tommy.

"Big deal," Tommy muttered. "I'd be down first if I had someone to *carry* me down."

Judy appeared as Tommy was tucking into his eggs. She was wearing a plaid skirt and pink sweater, her hair perfectly curled.

"I want to drive today, Judy," Tommy blurted around a mouthful of eggs as soon as she set foot in the kitchen.

"After you nearly killed us last time?" she said with a swing of her hair. "I don't think so."

"What's this 'nearly killed us' business?" Ray asked. "I thought it was just a close encounter with a pickup's wingmirror."

"It was!" Tommy protested. "No big deal!"

"It wouldn't have happened at all if you hadn't taken that corner like a stock car racer," Judy said.

"Judy drives," Ray affirmed.

"But that's not fair!"

"You'll get the car all to yourself after she graduates next year."

"And then I'll be in my junior year," Tommy muttered. "I need a car now, not next year."

"Why, so you can tear around like a maniac?" Ray pressed. "I've seen how the kids drive in this town. You'd think there'd be more deaths."

"Kids drive the same in Virginia."

"Hardly. These Californian kids are crazy, I've warned you about that before. Don't fall in with the wrong crowd."

"Why didn't we stay in Virginia then, if you're so worried about the kids around here."

Ray frowned. It was a petulant remark, spoken into his orange juice and the look in Tommy's eyes over the rim of the glass told Ray that he already regretted it.

"You know we moved here because of Mom's job," he told him. "We all have to make sacrifices. We're better off financially and it means the world to her, so just watch the lip."

"What means the world to me?" Claire asked from the doorway to the kitchen. She was dressed in her work clothes and was brushing her hair.

"Honey, you didn't have to get up," said Ray. "You worked late. You can have a lie in, can't you?"

"I wouldn't dream of it, Ray. I need to get back to the lab and continue my tests."

"Surely a piece of rock can wait around."

"What piece of rock?" Judy asked.

"Mom's working on that meteorite that landed the other night."

"Is it from outer space?" Tommy asked.

"Of course, it is, genius," said Judy. "That's why it's a *meteorite*."

"It's certainly the most fascinating find in our lifetimes," said Claire. "But I'd appreciate it if you kids said nothing about it at school."

Tommy and Judy gazed at her. "Why not?" they asked in unison.

"Well, we're not too sure what we're dealing with and the papers are hungry for news. So, until we know what it is that we have, I'd appreciate it if we kept a lid on things so there are no wild stories misinterpreting the facts."

"Sure, mom," Judy said.

"You kids had better skedaddle," said Ray. "And drive carefully."

"Huh! The way Judy drives, we get overtaken by old ladies walking their dogs," said Tommy as he swiped his lunch from the counter.

Ray poured Claire some coffee as Tommy and Judy headed outside. They heard the slam of the front door and the sound of the Buick starting up and rolling off down the drive. The only sound left was Rose babbling softly to herself as she pushed the last of her eggs around on her plastic Mickey Mouse plate.

"They hate it here," Claire said after a while as she sipped her coffee.

"What?"

"I heard what Tommy was saying. They hate that we dragged them here and they blame me for it."

"Oh, come on, Honey. They don't hate it and they don't blame you. Tommy was just venting as kids do. It takes time for them to settle in. New school, no friends, unfamiliar town. It's a lot to take in but they'll manage it. It's only been a few months."

"What about you?" she fixed her gaze on him, giving him no opportunity to look way.

"I'm happy enough."

"*Enough*?"

"Sure. It's taken some time for me to get adjusted too but look at us. Look at this house! Beats Virginia any day."

"You really mean that?"

"Claire, when you said you wanted to move back to California, I admit, I got the jitters. But if I hadn't wanted to come, I would have made my case plain as day."

"And the rest of it? Not just the move but ..."

"It's fine, honey. We don't have to go through all that again. I love spending the time with Rose."

She smiled. "What are your plans for today anyway?"

"I need to take the car down to Nick's garage and put some more air in the tires. Then Rose and I are going grocery shopping."

"Don't forget the Robertsons are coming for dinner on Friday."

"I haven't forgotten."

"What are you planning?"

"I thought I'd try my hand at a jellied veal ring."

Claire regarded him suspiciously. "Have you been looking at those recipes in *Family Circle* again?"

"What if I have?"

"You don't have to try and impress anyone, Darling. How about something simple like a baked glazed ham?"

"Oh, you're no fun. Fine. Baked glazed ham it is. But can I go crazy with the desert? *Family Circle* had a delicious looking fruit cocktail eggnog pie."

Claire held up her hand to halt him. "How about you just surprise me?"

"You bet."

"Wonderful, darling." She drank the last of her coffee and stood up. "Who'd have thought that I'd end up married to such an adventurous cook?"

"It's the only adventure left to me, honey. That and evading conversation with Mrs. Williams in the frozen foods section. Do you have to rush off right away?"

"Afraid so. Fred will be waiting for me. He's as excited as I am, and he won't dare take another look at the meteorite without me. I hate to keep the poor fellow on tenterhooks. I'll be home as soon as I can."

She set her coffee cup in the sink, kissed Ray on the lips and then went out into the hall for her keys. As the door slammed behind her, Ray turned to Rose and said; "Well, kid, it's just me and you again."

When he was done clearing away the breakfast things, he drove down to Nick's Auto Repair Shop. On the way he considered the conversation he had had with Claire. It wasn't that he minded moving to California, or even giving up his teaching job to become what they jokingly referred to as a 'kept man'. The thing was, it wasn't a joke at all. It was his life.

It wouldn't have been necessary if they had bought a property over in San Jose and Claire didn't have to drive eighty miles to get to work but they had their hearts set on a smaller, quieter town and Ralston High had a good reputation. In truth, he enjoyed keeping house, making sure there was always something good on the table and taking care of Rose. It would have suited him fine if it weren't for everybody else.

For most Ralston residents, the idea of a man staying at home while his wife went out to work was more than strange, it was *perverse*. But what did they know? In a town where most women were housewives and those who did work, fitted their jobs around their husband's careers, the existence of a female meteoriticist who worked over in the Ames lab for the NACA while her husband cooked and cleaned at home was akin to having a pair of Martians in their midst. But when they had got married, there had never been any question that Claire would give up her career. For the two of them to try and live off his measly teacher's salary was a laughable idea. But Claire left early and came home late. Someone had to hold the fort so it might as well be him.

His folks couldn't understand it of course, especially his old man who could barely look him in the eye anymore. It wasn't natural that his son should don a pinafore while his wife went off chasing a career. Claire's folks weren't a problem though; her mother had died before they had
met and her father, something of an oddball himself, had hardly been one to complain about his daughter upsetting the sanctity of tradition. He had got along with Claire's father fine. Until the old coot had been killed in an explosion in his lab in '52.

That had been an odd business. The official word was that he had been mixing a volatile compound in a coffee can and had dropped it but anybody who knew him knew that he was meticulous when it came to safety and, in light of the shady circles he moved in, foul play had always been suspected but never proved.

Shopping was the worst for Ray. In the confines of their home, he could almost feel that vacuuming, washing dishes and doing laundry were natural activities for a man. But the sidelong glances he got from the women as he led Rose around the grocery store, pushing a shopping cart of frozen steaks, comparing prices of canned goods and selecting the best detergents, were almost unbearable. He felt like some sort of traitor, although what or whom exactly he was betraying he could never quite put his finger on.

He liked Nick's garage though. Fixing the car was a man's job, even if he always did have Rose in tow. The smell of engine oil, the grubby, greasy surroundings and the opportunity for some manly wisecracking at least made him feel like he was doing something right.

Nick's Auto-Repair Shop catered to all automotive needs. As well as a service station, it had a mechanic shop and a junkyard out back filled with rusting hulks dating back to the bootlegging days. Ray lifted Rose out of the back seat and wandered inside. Some kids were tooling around with a '47 Chevy which had been chopped to within an inch of its life; the roof lowered so close to the hood line that the windscreen was a mere slit. The body had been dropped between the wheels so that it hugged the ground, the chrome stripped off, door handles removed, bare minimum of lights retained and the whole thing painted black with red and yellow flames along the sides. It was a beast, a Frankenstein's monster, and as the punk behind the wheel revved the engine to the whoops of his comrades, the roaring that filled the garage suggested that something salvaged from a much more powerful car now rattled and rumbled under the Chevy's hood.

"My nephew, Johnny," Nick explained as Ray stepped into the office and set Rose down on the edge of the countertop. "He does some work for me and I let him and his buddies fix up their cars here. It gives them something to do, somewhere safe to hang out. Keeps them out of trouble, teaches them a trade. At least, that's the idea."

Nick was a big man with a wide forehead and a pleasant smile. He had a good heart and a simple outlook on life and Ray found his views refreshingly tolerant.

"How's the wife, Nick?"

Nick sighed. "Holding out." Nick and Alice Short's three-year-old boy had died of pneumonia the previous summer. "She wants to try for another kid. Start over, y'know? Like it can undo everything if we can just start fresh. I keep telling her you can't trade one kid for another. Mikey is gone now and he ain't ever coming back." Nick's eyes looked damp but he fought the tears valiantly. "We had our shot with him and I just can't help but feel that if God meant for us to have a kid, then he wouldn't have taken Mikey from us. That's all there is to it but try telling Alice that!"

There was a squeal of rubber on asphalt as the kids in the Chevy peeled out, whooping and cheering. Ray shook his head in disapproval but said nothing.

CHAPTER 3

Before Judy eased the car around the corner and the blocky outline of Ralston High became visible, Tommy demanded to be let out.

"Are you for real?" Judy said. "Too embarrassed to be dropped off by your big sister?"

"Turning up on foot is better than being driven in by you. Now pull over and let me get out."

Judy obliged but, just as Tommy opened the door to get out, she leaned over, looped her arm around his neck and planted a big kiss on his cheek. "Be good at school today, little brother!"

"Lemme go!" Tommy cried, his face blazing red with embarrassment as he squirmed out of her grip. Some freshmen were gazing at them from the other side of the street. Judy laughed and Tommy slammed the door on her.

She left him on the curb and drove in through the school gates, circling the building to the student parking area. It was heaving with kids, some loitering, swinging their schoolbags, some horsing around while others backed up and down in their cars, squabbling over parking spaces. Judy nipped into a handy spot that nobody seemed to have noticed and got out. She headed over to the steps and found Susanne sitting on a wall, calculus book open on her knees as she crammed in some last minute studying for the test.

Even after four months, Susanne was the only real friend Judy had made at Ralston High. It was tough moving to a new school in the middle of your senior year when everybody had already broken into their cliques years ago. The first few days, she had felt totally adrift and without a soul to talk to. It made her miss her old high school in Virginia all the more. There, she had been popular and always had girlfriends to call or meet up with. Whenever she thought of all the friends she had left behind, she almost cried. But that would never do so she forced her feelings down into her gut and fought each day as it came.

Then, Susanne Crane had come to her rescue; a plain-looking girl in red-rimmed cat-eye glasses who was in several of her classes. Susanne had been her savior, but Judy was quickly disappointed that she never introduced her to any other girls. It was only after knowing her for a week that Judy realized Susanne was just as friendless and lonely as she was. Susanne had recognized a fellow loner and had made a grab for her like a drowning sailor grasping at a life raft. She was nice and all, if a little dull, but Judy knew Susanne would never be her ticket to breaking into a hip crowd. She had to face it, her social life had peaked with Susanne and she would be lucky if she made even one other friend by the time they graduated in the summer let alone a date for the prom.

"Ready?" Judy asked her.

Susanne sighed. "No. I was up all night studying and I couldn't eat a bite of breakfast I was that nervous."

"Relax," Judy told her. "It won't be that bad."

"It's all right for you to say, you've got a brain for this stuff. You'll pass, no problem. Calculus just isn't my bag."

A hot rod roared into the parking lot and kids scattered, some whooping with glee as the powerful engine growled and bellowed. A scrawny kid who had just parked his grandad's clunker hurriedly backed it out and gave up his spot for the thundering auto shop creation. The doors opened and three greasers spilled out accompanied by two girls wearing tight sweaters and a lot of makeup.

"Isn't Johnny Packer just boss?" Susanne said dreamily as she gazed at the leader of the pack; a tall youth with an oily rockabilly haircut, satin jacket and black Levis with the hems rolled up to show off his heavy workman's boots.

Johnny Packer was the local tough guy. He and his pals – known as the Black Camelots – could be found most Saturday nights roaring up and down 10th and 11th street in their souped-up machines making life hell for other drivers. They claimed to be a hot rod club but nobody was fooled. The Black Camelots was a gang with all the trimmings; satin jackets, dumb initiation rites, illicit business activities and intimidation tactics used on anybody who didn't play ball.

"I think he's a dumb thug," said Judy sniffily. "I much prefer smart guys who dress well."

"Well, you're probably right," said Susanne with a shrug of her shoulders, but her eyes didn't leave the swaggering form of Johnny Packer until he had disappeared inside.

"Come on," said Judy. "That's the bell. First period math awaits."

Susanne groaned and they went in.

Judy had been right; the test wasn't so bad. Although, as Susanne had said, she had a head for math. She had inherited her mother's skill with numbers and a calculus test posed no real problems. The rest of the class didn't look so pleased with themselves as Mrs. Williams collected their test papers.

"How'd it go?" Judy whispered, turning around in her seat to speak to Susanne behind her.

"Okay, I guess," Susanne replied. She just looked relieved that it was over.

"Not as bad as you thought?"

"No. But I think I flunked a couple of questions."

"Don't worry. I'm sure you did fine."

Judy and Susanne sat together in the cafeteria during lunch as they always did, just the two of them at a table, tucked away from the attention of anybody. As Judy inspected her dad's best effort at a peanut-butter and jelly sandwich, she saw Susanne's gaze fixed on a group several tables over.

"Oh, wowzers!" she exclaimed in a whisper. "Look at Connie Lund! How does she get everything to match so perfectly?"

Judy craned her neck to take in the sight of Connie Lund's pastel pink Angora sweater, immaculate blonde curls held up with a matching bow, pencil skirt and black saddle shoes that didn't have a single scuff. Her three friends were also immaculately dressed. They even seemed to match each other as if they had a coordinated dress plan.

That wouldn't have surprised Judy. Connie Lund and her three friends were the most closed and exclusive clique at Ralston High. Susanne had given her the skinny on them the first day they had met. Connie Lund's father was some real estate tycoon with a mansion in Palm Springs. Her friends – Karen Wood, Heather Marshall and Trudy Braddock – all came from money too and dressed the part.

Susanne looked down at her own drab blouse and felt skirt in misery. "I could never look that pretty ..."

Judy cleared her throat for want of something to say. Susanne was pretty enough but didn't exactly dress to impress. 'Old fashioned' would be a polite way of putting it. She focused instead on stopping the jelly oozing out of her sandwich as she ate it.

Mrs. Williams marked the papers over lunch and posted the results on the noticeboard by the trophy cabinet. Before the sixth period, a large group of students had gathered around it and were clogging up the hallway as they pushed and jostled to see their scores. Some were pumping their fists in the air with glee while others sighed and rubbed their foreheads in frustration.

Susanne and Judy pushed their way to the front and eagerly looked down the list for their names.

"I got a seventy-two!" said Susanne. "That's better than I thought! How about you?" She followed Judy's gaze. "Ninety-eight! That's incredible!"

They removed themselves from the crowd. Judy was happy with her result but envied Susanne's joy. The test had occupied Susanne's brain all week, driving her to distraction while Judy, if she was perfectly honest, had barely studied for it. Susanne's mom had even been concerned because her daughter was in such a flap while Judy's parents had completely forgotten about it. They hadn't even wished her luck that morning. What was a ninety-eight for someone who knew they were going to ace the test? Wouldn't it have been much better to get a seventy-two if you were worried you were going to fail? It didn't seem fair that a higher score should be less exciting but there it was.

"Ninety-eight, that's not bad," said a deep voice.

Judy turned around and saw Marty Landers, a boy from her math class leaning against the trophy cabinet. He was tall with close-cropped golden hair and a face that looked like it should be on the movie screen.

"Thanks," she found herself saying.

He smiled. "Top of the class, in fact. I checked."

"Top?"

"Sure. You got the best score out of all of us. Congratulations."

"Thank you." She felt flustered at this sudden and unexpected social interaction and fumbled for something else to say. "How about you?"

"He shrugged. "Eighty-two."

"Well, that's pretty good."

"Yeah, my folks'll be happy. But I'm way behind you. In fact, everyone is."

Judy felt a giggle rise in her throat and fought against it, not wanting to sound like a silly little girl. It caught in her throat and came out as a strange gurgle.

"Pardon?"

She made a pretense of coughing. "Nothing. Just clearing my throat."

"Well, see you around."

"Yes. Bye."

She watched him go and Susanne, who had been silent throughout the exchange, sidled up to her. "Is Marty Landers a 'smart guy who dresses well'?" she asked, nudging Judy in the ribs with her elbow.

"Oh, stop it!" Judy hissed. She felt her face burning. Marty Landers *was* smart. He dressed pretty well, not flashy or anything, but neat and tidy. And he was *very* handsome.

Suddenly, Judy felt a lot happier about her score on the test.

When school was out, Judy and Susanne walked out together. They passed Connie Lund who was sitting on a low wall with her three friends.

"I saw you aced that test today, Weldon."

At first, Judy wasn't sure who had spoken and, looking around, saw that it had been Connie who looked at her with a cat's smile, her friends mirroring it as if they were all in on the joke.

"Pardon me?"

Connie blinked her long lashes slowly as if with great patience. "I said, I saw you aced that calculus test today. Top of the class. Nice going."

"Well ... thank you," said Judy, feeling well and truly out of her depth. Marty Landers congratulating her was one thing, but Connie Lund?

"Quite the brainiac," said Connie. "We've had our eye on you for some time. You're smart, that's clear. Straight A's. What does your father do?"

The question was so unexpected and abrupt that Judy felt herself quite unprepared to answer it. "My father ...? I ... ah, he ... he's a schoolteacher."

It was only a white lie. He *had* been a schoolteacher, but Judy couldn't quite bring herself to tell the daughter of Arthur Lund, the real estate mogul that her father did ... well, *nothing*.

"A schoolteacher," Connie Lund repeated, tonelessly. The eyes of her friends darted to one another, and Judy was afraid they were going to burst out laughing. But no permission from their leader was forthcoming so not so much as a smile crossed their faces.

"My mother is a scientist," Judy said by way of making up for lost ground.

"A scientist. Really?" Now that had impressed them. Eyebrows were raised and the four girls had straightened their postures a little, giving her their full attention. "You mean she *works*?"

"Oh, sure, over near San Jose. At the NACA laboratory."

"The NACA laboratory. Interesting. What does she do there?"

"Well ... she studies meteorites."

"Meteorites?" asked one of Connie's friends. "Like the one that landed the other day?"

"Yes. As a matter of fact, she's studying that very one right now." She knew she was disobeying her mother in telling them this even as the words came out of her mouth but she couldn't help it. Connie Lund was talking to her! Connie Lund was showing an interest in her! She had to give them something.

"Listen," said Connie, leaning closer as if about to impart some top-secret information. "My girls and I like to hang out at the coffee shop on the corner of H and 11th on Saturdays. Do you know it?"

"Yes," Judy lied. She didn't go out on Saturdays and wasn't all that familiar with Ralston's coffee shops and cafes.

"Come along this Saturday."

For a moment Judy froze. She had lost all powers of speech. *Connie Lund wants me to hang out with her?*

The look on the girls' faces told her that an answer had better be forthcoming so she willed her vocal chords to get off their keysters. "Sure! I'd love to! Thanks!" She turned to walk away, not wanting to ruin what was the most wonderful afternoon of her life by saying something foolish. "Um, bye!"

"Eight o'clock!" Connie called after her.

"Eight o'clock!" Judy repeated before hurrying on.

She nearly bumped into Susanne who had been waiting at a safe distance. Her jaw nearly reached down to the frilly front of her blouse. "What," she exclaimed, "was that all about?"

"Connie Lund," Judy began, unable to keep the excitement out of her voice, "wants me to meet her at a coffee shop on Saturday!"

"You are *kidding*!" Susanne nearly squealed.

Judy couldn't stop herself from grinning, amused at Susanne's joy on her behalf. After all, Connie had said nothing about Susanne and Judy wouldn't dare bring her along uninvited. She felt a little bad that Susanne hadn't been asked too, but really, what could she do about that? She didn't let the small stab of guilt ruin her mood. Things were finally looking up for her.

CHAPTER 4

Tommy ducked as the fist whistled towards his face. He felt the breeze of it ruffle his hair as he brought his own fist up and slammed it into Tyler's gut, making the bigger boy double over, the wind knocked from him.

"Bastard!" Tyler Weston gasped as Tommy stood back to allow his opponent the opportunity to give up.

He didn't and, as soon as Tyler had regained his breath, he launched himself at Tommy.

Knocked from his feet, Tommy was slammed into the locker behind him with a loud crash that echoed down the hallway, drawing yet more kids to the already sizable ring of spectators who whooped and cheered. A hallway fight was always entertaining.

Tyler had Tommy around the middle and was wrestling him to the ground. And Tyler was a good wrestler. He was on the school team. Tommy knew nothing about wrestling but he was good with his fists. He didn't have much reach with Tyler pressing him against the lockers, trying to flip him over, so he raised his right arm and brought his elbow down hard on Tyler's neck.

There was a groan of sympathy from the crowd and Tommy couldn't tell if it was for him or Tyler because now Tyler was mad as hell and doubled his efforts in bringing Tommy down. If that happened, Tommy would be dead; a puddle of red mush on the waxed hallway floor. He had nothing to lose now and so kept up a barrage of blows on Tyler's head, neck and shoulders with his elbows.

"Just what is going on here!" bellowed Mr. McVey as he waded through the crowd to separate the two boys. Kids scampered out of his way and Tommy felt a meaty fist seize him by his shirt collar. A similar fist held Tyler at arm's length and Tommy was worried the six-foot five geography teacher was going to slam the two of them together.

"Okay, tough guys, let's take a walk to the principal's office!"

As Tommy sat outside the frosted glass door marked 'Principal's Office', he kept his glaring eyes fixed on Tyler Weston in the seat opposite him as if daring him to launch another attack.

A couple of other boys were awaiting Principal Johnson's pleasure. Tommy knew them as the inseparable pals Donnie and Burt. He had a couple of classes with them, but they hadn't been around today, leaving no wonder as to why they were currently warming a sinners' seat apiece.

The door opened and Mr. McVey sauntered out, glaring at Tyler and Tommy before heading off to continue his patrol.

"All right, Weston," called Principal Johnson from within. "Get in here."

Tommy watched Tyler slouch into the office, shutting the door behind him. He hoped that whatever heat Principal Johnson would put down on them would be mostly used up on Tyler. It *was* his fault after all. He had goaded him into swinging a punch at his grinning mug and he had been working up to it for four months.

Even on his first day at Ralston High, Tommy knew Tyler would give him trouble. He was a smug rich kid who swaggered about with his letterman jacketed crew like they owned the place. Tyler had quickly found out that Tommy's dad stayed at home while his mom worked and this was a source of endless amusement for him. What started as vague wisecracks soon turned into open insults which drew in a few others, making Tommy a class laughingstock.

Not that he was the only kid who suffered – Tyler made life hell for anybody at the slightest excuse – but that wasn't much consolation. It wasn't as if any of his fellow schoolmates would dare come to his defense. They were just happy it wasn't them this time. But now Tommy had had enough. Tyler had opened his big mouth once too often and Tommy had planted his fist in it. And here he was.

"Looks like you just about creamed Tyler Weston," said Donnie, lounging in his seat, thumbs jammed through the belt loops of his black Levis. Both he and his buddy Burt were dressed like greasers; turned up jeans, black boots and white tee-shirts.

"Nice going," said Burt. "That kid needed some attention."

"I notice he doesn't give you guys any trouble," said Tommy.

Donnie and Burt grinned at each other. "No. He don't. He wouldn't dare,"

"You guys are in the Black Camelots, aren't you?" said Tommy, leaning forward and keeping his voice low. He didn't know why he did that when it was hardly a secret. The gang wore its name on their satin jackets and he had seen Donnie and Burt put theirs on as soon as school was out.

"Yeah?" Donnie said. "What of it?"

"Nothin'. Do you know Johnny Packer?"

"Does the pope know Jesus?" Donnie said. This made Burt crack up. "Yeah, we know him. Why?"

"Seen him around. Seems to be the big man in town."

"He is. He's club president of the Camelots."

"That's a swell rod he drives. What's he got in it, a flathead V8?"

Donnie and Burt raised their eyebrows at him. "You know engines?"

"Sure. I tinker around."

"What have you got?"

Tommy cleared his throat. "Well, nothing right now. I had to sell my '31 Coupster when we moved here from Virginia. I'm looking around to buy but I haven't made my mind up yet."

"A Coupster, huh? Nice. What did you drop into it?"

"An SBC."

"I put an SBC in my Ford pickup. Man, that baby can nearly climb trees!"

The door to the principal's office opened and Tyler Weston propelled himself out of it while Tommy was summoned to take his turn. He was almost glad. He could shoot the breeze about cars all day but a couple of greasers like Donnie and Burt might cotton on to the fact that he had never owned anything more than a Vesper in his life.

Principal Johnson was an elderly, mild mannered man who would have been eaten alive by the students of a tougher school. But Ralston High was pretty soft and today's fight was the most trouble it had seen all year. Nevertheless, Principal Johnson was dutybound to lay down the law and he beckoned Tommy forward with a gnarled old claw of a finger.

"Close the door, please," he said.

Tommy did so and approached the desk.

"Now, you're new to this school so I understand that you've had a hard time fitting in," Principal Johnson began. "But that does not excuse your using your fists to settle an argument in the school hallways. I know you're not a bad kid. Your teachers tell me you're doing just fine academically and your behavior on the whole is very good. So don't let yourself be pulled down to the level of Tyler Weston."

"Yes, Sir," was all Tommy could say.

"All right, get back to your classes."

Not quite believing his luck, Tommy made for the door. Principal Johnson followed him out and levelled his frown on Donnie and Burt. "All right, you two class cutters. You know the drill. Get in here."

That Saturday, Tommy met some of the kids in his grade at Jake's Drive-In; a popular haunt for sophomores on 10th street. Hot rods and roadsters were parked in the lot out front and were waited on by car hops while kids hung about, admiring engines and horsing around, mouths full of fries. Inside, the jukebox was jumping to the sounds of Fats Domino and the dance floor seethed.

Tommy sat with Chet, Benny and Benny's girl, Dot, in a booth by the window as they slurped milkshakes. Chet and Benny were the only two kids Tommy counted on as friends, but they weren't gear heads, not by a long shot. Chet drove an old Ford roadster that hadn't even been souped up while Benny borrowed his parents' '55 Packard. They were okay guys but were more interested in dancing and pinball than the cars out in the lot and Tommy longed to be out under the streetlights with the other kids, his head under a car's hood, trading tips and secrets.

The conversation had turned to the meteorite and in particular what the papers were saying about it.

"My pop says it isn't a meteorite at all," said Chet. "He read that it's a Russian satellite that malfunctioned and came crashing down."

"In Northern California?" said Benny. "Ain't that a little far from home?"

"Satellites go around the earth, dummy," said Chet. "There's probably fifty of 'em above our heads right now, listening to this very conversation!"

"Oh, don't say that!" said Dot. "I'll have nightmares. Doesn't it just make you feel icky?"

"He's kidding you," said Tommy. "The Russians don't have that kind of technology. Nobody does outside of science fiction magazines. There's nothing up there but space and meteorites."

"Oh yeah?" said Chet. "How do you know so much about it?"

"His mom works for that space lab," said Benny.

"Right!" said Chet, suddenly remembering. "Hey, has she told you any secrets? Like what the Russians are doing?"

"No, and if she did I could hardly tell you. It would be top secret."

"Yeah, the FBI would whack him," said Benny with a grin.

"Look, the papers have got it wrong," said Tommy. "It's a boring old hunk of rock that fell down. I know because my mom is studying it."

"No kidding?" said Benny.

"Oh, great," said Chet, looking over at the door. "Here comes trouble."

Tommy glanced over his shoulder and stifled a groan. Tyler Weston and two of his buddies had appeared, their eyes scanning the joint. Tyler's eyes met his and the heat could almost be felt across the crowded room.

"He's coming over," Benny said helpfully.

"Weldon, whaddya say?" said Tyler, planting a heavy hand on Tommy's shoulder. "Did you bum a ride here from somebody? It's a long walk from your end of town."

Tommy didn't answer and hoped Tyler would move on even though he knew he wouldn't.

"You know, old man Johnson sent a letter home to my folks," said Tyler. "Did your folks get a letter?"

"Nope," Tommy said with as much carefree innocence he could muster.

"Well aren't you just the teacher's pet?" Tyler snarled. "You've even got old man Johnson doing you favors."

"Listen, Tyler. You started that fight and I would have beat your ass if it hadn't had been for Mr. McVey so just clam it!"

Tyler and his pals grinned at one another and Tommy knew he had fallen for their plan to get him riled up. "Tough talk, Weldon," Tyler said. "You looking for a rematch?"

Tommy glanced at Tyler's buddies. They were also on the wrestling team. He sure had brought backup.

"I'm talking to you, Weldon!" Tyler snapped.

The dance floor cooled off as heads started to turn in their direction.

"Why don't you get lost, Tyler?" Chet said.

"I don't remember asking you anything, dork," said Tyler. "Let the tough guy speak for himself. Or is he just like his old man? A queer in a pinafore?"

Tommy stood up suddenly, overturning his empty milkshake glass as he did so. It didn't break but it made a clatter loud enough for Jake, the proprietor, to come hustling out of the kitchen, his face red.

"What's going on here, boys? I'll have no trouble!"

Tommy glared up into Tyler's eyes and the two of them stood a foot apart, the air around them crackling with energy. Jake sized up the situation and thankfully took Tommy's part.

"All right, Tyler, you can't come in here stirring up trouble. Take a hike, the three of you!"

"We were just leaving anyway," said Tyler. "I only came in to deliver a message." He glared at Tommy. "You are gonna get yours, Weldon!"

The three of them sauntered out and, as another tune kicked up on the jukebox, the place started moving again. Jake frowned at Tommy and his friends as if to warn them that they were on thin ice, before heading back into the kitchen.

"Man, I thought you were gonna slug Tyler just then," said Benny.

"I wanted to," Tommy replied.

"And no one would have blamed you," said Chet. "But pick your battles, Tommy. He and those two apes would've creamed you."

As the evening wore on, everybody lightened up apart from Tommy. He sat in the booth and watched Benny and Dot dance while Chet put the movies on a girl in a pink poodle skirt with a flamingo on it who sat with her friends in a booth on the other side of the room. By the time Tommy's watch showed midnight, he knew he had to head for home. Benny and Dot were getting ready to leave too.

"Hey, can I get a ride home with you guys?" he asked. "You can drop me off on the corner of Rose Avenue. It wouldn't be too far out of your way."

"Rose Avenue?" Benny said. "That's the other side of town! I've got to get Dot home by one or her father'll have my hide for a lounge rug. Sorry, Tommy. Ask Chet, he lives your end of town."

Tommy waited until Chet was done distracting the girl in the pink skirt from her friends and groaned when he came over with her in tow. They looked like they were getting ready to leave together.

"Any chance of a ride?" he asked Chet, knowing it was futile.

"Sorry, Tommy. I just promised Susie here that I'd take her for a ride down the strip before dropping her off. I'd let you come along, really, but my roadster only has two seats."

"He can go in the trunk!" giggled Susie and Chet guffawed. Tommy didn't find it funny.

"Sorry, pal," Chet whispered in Tommy's ear as Susie took out some lipstick from her purse and applied a fresh coat. "I'm on to a winner here. You understand, right?"

"Right." Tommy watched them go. He gritted his teeth. What a lousy situation! He was doubly angry because Tyler had been absolutely right. He *had* bummed a ride from somebody. His sister. She was hanging out with her dumb friends at some fancy coffee shop all the way down on the corner of H and 11th. He had hoped to get a ride home with Chet or Benny, but they had ditched him, leaving him with no alternative but to hoof it over to H street and get a ride back with Judy. Finding himself suddenly alone in the booth, he decided it was time to hit the road.

The evening air was warm and the streetlights buzzed as he crossed over to 11th and began the long trek down its length. He peered in through store windows at dimly lit dress mannequins that stared back at him with blank faces. Radios and television sets sat on their polished mirror pedestals under low-hanging lamps. There were few pedestrians about but plenty of cars cruised up and down the strip. One of them, a rod with a powerful engine, lurched suddenly towards the sidewalk so that its front and back right wheels rode up onto the curb. It was a burgundy Model A with the hood removed. Tommy knew that car.

Tyler and his goons climbed out of it and blocked the sidewalk. "You're going nowhere, dickface," said Tyler.

Tommy knew he was trapped. It would do no good to run; these varsity athletes would chase him down before he reached the end of the block. They hemmed him in, forming a semi-circle around him. Tyler's friends grabbed an arm each and they began hauling him into a nearby alley.

It was dark in the alley and refuse lay piled up against the walls. Tommy found himself pinned up against the brickwork.

"Hold him steady," said Tyler as he balled up his fist.

Before he had a chance to swing it, Tommy lashed out with both feet, catching Tyler in the chest, knocking him backwards.

"Hold him, damnit!" Tyler cried.

A fist to the ribs from one of his captors made Tommy screw up his face in agony. Sturdy legs grappled with his own so that he couldn't kick out a second time. Tommy shut his eyes and prepared for the impact of Tyler's fist.

The blow never came. The party in the alley had grown in number and, as Tommy opened his eyes, he saw that Donnie and Burt were there, shoving Tyler away from them. He felt his captors release their grip on his arms as they rushed forward to aid their leader. Fists smacked against flesh as the greasers and the jocks duked it out in the alleyway.

Tommy pushed himself away from the wall and launched himself at Tyler. The bigger boy wasn't ready and was knocked off his feet, landing heavily on the garbage-strewn ground. Tommy straddled him and began to strike him again and again across the face with his fists.

Donnie and Burt were outweighed by their opponents and the fight might have gone badly for them but Donnie had pulled a length of chain from his jacket and was swinging it around in an arc. Burt had pulled a switchblade and the two jocks backed off nervously.

One of them stumbled against Tommy and shoved him roughly off Tyler. Tommy rolled and came up swinging, catching the boy who had shoved him on the lip.

That was enough for them and they split, hauling the bloodied Tyler to his feet and half pushing, half dragging him out of the alley, back to their car.

Donnie, Burt and Tommy followed them out of the alley and watched them scramble into the car and peel out, one of Tyler's buddies behind the wheel with Tyler lying on the back seat. Further along the sidewalk, Tommy saw a chopped Ford pickup parked on the curb.

"Gee, thanks, guys," he said. "I thought I was a gonner."

Donnie grinned. "Yeah, we thought you were too, that's why we decided to pull over and give you a hand."

"We were cruising past and saw Tyler and his apes drag you into the alley," Burt added.

"You did pretty good," Donnie said to Tommy. "Tyler's gonna have a face like a hamburger for a week or two."

"Say, why don't you ride around with us for a bit?" said Burt. "We can have a few laughs."

"I gotta be home before midnight," said Tommy.

"Another time, then."

"Sure."

"How are you getting home?" asked Donnie.

"I'm meeting my sister. She has the car tonight."

Donnie laughed. "Man, you really need to get yourself some wheels."

CHAPTER 5

It had been over a week since the meteorite had landed. The initial excitement had died down, despite a brief flare in interest as a ludicrous rumor of a Soviet satellite began to circulate in the newspapers. Claire had got no closer to identifying the sample she had taken and was still puzzled by the strange, regular depressions in the meteorite's cavity. She had sent off her results as well as some samples and a few photographs Fred had taken to a number of authorities including the pioneer in her field, Harvey Nininger.

Claire had many of Nininger's books and had even attended some of his lectures. It had been due to his efforts that meteoritics had progressed from an eccentric interest to a serious science and he had assembled the largest collection of meteorites in the world at his museum in Arizona. She had also contacted a geologist called Jeremy Norton who was an old friend.

Claire and Fred were continuing their research into high-speed impact by measuring the penetration of small spheres into copper targets when the phone rang in her office. It was Jeremy.

"Hi, Jerry, good to hear from you," said Claire, settling into her seat. Fred had followed her in, eager to hear what the geologist had to say about their mysterious meteorite.

"Claire, what the hell did you send me?" was Jerry's opening statement.

"That's why we sent it to you. We have no idea."

"Well, I agree with your results and share in your defeat. I'm utterly stumped."

"But the depressions ..."

"Yes, the depressions. Well, at first, I was inclined to believe that they were the impressions of concretions or nodules – that is to say, mineral deposits – in the rock. It's not uncommon to find such depressions in sedimentary rock where the concretion has fallen away."

"Have you ever seen a pattern of concretion or nodule impressions so ordered and similar in size?"

"No. And that leads me to, what I can only say with some apology, is my conclusion, though it's one I do not understand in the least. I mean to say that these impressions are not of mineral deposits, but fossilized eggs."

There was a silence as Claire took this in. She held Fred's eager gaze, unable to convey with her eyes the gravity of what Jerry had just told her.

Fossilized eggs. In a meteorite.

"Are you absolutely sure?"

"Historically, concretions have often been misidentified as fossilized dinosaur or turtle eggs due to their round or oval shape but this pattern in the rock, this regularity in size, I just have no other explanation to offer than the natural perfection of biology. Something laid its eggs in some distant part of the universe God knows how many millennia ago, and now, a piece of that place, fossilized eggs included, has made its way to Earth. Do you know what this means, Claire?"

"Yes ..." she managed.

"It's more your field than mine of course, but damn me if I'm not as excited as a schoolboy! You said that a piece of the rock had cracked off and fallen into the water revealing the cavity. Did you recover the other piece?"

"It was right there in the water, with the same impressions; a mirror if you like, of the opposite side of the cavity."

"But the fossils themselves!"

"We saw none. Whatever made those impressions must have fallen into the water too. My original theory was that the impressions were made by bubbles of trapped gas, so I thought nothing of it but ..."

"Claire, we need to find those fossils!"

"I know. I'll do my best. Thank you for your help."

"Think nothing of it. Promise me you'll send me one of them when you do find them?"

"I'll see what I can do. I'll call you anyway."

They said goodbye and Claire hung up the receiver. She waited a while before looking up at Fred who was regarding her was barely concealed agitation.

"Well, come on, Claire, don't keep me waiting! Jerry obviously found something."

"Yes, he did. And now *we* need to find something."

"What?"

"Eggs."

Fred was silent.

"That's right, Fred. Those impressions were made by fossilized alien eggs. They must have fallen loose when the meteorite cracked open and fell into the reservoir."

"I don't believe it," Fred managed.

She laughed. "Neither can I!"

"We'll be famous! It's the scientific discovery of the twentieth century! Claire, we've found the existence of alien life on other planets!"

"I know, I know! But before we start celebrating, we need to find them. Without the fossils themselves, all we have are a sign of alien life but if we can find just one of those little suckers, we will be holding the fossilized remains of extraterrestrial life itself!"

Fred bit his knuckle in barely restrained glee. "I'll get my coat. We can make it to the reservoir before dark and it's almost time you headed home anyway. I'll follow you in my car so I can drive myself back to San Jose."

"Fred, if we find what we're looking for, you can come back to my place and we'll crack open that bottle of champagne Ray and I were saving."

"You're on!"

They quickly packed up for the day, unable to get out of the lab quick enough, and headed down to the lobby. Once the doors of the elevator closed on them, Claire said to Fred; "Not a word of this to anybody. Not until we can put together a proper paper."

"I agree," Fred replied. "It's far too outlandish. Nobody will believe us until we have absolute concrete proof. But when we do ... Boy this is going to explode!"

Claire nodded but said nothing. Fred was right. She couldn't afford to tell anybody at the NACA, not with her history. Oh sure, she could see their faces now; 'that's what you get when you bring in meteoriticists to work on space flight research, and one of them the daughter of John MacReady no less! She hasn't been in the job six months yet and she's already babbling about Martians!'

It was incredible how skeptical they could be of new ideas. Claire was sometimes amazed they had got anywhere in this country. Years ago, many of the same people she worked with now had thought her father was wasting his life developing rocket propulsion with the aim of utilizing it for space exploration. His theories drew derision and mockery by his peers who felt that such ideas should be left between the lurid covers of *Astounding Stories*. Now, five years after his death, it was one of the most important projects with government funding in the country. *Five years too late.*

Not that she had ever shown any interest in the pursuit of alien life. She was a meteoriticist, not an astrobiologist. Yet here they were with potential evidence; evidence she intended to handle like a ticking timebomb until the time was right.

As they entered the lobby, the receptionist hailed them over. A man with a camera satchel slung over his shoulder stood nearby, his eyes keen behind black-rimmed spectacles. Claire immediately recognized him as the press. A security guard loomed in the corner of the room, watching the small reporter closely.

"Dr. Weldon," the receptionist said. "This man has been waiting for you. He has been with Director Allen. I told him that you work late, but …,"

"Ah, Dr. Weldon," said the reporter. "Mark Peters. I'm from the San Francisco Chronicle. The head of your division, Mr. Allen, was kind enough to talk to me about your work here, but it was really you I was hoping to run into. Could you spare a few moments to talk about the meteorite you are currently studying, if indeed it is a meteorite at all …"

He left the sentence hanging, purposefully, his notebook in his hand.

"I really am in a hurry," Claire said.

"Just a few words, please. It would certainly put a lot of folks' minds at rest, what with all the hubbub that it might really be a piece of a Soviet satellite."

"It's no satellite, Mr. Peters," Claire answered. "It's a meteorite, plain and simple."

"I'm given to believe that objects entering the Earth's atmosphere go under extreme pressures and heats. Might it not be possible for a hunk of metal to appear to be a meteorite after it partially burns up in the atmosphere and then thumps into the side of a mountain?"

"I know my work, Mr. Peters," said Claire frostily. "It's a meteorite."

"Well, my sources give the impression that you don't know exactly what it is. Is that a fair assumption?"

Claire glared at him. "What sources?"

He grinned. "I'm not at liberty to say."

"It does present some questions, yes," Claire admitted. "And so far, we don't have all the answers, but it won't do to let wild imagination fill in the gaps science is working on."

"But the proximity of the fall to the Ames laboratory – home to our own space program – is a little convenient, wouldn't you say?"

"I wouldn't say it had any bearing on the matter."

"But you must agree that it isn't hard to imagine the following scenario; that a Russian probe was spying on you fellas ..., oh, and ah, *gals*. Something went wrong and it crash landed in the Sierra Nevada foothills."

"Ridiculous. It is no Soviet technology, I can tell you that much."

"Though of course, you might say that."

"What's that supposed to mean?"

"Oh, just that if the NACA isn't covering something up, then perhaps you are."

"Me?"

"The Chronicle is aware of who your father was, Dr. Weldon. What he was implicated in. Some say the apple never falls far from the tree ..."

"Listen, pal," Fred cut in. "We've told you all we're going to. Now you can write what you want but if you print any of your loony ideas, then it won't be the truth you're printing, but fantasy. And you'll be held to account for it."

"Is that a threat, Sir?" Peters asked, grinning widely.

"Come on," said Claire. "Let's get out of here."

They left the reporter smirking in the lobby as they headed out to the parking lot.

"Why did Allen agree to talk to the press anyway?" Claire grumbled as she unlocked her car door. "Is there no secrecy surrounding our research for the government?"

"It's politics, Claire," Fred said with a shrug of the shoulders. "And it's not the first time the press have been allowed to make a nuisance of themselves around our 'top secret' work. If the Soviets want to keep their space program a matter of military secrecy, then we, in direct contrast, must show openness. The American space program is an extension of our values apparently, and our end goal must be seen as freedom in space, not conquest of the skies. It's what sets us apart from them, at least in the public's eye."

They got in the car and Claire revved the engine. She took them out of the gate and onto the highway a little too fast for Fred's comfort by the way he squirmed in his seat. She was seething. That odious little journalist's comment about her father had been an attempt to get her to let something slip in anger. Well, she was angry all right, but there had been nothing to let slip, at least nothing about Russian satellites.

To suggest that she might be covering something up because of what her father had been accused of made her blood boil. They had never understood him. Neither had she, but she knew him well enough to know that he had been no spy. That's what they had accused him of. It was how they got rid of him in the end. His past association with refugee scientists from Europe back in the thirties had spoken against him. He had shared many of their socialist sympathies but he was no communist. He had been an individualist who despised totalitarianism in its fascist and communist flavors equally.

It had all been an excuse anyway. Even his most outspoken critics hadn't really believed he was a Soviet spy, Claire was convinced of that. It was his involvement with that damned lodge and its black magic charlatans that had really spooked them. America's premier scientists acting like a bunch of frightened old maids! But truthfully, it had spooked Claire too. It had spooked her for nearly all her life.

An old memory came back to her as she gripped the steering wheel and focused on the road ahead. She had been perhaps nine years old. Her parents were part of a wide social circle and often held parties at their Pasadena mansion. Claire used to sit at the top of the stairs in her nightdress and listen to the soft jazz music and the clink of cocktail glasses below. When she grew tired, she would go back to bed, content that she was surrounded by laughter, warmth and happiness.

One night, she woke up and could hear the jazz records still playing but other than the music, there was nothing but silence throughout the house. She got up and tiptoed to the top of the stairs. A dim light showed from the living room. Treading the stairs carefully, she went down and crept to the doorway that led to the living room.

The sight that met her eyes was not one she had understood then, but she had carried it with her always, like a haunting. Everywhere she looked she could see bare, pale flesh. There were about ten or fifteen people in the room, her parents included, all of them naked and lying in strange positions, strewn across every piece of furniture. At first, Claire thought they were dead, stricken down by whatever poisonous fumes she could smell in the air, but no, they were all moving, writhing like beasts, limbs locked in deathly embraces.

Her mother lay on a divan beneath one of the newer members of their circle, a man Claire didn't recognize. The man's buttocks were rising up and down and her mother's face was wracked by, what Claire had thought then was pain but knew now had been ecstasy. Her father stood behind a woman whose name was Mary and had always been very kind to Claire. Now she was bent forward over the grand piano, her rigid fingers clutching futilely at its glossy lacquered surface.

As she watched, Claire felt her entire world fall out from under her. These people she knew, her parents whom she loved, were there before her but she didn't recognize them as people anymore. They were something more primal than that, alien beings, ancient and strange; things she didn't understand.

"Claire, watch your speed!" Fred said to her. "I want to get to those fossils too, but we won't get there any quicker if the cops pull us over."

Claire blinked out of her reverie, glanced at the speedometer and eased her foot off the gas. "Sorry, Fred. Just a little eager I guess."

Darkness was fast approaching and by the time they had wound their way up into the foothills of the Sierra Nevada, Claire knew they were going to be searching the water by torchlight.

CHAPTER 6

The first indication to Ray that something was wrong happened when he and Rose were doing the dreaded weekly grocery run. He always tried to get it done as quickly as possible, zipping up and down the aisles of frozen and canned foods with Rose sitting in the trolley seat thinking it was all great fun.

Paying was always the worst, especially if there was a cluster of women in front of him fumbling about with their coupons and gossiping with each other and the checkout girl. They always stopped whenever he approached to put his groceries on the conveyor belt and eyed him sidelong. He heard their comments as they headed outside; 'Could you imagine if my Bob did the grocery shopping? Or your Dan?', 'I know, and taking care of the baby too!', 'Wife *works*, you know.'

They thought he couldn't hear them, or perhaps they knew and didn't care. Either way he felt each comment as a stab and twist of a knife to his male pride, or what was left of it.

This time something else had their full attention and for once, they didn't pay him a glance. Three mothers were talking and regularly nodding their heads in the direction of a girl playing on the street outside the store.

"I just don't know how seriously I should take it all," one of them was saying. "All children play make-believe, of course, but she is just so adamant that I really believe she is convinced little Patches is back."

"Well, it was only last summer that the dog was run over," said one of the other mothers. "And right in front of Nancy too. That's sure to have an effect on a child. She must miss him so."

"But why wait nearly a year to start pretending Patches is still alive, that's what gets me," Nancy's mother replied. "She was distraught last night when Dan locked the back door. Patches was still in the yard, Nancy said, and she raised hell when we wouldn't let her out to call him in. Dan told her to stop playing silly games but she wouldn't. He wants her to see a doctor but I'm not sure. In all other respects, she's absolutely fine, it's just this invisible dog business that has me worried."

"Oh, where's the harm in it?" sad the third mother who had, until now, kept quiet. "She's just a kid playing make-believe. Let her be a child while she can. There's enough badness in the world right now without taking that little joy from her."

The three women shuffled out of the store, unaware that Ray had been listening in on their conversation. When he stepped out onto the sidewalk, one arm loaded with paper bags brimming with groceries, the other holding Rose, he caught a glimpse of little Nancy and her mother heading down the street. Nancy was skipping behind, turning around every so often to smile at something that wasn't there, acting for all the world as if a little dog was following her.

He didn't think much on it and had nearly forgotten the episode until he rolled into Nick's garage to fill up the tank. Nick himself came out with apologies that the usual pump attendant was sick. Nick looked pretty sick himself. His face was pale and he had tired circles around his eyes.

"Everything all right, Nick?"

"Not exactly, Ray, no."

"What's up?"

"It's Alice. She's not well." He spoke in a low voice, as if fearful of being overheard.

"Nothing serious, I hope?"

"Physically, she's in great shape. Better than usual in fact, now that her appetite is back."

"Well, that's something."

"Sure. But it's her mind that bothers me."

"How so?"

Nick sighed. "I don't know, Ray, I just don't know. I should be happy, I guess. I mean, she's eating well, sleeping through the night and generally seems her old self, you know, from *before*. But she's got this crazy new obsession."

"Grief is a funny thing, Nick. Takes on all forms. Maybe a hobby is what she needs and, by the sound if it, it's doing her a world of good."

"Ray," Nick said, fixing him with a grim stare. "She thinks little Mikey is with us."

Nick frowned, not quite knowing what to say. "You mean, like his ghost?"

"No, not a ghost. But *alive*. There in the house with us."

Ray was stunned.

"As far as she's concerned, it's as if he never died. She won't hear of it. She sets a place for him at the table, even cooks enough food for him. Then, when she cleans up, she empties his plate into the garbage and acts like he ate it all. She carries out conversations with him, while I'm sitting right there wondering if she's a candidate for the funny farm! I can't take it, Ray!"

"Nick, this sounds like some sort of delayed part of her grieving process. Have you considered taking her to see a doctor?"

"Yeah, I've considered it. But I can't stand the idea of her being carted off to some nuthouse. I already lost my boy, I can't lose Alice too!"

"It may not come to that. Like I said, I think it's some psychological way of dealing with Mikey's death. A professional could help her through it."

"I guess. I'll tell you one thing, we can't carry on like this! She's knitting him sweaters and tucking him in at night. Talking all day to him. It gives me the creeps!"

Another customer pulled in behind Ray's car and Nick hurried over to attend to him. Ray pulled out onto the road and headed for home.

He couldn't stop thinking about Nick's wretched situation all day. He liked Nick and it pained him to think of him having to deal with whatever breakdown his wife was going through. But there was more than that; he also thought about little Nancy and her invisible dog. A child playing make-believe was hardly the same thing as a grown adult having delusions about her dead son. And yet, the more Ray thought about it, the harder he found it to distance the two cases. Both Nancy and Alice were mourning the loss of a loved one and were imagining away their pain. But how hard were their imaginations working? Where did make-believe end and insanity begin?

The Robertsons had invited them to a barbecue that evening to repay Ray for his baked glazed ham. It wasn't an invitation Ray had been looking forward to with relish. Ann Robertson was a meticulous perfectionist who prided herself on keeping a much better house than Ray did and her husband Jerry was a condescending braggart who always seemed to have a wisecrack ready for Ray. The fact that he did the housework while Claire brought home the bacon never failed to raise the corner of his mouth in a half-hidden smirk. Oh, it was all dressed up in politeness and the Robertsons put on a very good show of being their friends but the sneers were always just beneath the surface.

If Ray could have his way, they'd have nothing to do with them at all but it was Claire who insisted that they maintain the façade of friendship. They were their neighbors, after all, and wasn't that what neighbors were supposed to be? Friends? Invite each other to dinner? Chat over the garden fence about new cars, job promotions and how wonderful their kids were? The Robertsons had one daughter who had got married last year to a successful attorney in Los Angeles, a fact which was brought up time and again.

Ray despised it all but did it for Claire. So when Claire came home late that night, apparently having forgotten all about the barbeque, he was not best pleased.

"I had to fence with them both in your absence," he said to her in the kitchen while Fred hung around awkwardly in the living room. "Jerry is bad enough but without you there, Ann had nobody to gossip with so I found myself surrounded. And the kids were no help. They just moped around before slinking off claiming that they had homework to do. I should be so lucky."

"I'm so sorry, Darling," Claire said. "We've had a very exciting day and I suppose we just got carried away. Fred and I had to go back to the reservoir and ..."

"Thank God it was only a barbecue and not another dining room party or I'd never have got away," Ray continued. "I've had just about all the snipes from Jerry Robertson that I can take."

It was nearly eleven and the kids were in bed. Ray poured a scotch for Fred and began making up a bed on the sofa. Claire was still dressed in her work clothes and they both looked tired and disappointed.

"What was so exciting that you just had to drive up to the reservoir again?" Ray asked.

"It's unbelievable, Ray," said Claire. "Eggs. The meteorite contained fossilized eggs."

Ray glanced from Claire to Fred, not sure if he was getting the joke. "Eggs? You mean ..."

"*Alien* eggs, yes. They must have fallen out of their depressions and into the water when the smaller part of the meteorite cracked upon cooling. We went back to the reservoir to retrieve them but without any luck. We searched the water surrounding the meteorite, but it was too dark to see properly."

"They could have been taken as souvenirs," said Fred. "That old rock has had plenty of sightseers, I gather."

"Yes, but it would be strange if all of them had been taken and not a word about them was printed in the papers. If somebody found them then surely they would be keen to find out what they were and would have pursued the same avenues we have."

"Maybe they rolled into deeper water," said Ray.

"Perhaps," said Claire, biting her lip. "Tomorrow is Saturday. I want to go back at first light and try again. We've just got to find those eggs!"

Chapter 7

Nearly two weeks had passed since Connie Lund had invited Judy to hang out with her and her girls at the coffee shop and things were going swimmingly. Judy had been far more nervous about meeting them than she had been about the calculus test. What if she said something silly and they laughed in her face or made fun of her? The only thing worse than that was the idea that they might save it and laugh behind her back while pretending to be her friend. She would just want to die if that happened.

After dropping Tommy off first at Jake's Drive-In, she had made her way over to the corner of H and 11th. The coffee shop was a new Italian place and was as clean and shiny as a brass tack. She had found Connie and her friends sitting in a booth by the window, sipping large cups of steaming coffee with foamy cream on top, dabbing daintily with their napkins at the milky moustaches each sip left.

As she approached the booth, Connie stood up and kissed Judy on both cheeks. The other girls did the same, leaving her head spinning, unused to such a custom.

"That's what they do in Paris," Connie explained, sensing her bewilderment. "Mother went there last year and told me all about it."

They sat back down and one of the girls – Judy thought it was Heather Marshall – scooted over to make room for her. Connie hailed an attractively dark boy working at the counter and an identical cup of foam-topped coffee promptly appeared before her. Judy thanked the boy and took a tentative sip. If this was coffee, then she had been missing out. She was used to the black, strong stuff her dad made which she didn't really like but drank when they had company in an effort to appear sophisticated. But this, smooth, milky stuff was so much easier on the palette with none of the bitterness she always expected in coffee. She was aware of the other girls watching her.

"Pretty good, huh?" said one of them, either Trudy or Karen, Judy wasn't sure.

"It's delicious!" she replied. "What is it?"

"A *cappuccino*," said Connie. "It's Italian."

"This is the only place that does it," said one of the other girls. "That's why we always come here."

"You don't go to any other places?" Judy asked. "A lot of kids go to the drive in."

Connie and her friends shrieked with laughter and Judy felt she had made some sort of faux pas.

"The drive-in, she says!" giggled one of them.

"We prefer a little more sophistication than juke-boxes and greasy food," explained Connie. "You're new to the gang so it's understandable, but we belong to a more select crowd."

"Our fathers are members of the Del Rio country club," said the one Judy thought was Heather.

"We go up there at least once a month," said Connie. "Is your father a member of any country clubs in Virginia?"

"Um, no."

"Well, I'll have you put down as a guest the next time we go up. You'll love it."

"Really? Oh, that's very kind!"

"We think you've got the makings of a member of our crowd. There are a few little kinks that need ironing out first, of course."

"Kinks?"

"Oh, just a few little things." Her eyes looked Judy up and down. "That cardigan, for example. But don't worry, we'll take you shopping one day before we all go up to the county club and you'll fit in, you'll see."

"Is she going to join the prom committee?" one of the girls asked.

"I've given that some thought too," said Connie, smiling at Judy. "If you're prepared to give up some of your evenings, that is."

"That prom committee?" Judy said. "Isn't it a bit early to be thinking about the prom?"

"Not for the ones organizing it. And this year it's going to be just perfect as we're in charge. Well? What do you say?"

"Oh, I'd love to!"

"Then consider yourself on the committee."

The evening continued in this pleasant manner until, just her luck, Tommy appeared at the window, right by their booth, peering in like a hungry orphan in a Charles Dickens novel. He spotted Judy and came in. Judy could have just died.

"Ready when you are, Sis," he said, ambling over to their booth, his leather jacket and dirty jeans drawing stares from the polite clientele.

"Ready for what?" Judy snapped. "I thought you were getting a ride back with one of your friends."

"They ditched me for a couple of broads."

"Is *this* your brother?" Connie asked in the tone of voice one uses when commenting on a dead rat in the street.

"Yes," said Judy, feeling the ground she had gained with Connie slipping with every moment her brother loomed over them. "I gave him a ride into town." She turned eyes of fire on her brother. "You'll just have to wait outside. We're not done here."

"No, I think we may as well call it a night," said Connie. "Come on, girls."

They left their coffees and rose, as one, filing out of the booth. When they stepped out onto the sidewalk, they all kissed each other goodnight. Judy could feel

Tommy's eyes widening and silently begging him not to open his mouth.

"*Kisses*?" he said as the other girls left.

"Shut up," Judy told him. "It's a French thing. You wouldn't understand."

Despite the embarrassment of Tommy showing up, Judy was pleased with the evening and, as the following week rolled by, she felt that her life was definitely on the up. Not only was she making good ground with Connie's gang, but she had even started dating.

Martin Landers, she had discovered, worked at the stationary store on 10th street. She had gone in to get some school supplies the following Saturday and found him holding the fort while Mr. Jessop was out to lunch. He looked even more handsome in his work clothes, shirt sleeves rolled up above muscular forearms that bulged as he carried boxes of supplies in and out of the storeroom.

"Oh," she said, as casually as she could manage. "I didn't know you worked here."

He smiled. "Come to stock up? We have a discount on fountain pens. We also have half off rubber stamps which, thanks to a fault at the factory, say 'Aproved' instead of 'Approved'."

Claire laughed. "I'll pass, thanks. I'm just here for some notepaper."

"Sure? We have a whole box of the things out back and old Mr. Jessop wants them shifted." He grinned at her.

She smiled back. "Gee, it must be swell having a Saturday job. A little extra pocket money. I would like to get one, but my folks think it would eat into my studying time too much."

"Maybe it would. You're top of the class. Your folks sure wouldn't want those grades to slip."

"Oh, I'd be all right. You're managing it."

His face fell a little at this. "Because I have to. And it's not just a Saturday job. I work three nights a week after school too."

She must have looked shocked because he explained further, "Money is a little tight at home. I help out where I can."

"What do your folks do?" She regretted the question as soon as she asked it. It was something Connie Lund asked people because she could afford to.

"It's just me and my dad. My mom died when I was five."

"Oh! I'm sorry ..."

"It's fine. We make do. But my dad doesn't exactly make much. He's a janitor over in Creekside. I hear your mom's a scientist."

"Yes." She felt like such a spoiled fool. Here she was saying how wonderful it would be to earn some pocket money with a Saturday job while poor Martin had to work four days a week to help his father make ends meet.

"That ... must be interesting," Martin prompted.

"Oh, not really. She studies meteorites."

"Wow, like the one that landed a couple of weeks ago?"

"Yes. But I'm not really supposed to talk about it."

"Top secret stuff, huh? Well, I promise not to ask any questions. If ..."

"If?"

"If you let me take you out for a hamburger some time."

She blushed. "Sure, I'd like that."

"How about tonight?"

"Tonight?" This was all happening so fast.

"I punch out at five. I can pick you up at, say, nine and we can take a drive."

"That would be wonderful!"

He beamed. "Nine o'clock it is, then!"

Donnie Kowalski lived on a small farm west of the Golden State Highway. His folks were simple, hardworking types but the poverty of their situation was embarrassingly apparent to Tommy the first time Donnie drove him and Burt out to that old farm, his souped-up pickup truck kicking up clouds of dust as it roared up the dirt track.

Donnie's garage was a disused barn that was coming apart at the joints. It seemed to double as Donnie's workshop and bedroom evidenced by the army cot at the far end, the doorless wardrobe and the collection of comic books, model cars, and combs on some hanging shelves.

Tommy started hanging out on Donnie's farm most days after school and they would tinker with his pickup truck and horse around. Sometimes Donnie's mom would come over from the house with lemonade. They occasionally took his Daisy air rifle out and shot at tin cans and whisky bottles behind the barn. Tommy loved it. There was a feeling of freedom out here beyond the highway where there was nothing but farmland for as far as the eye could see. Here there was room to breathe, miles away from the cookie-cutter houses of suburbia with their neat lawns and nosy adults always keeping an eye on things.

Donnie and Burt quickly became Tommy's best friends and he forgot all about Chet and Benny and the insufferably dull Dot. On Saturdays, when darkness approached and they tired of hanging out on the farm, they would clamber into the pickup truck and shoot into town where they would cruise up and down 10th and 11th street, seeing who was out and about. Tommy got to meet some of the other Black Camelots who hung out at a hamburger stand. They were a good bunch and, although he was just a hanger-on, Tommy felt like he belonged to a crowd. Roaring around with Donnie and Burt who always wore their satin jackets, he felt like one of the town's tough guys. The kind of guy creeps like Tyler Weston wouldn't even consider tangling with.

Tommy made no secret of his desire to earn his own jacket and become an official Black Camelot, often pestering Donnie and Burt on how it could be done and what he had to prove. They just laughed and told him these things took time. He had yet to meet 'the boss', Johnny Packer, and until that happened, he was strictly an associate.

But, one Saturday afternoon which they had spent tooling around with a new intake manifold on the pickup's engine, Donnie announced that they had to skedaddle if they were going to make the meeting.

"What meeting?" asked Tommy.

"Johnny's called a meet at the clubhouse tonight. Seven o'clock. We'd better move if we're gonna get cleaned up and into town."

Tommy's heart sank. It was Saturday night and he'd been looking forward to cruising around with Donnie and Burt.

"Don't look so glum, chum," said Burt, thumping him on the shoulder. "You're invited too."

"I'm invited?" asked Tommy. "To the meeting?"

"Sure. We've told Johnny all about you and he wants to take a look at you."

"If you play your cards right tonight," said Donnie, "you might make prospect."

"No kidding?" Donnie exclaimed. A prospect was definitely a step up the right ladder.

They were cleaning the oil off their hands and combing some pomade into their hair when Mrs. Kowalski came into the barn with a tray of lemonade.

"Mom, it's a little late for lemonade," said Donnie. "Anyway, you brought us some today already."

"Just thought you boys could do with a refresher."

"We're heading into town now. Hey, Mom, you're spilling it!"

But she wasn't spilling. The lemonade was in its jug but Mrs. Kowalski was standing in a pool of liquid nevertheless. The light of the dim hanging bulb in the barn had prevented them from seeing it before, but she was soaked to the skin. Water dripped off her frumpy, floral print dress.

"Um ... Mom?" Donnie asked. "Are you ok? Why are you all wet?"

"Oh, I took a foot wrong by the canal and fell in," she replied. "I'm all right though. Listen, why don't you boys stay in tonight?"

"You *fell* in the canal?" Donnie asked, a look of concern on his face. One of the lateral irrigation canals ran underneath the highway and passed through the Kowalski farm, its still waters bringing life to crops many miles to the west. "Why don't you go change your clothes? You're dripping water all through here."

"I really would prefer it if you stayed home tonight, Donnie."

"Can't, Mom. The Camelots are having a meeting in town. I won't be back late. So long."

They got into the pickup truck and Donnie gunned the engine. They rolled out of the barn, leaving Mrs. Kowalski staring after them, the tray of lemonade still in her hands.

"Your mom was sure acting weird," said Burt as they headed into town.

"Yeah," said Donnie, his eyes on the road ahead. "How she fell in the canal, I don't know. It's not like she's a drinker. My old man on the other hand, I could believe *he* fell in the canal, but not Mom."

The Camelot's clubhouse was a shack behind Nick's Auto Repair shop that was really part of the junkyard but Nick, having no use for it, had given to Johnny and his buddies to use. They had put a pool table in there and a couple of busted sofas. Some of the wrecked cars had been cleared to the side of the building to afford parking space for the gang's hot rods. When Donnie, Burt and Tommy got there, they found the place jammed with cars.

"Full house," said Burt as Donnie parked.

They got out and headed over to the entrance to the clubhouse where several Camelots were standing around smoking and shooting the bull. The only other person besides Tommy who wasn't wearing a satin jacket was a skinny, unhealthy-looking man with scruffy hair and a tatty shirt. He looked like a hobo but seemed to be on good terms with the gang who were horsing around with him.

Tommy was regarded with critical eyes as they joined the crowd at the door although no questions were asked. He knew most of them by sight and they didn't seem surprised to see him. The door to the clubhouse opened and a large gang member Tommy hadn't seen before emerged. He had a pug face and his hair was cropped into a flattop.

"All right, you bums, get inside. The meeting's about to start." He took one look at Tommy and added; "Who's the eyeballer?"

"His name's Tommy," said Donnie. "Johnny wants to take a look at him. He's okay."

"*Johnny* will decide if he's okay," the big man said. "I'm Mack, the club's vice president. Get yourselves inside. Not you, Archie!" This last was directed at the skinny hobo. "You know you're not allowed inside the clubhouse. Scram!"

"Mack," said the skinny man, "could you lend me a few bucks? I'm short and I need a hit tonight or I'm gonna go into breakdown mode."

"I already lent you some dough I haven't seen back yet," Mack said. "No more handouts til you pay what's owed."

"Please, Mack! I gotta score lined up, a real pretty one. I can pay you back what I owe plus interest. I just need you to help me out tonight!"

"Nothin' doin'. Now you best get gone before Johnny comes out here. You know he doesn't like you hanging around. Move it!"

With sagging shoulders, Archie slumped off.

"Archie's a hophead," Donnie explained to Tommy as they went inside. "He's always scrounging for dough to get his next fix. His old lady kicked him out a few weeks ago. He's on his ass."

The room was crowded and gang members piled onto the sofas while others leaned against the walls. A single easy chair at the head of the room remained vacant. A door to a backroom opened and Johnny Packer sauntered in followed by a smaller kid with a sour mug. Johnny sat down in the vacant chair while the kid perched on the edge of the pool table.

"All right," Johnny began, commanding instant silence from the room. "Before we get down to business, I understand Donnie here has an associate he wants to put forward for prospect."

Tommy swallowed as the entire room turned to look at him.

"This here is Tommy," Donnie said. "He's been helping me fix up my pickup. He's a good kid, good in a brawl too. You should have seem him lay into that punk Tyler Weston and his pals. We helped him out, of course, but he was doing pretty good."

"Tyler Weston?" Johnny asked. "I don't know him."

"He's a Junior," piped up Burt. "Has some classes with us. Thinks he's a tough guy 'cause his daddy's rich. He's a creep."

"All right," said Johnny, eyeing Tommy. "We need good brawlers in this club. We don't go asking for trouble, but we answer if it comes knocking. You got a rod?"

Tommy cleared his throat. "Uh, no, not at the moment. I had to sell my Coupster when we moved here from Virginia. I'm just trying to get the dough together to buy something." It was the same lie he had fed Donnie and Burt on the day they had met outside old man Johnson's office. He had to run with it.

"Coupster, huh? You race it?"

"Sometimes."

"You good?"

"I do okay."

"Well, we're an automobile club and we need members who are better than 'okay'. We're gonna test you out sometime but we have more pressing concerns at present. Stick around and learn from Donnie. He was only a prospect for a month 'cause he's hip. He knows the score. All right, next item of business." He reached into the pocket of his jacket and pulled out what looked like a photograph. "I have here a pornographic picture of a girl."

There were wolf whistles around the room and pleas for him to pass the picture around.

"Can it!" Johnny thundered. "This ain't no regular broad. This here is Chuck's sister."

A silence fell over the room that was deafeningly uncomfortable. Several pairs of eyes flitted to the kid sitting on the edge of the pool table. Tommy guessed that was Chuck.

"Now, as we all know, Chuck's sister ain't got great taste in men, running with one of the Jungle Dukes. She even let them dope her up on their junk but what we only just found out is that they're taking blue pictures of her and selling them for five bucks a stack."

There was angry grumbling at this. The Jungle Dukes, Tommy knew, were a rival gang that operated out of Stockton.

"This, my friends, we cannot abide," affirmed Johnny.

"Hell no!" somebody cried.

"Chuck here has to live with the knowledge that his sister is being used like a cheap whore!" said Johnny. "And his folks don't even know where their little girl is."

"A rumble!" somebody shouted.

"Snatch her back!" said somebody else.

"Nah, they're being too careful for that," said Johnny. "If we blaze into Stockton and start cracking skulls, we're just gonna end up in jail and still not know where Marie is. They've got her someplace and we need to use our heads. Now, I've been using our connections in Stockton and the words I'm hearing have something to do with an abandoned farmhouse out by Del Rio way. But I want to know if she's there before we storm the place. Donnie?"

"Yes, Boss?"

"I want you and Burt to handle this. Take the new fish with you, make sure he pulls his weight. Find out if Marie is there and report back to me without being spotted. This is a plainclothes job. Lose the jackets once you're on the road."

"Sure, Boss!" Donnie batted Tommy on the chest and whispered to him; "First job, Prospect! We gotta pull this off with no hitches."

Once the meeting was over, the gang dispersed out into the yard. A beer keg was opened and plastic cups were filled and passed around. Tommy found one being pushed into his hand.

"Bottoms up, Prospect!" said Donnie with a wink.

Tommy shrugged and took a gulp. He wasn't used to beer but he felt like he could get used to it pretty quick.

Several girls appeared. Apparently they had been confined to the back room while the meeting was going on. A record player was brought out and Bill Haley & His Comets lit up the scrapyard to much acclaim. The gang was buzzing and many oaths were sworn against the Jungle Dukes.

"Man, when we bust Marie Giorgino out, those Dukes won't know what hit 'em!" said Burt, pounding his fist into his palm.

"You leave the tough stuff for the big boys," said Mack, lounging against the door of his black '55 Chevy, his arm around a girl. "Your job is to confirm that she's there. Johnny gives the say so on when we move."

"I know, I know," said Burt. "They just make me mad, y'know?"

"Who can blame you?" said another gang member. "Those punks have had it coming for a while now. Johnny's mad as hell at how they've been pushing their junk here in Ralston. This is our turf and we don't deal hop! And now this business with Chuck's sister!"

"They'll get what's theirs," said Johnny, sauntering over. He was smoking a large cigarette that smelled sickly sweet. Tommy had the idea that it wasn't tobacco.

Thunder rumbled overhead. Spots of rain pattered down on the roofs and hoods of the cars, splashing into the dry dirt, turning it muddy.

"Ah, shit!" said Mack. "C'mon, let's take this party indoors!"

As everybody hustled in, carrying the keg and record player with them, Donnie slapped Tommy on the shoulder. "Drink up. We'd better hit the road."

"We're not staying for the party?"

"Trust me, these parties carry on late and get wilder by the hour. Another time. We gotta head out early tomorrow and find this broad."

"Yeah, if we screw this up, Johnny will kill us," said Burt.

They piled into Donnie's pickup and hit the road.

CHAPTER 8

Claire and Fred spent the whole of Saturday morning searching the reservoir for the fossils. With the sun beating down on its crystal waters, they found themselves much more optimistic as they probed the sandy bottom of the shallows, their pantlegs rolled up to their knees as if they were children fishing for crabs. Some families were picnicking on the grass further down and out on the water, kids in motorboats zipped back and forth. They stuck to the shallows, combing every square inch of sand for twenty yards on either side of the meteorite but with no luck.

"If they've rolled deeper then we've no chance of retrieving them without a diver," said Fred. "And then there'll be all sorts of questions to which we don't have any good answers."

"I know," said Claire. "I just don't see how they could have vanished like that." She became aware of a man making his way towards them. He wore a sun hat and carried a large amount of equipment including a cooler box slung around his neck.

"Found anything interesting?" the man called out to them. "I can tell you're looking for something because I am too. Beautiful day for it."

When Claire and Fred were slow in responding, the man thrust out his hand in greeting. "Andy Willard. I'm a marine biologist."

"What's a marine biologist doing at a reservoir?" Fred asked, shaking Andy's hand.

"Well, that's the real question sure enough, and one that I keep asking myself. You see, I'm looking for something rather special and I don't even know if I'll find it here. Last week, a farmer found something down in the irrigation canals that run through his land. Something that has no business in fresh water. At first, he thought it was a ...” he faltered a little here and the color rose on his neck, “well, a *condom*, begging your pardon, ma'am. A friend told him it was an egg casing but bigger than what you would get from carp, catfish, or bluegill. He asked around and a mutual friend put him in contact with me. I asked him to send it to me. I haven't been able to identify it, but it seems to be some undiscovered subspecies of freshwater cephalopod.”

“Cephalopod?” Fred asked. “You mean squids and octopuses and such?”

“Exactly. Only, all cephalopods are saltwater creatures. They don't have sodium pumps to help them cope with osmotic change in freshwater. If there really is some new species of cephalopod in Ralston's irrigation canals, then it will be a landmark discovery! I figured that if it got into the irrigation canals, then it probably came from the reservoir.”

Claire and Fred looked at each other uneasily and then, entirely involuntarily, back at the broken meteorite. Andy followed their gaze, then regarded them curiously.

“You didn't say what you two were looking for, but I'm guessing it's not cephalopods,” he said.

“No,” Claire said, forcing a small laugh. “We're meteoriticists. We're looking for any fragments that may have broken off the meteorite.”

“Say, this town's become quite a sensation. They're still talking about this old hunk of rock in San Fran. At least I can see that it's no downed Soviet satellite.”

“No,” said Claire. “But tell me more about this egg casing. You said it was large.”

“About four inches across and believe me, that's big! The eggs of the giant Pacific octopus are only millimeters long upon hatching. Whatever came out of that thing will be a big sonofabitch.”

"Could something that size survive in the irrigation system?"

"Well, there's plenty of fish in the canals and now that irrigation season has started, the waterways are full of spring melt from the Tuolumne River meaning that there's enough depth for it to conceal itself. But something that big can't stay unnoticed forever. I'm guessing it's a newcomer. I don't know where it came from but it sure isn't native to the Ralston Irrigation District!"

They said goodbye and left the man to his tests. Neither spoke as they headed back to Claire's car and only once they were both seated, their damp calves drying against the vinyl seats, did they break their silence.

"What do you think, Claire," said Fred. "Is it possible?"

"That the eggs we're looking for, the eggs from the meteorite, aren't fossils at all but actual eggs containing lifeforms? I don't know what to think, Fred."

"Hell of a coincidence otherwise. Fossilized extraterrestrial life *and* a new species of squid in the same month? That Andy character was right, this town is quite the sensation."

Claire looked out of the window at swimmers and picnickers returning to their cars wearing the big smiles of those who have enjoyed their day in the sun. It *couldn't* be possible.

"Let's just theorize for a minute here," said Fred. "If some alien species wanted to send its eggs to a distant planet, what better way than to conceal them within a meteorite that would protect them from the intense heat of entry."

"Listen to yourself, Fred," said Claire. "You're suggesting an alien species that is too primitive to devise space travel is somehow able to bury its eggs inside a rock and send it across the galaxy. It's absurd! No, the eggs had to have been laid thousands of years ago, millennia even, and then, whatever planet they called home was destroyed and a piece of it was sent hurtling through the freezing depths of space, to land here, countless eons later."

"And then the eggs hatched."

"We don't know that."

"Exactly. We don't know anything about this species such as how long its incubation period is. I've heard that octopuses guard their eggs for several years before they hatch. Our marine biologist friend could tell us more about that, I'm sure."

"Are you suggesting we talk to him, let him in on this?"

"As crazy as it sounds, I think we might be looking for the same thing. This is getting too big for us anyway. We might not be looking for eggs anymore."

The thought both thrilled and frightened Claire. "All right. Let's go back and talk to him."

They found him in the parking area, packing his gear into a beat-up old RV. He seemed surprised to see them.

"Mr. Willard," said Claire, "I wonder if we might take a look at the egg casing, if you still have it."

"Sure I have it," said Andy. "Although I don't know what interest it has for a couple of stargazers but you're welcome to come in and take a look. You'll have to excuse the mess."

"You have it here, in your RV?" Fred asked incredulously.

"Yep. This old baby is my home and lab in one. Where I go, it goes." He clambered up the short stepladder and beckoned them to follow him.

Claire and Fred did so and found themselves in a small kitchenette that held more scientific instruments than culinary mod-cons. Looking down the birch-paneled length of the vehicle, they saw a sleeping quarter at the rear with a bunk strewn with discarded clothes. The other end of the RV, past the kitchen and tiny bathroom, was entirely taken up with a miniature laboratory complete with water tanks, microscopes, racks of bottles and beakers and even a small library.

"Wow, you really are all set here," said Fred in admiration.

"Beats having a mortgage," Andy replied with a grin. "And I can go wherever I need to at short notice. Take a seat, please. I'll put some coffee on."

As Claire and Fred sat down at the folding table, Andy began rummaging around the kitchenette and soon had a pot of coffee on the boil. He then beckoned them into the lab portion of his home, and they followed him into the fluorescent-lit fore of the RV.

Andy opened the lid of a refrigerated box and drew out a glass bottle containing something immersed in liquid. He placed it on the inspection bench and popped the overhead lamp on. The three of them leant forward to examine the preserved egg casing.

"Mr. Willard," said Claire. "What would you say if we told you that whatever species hatched from this egg came not from earth, but from somewhere else?"

Andy chuckled. "What, like outer space?"

Claire and Fred said nothing.

"Jesus, you two aren't kidding? I thought that was one of your meteoriticist jokes."

"We weren't completely honest with you earlier," Claire admitted. "We weren't looking for broken fragments from the meteorite. We were looking for the fossilized remains of what we believed were eggs trapped inside the rock. Now, in the light of your suspicions, we are beginning to think they weren't fossilized at all but ..."

"Dormant," Andy finished for her.

"I'm given to believe that the incubation period of some cephalopods is extraordinarily long," said Fred.

"That's true," said Andy. "A female octopus gives birth only once in her lifetime. She guards her eggs until they hatch which can take months or even years depending on the species. I read about one deep sea octopus that guarded her nest for four years."

"Four years?" Claire exclaimed.

Andy nodded. "The mother dies once the eggs hatch. She doesn't eat, you see, and eventually starves to death. She only survives long enough due to her slow metabolic rate and the cold temperature of the deep. It's kind of like hibernation."

"And in the coldness of space," Fred mused, as he gazed at the thing in the jar, "who knows how long the mother of this thing might have hung on to her nest. Or how long her eggs have lain dormant, in frozen incubation as they travelled through space, waiting for just the right planet with just the right conditions."

Andy was watching Fred talk, breathless with excitement. "I would very much like to take a look at this meteorite," he said.

Leaving their coffee, they took him to see the meteorite and showed him the circular depressions which exactly matched the dimensions of the egg case.

"Looks like there were about twenty or so eggs in here," said Andy, stooping down to peer into the meteorite's cavity. "And they all dropped out into the water."

"Meaning there could be more than one of these creatures out there," said Claire.

"Not necessarily. The eggs of some species have only a one percent survival rate. The hatching and survival of just one of these creatures in an alien world with a different temperature, atmospheric pressure not to mention an unfamiliar diet is nothing short of a biological miracle."

They went back to the RV and, finding their coffee cold, decided to head into town and stop at a diner. As they had their pie and coffee, they discussed some theories and what they were going to do next.

"Who on earth can we go to with this?" said Fred. "We might be meteoriticists but this is a little out of our line of work."

"The military perhaps?" said Andy.

"Perhaps. But would they believe us? And once word gets out that we made a call about an alien in Ralston, we'll have every reporter and journalist in the country descending on the town looking for aliens in its canals."

"Agreed," said Claire. "People would be out hunting for it. It would be finders keepers and the thing would probably be shot by some overzealous farmer before we get a chance to study its behavior. No, we must keep a lid on this for the time being until we know what we are dealing with. Then we can think about making headlines."

Claire went home and had dinner with Ray and Judy. Tommy was with his friends on some farm out on the town's outskirts. Judy had a date that night. She was glad Judy and Tommy seemed to be making something of a social life for themselves, even if Ray had his concerns about the crowd Tommy was hanging out with. It was Judy's first date since the move and Claire couldn't be happier for her.

Once Ray's meatloaf had been eaten and Judy had vanished upstairs to get ready, Claire and Ray sat in the kitchen and drank their coffee while Rose sat in her highchair and played with what was left of her carrots.

"Ray," Claire said, "I need to discuss something with you, and I need it to remain between us. Not that it's a big secret or anything but I just don't know how to keep quiet about what I've learned today without my head exploding."

"What is it, Honey?"

"You know those fossilized eggs from the meteorite Fred and I have been looking for?"

Ray nodded.

"Well, today we met a marine biologist who has a broken egg casing that matches the depressions in the rock. He thinks it's from some kind of cephalopod." At Ray's blank stare, she elaborated; "Like an octopus or a squid."

"I know what a cephalopod is, Claire. You're not the only person in this house with a college degree. I was just trying to make the connection. This marine biologist thinks that this egg casing is one of the fossils from your meteorite?"

"They may not have been fossils."

"Eggs then. Eggs with life inside them? In a meteorite?"

"I know it sounds crazy, but Fred and I believe it to be true."

"But, Honey, alien life on a meteorite? Is that even possible?"

"Possible, certainly, although not many in my field would be prepared to believe it."

"But absence of evidence isn't evidence of absence you figure."

"It's more than that. I'm not just talking about fossils or bacteria or microorganisms, not *traces* of life but *life itself*, in the form of eggs, and we believe one of them has hatched here in Ralston."

Ray set down his coffee cup slowly. "Are you talking about an actual alien hatching from an egg?"

"Yes. Either in the reservoir or the egg passed through the dam and hatched in the irrigation system. We have reason to believe that it's out there, roaming the canals. Ray, if we could capture this thing, well ..., I don't have to tell you what that would mean."

"Fame and fortune aside," Ray said calmly, "is this thing dangerous?"

"We have no idea. It must be incredibly resilient, whatever it is."

"Don't you think people should be warned? It might be crawling with foreign bacteria."

"I know but we can't cause a huge panic over this. It might all be a wild goose chase or a hoax or something."

Ray regarded her quizzically. "Do you think it might be?"

"No. I'm telling you this because I'm at a bit of a loss as to exactly what I should be doing." She set her coffee cup down a little too hard and spilled some. Then she drew a cigarette out and lit it with shaky hands. She was emotional and exhausted.

Ray sighed and got up. He walked around the table and stood behind her, his hands massaging her tired neck and shoulders. "I don't know much about aliens, but I do know you and this is what you're going to do. You're going to put Rose to bed while I clear up and then I'm going to mix up a couple of Tom Collinses and we're going to drink them out in the yard and look at the stars – not talk *about* the stars, mind you, just look at them – until Judy's date picks her up at nine. Then we're going to go up to bed and take advantage of a nearly empty house."

Claire smiled and held the hands that massaged her neck and kissed them. "Thank you for being such a rock, darling."

If Judy had been nervous at meeting Connie and her friends, then she was doubly so at going on a date with Martin. She hardly ate a bite of dinner and then spent at least an hour in front of her mirror making sure her hair and makeup were just right. As nine o'clock approached, she sat in the living room half watching *Country Music Jubilee* while Dad pottered around in the kitchen, cleaning up after dinner. Mom was putting Rose to bed and Tommy was out with his greaser buddies fixing up some old heap in a garage somewhere.

When the doorbell rang, nine o'clock on the dot, she nearly leapt out of her skin. Dad invited Martin in, of course, and Judy cringed as they made small talk and a promise was exacted from Martin that he would have her home by midnight. Then, leaving Dad on the doorstep, they headed out for the evening in Martin's '55 Ford Customline.

They ate at a quiet hamburger stand on the edge of the city before heading out for a moonlit drive. Martin knew a spot by the reservoir where they could look at the stars. He was acting the perfect gentleman and Judy wasn't worried that he'd so much as put his arm around her.

They parked up beneath the trees and watched the moonlight play on the still water. Martin flipped on the radio. Tab Hunter's *Young Love* was playing, and it set the mood beautifully. They talked about school and their folks. Judy mentioned that she was fast becoming friends with Connie Lund. Martin frowned at this.

"That doesn't seem like your kind of crowd," he said.

"Why on earth not?" she demanded, feeling a small sting of insult.

"I don't know. Connie Lund ..."

"She's asked me to be on the prom committee."

"Just be careful, Judy."

"Why should I be careful?"

"I just have the feeling that she's bad news."

"You don't even know her," Judy replied sniffily.

"All right, I'm sorry. Let's change the subject."

"Yes, let's."

"So, prom, huh?"

"Yeah ..."

"*Senior* prom. The biggie."

"Yeah."

They were close now, their shoulders nearly bridging the gap between the seats. He had his head turned towards hers and the space between their lips seemed both close and yet devastatingly far at the same time. She searched his blue eyes and saw that they were flecked with gold motes.

"Judy?" he asked.

"Yes, Martin?"

Young Love faded out and the jockey's howling voice filled the car with his horseplay, ruining the moment. Martin turned away from Judy and fiddled with the volume. He checked his watch. "Wow! We should be heading back. I don't want to drop you off late or your pop will never let me take you out next time. Uh, that is, if you want there to be a next time?"

Judy smiled. "Yes, I'd like that." *Next time he might actually kiss me.*

As they drove back towards Ralston, the Ford's headlights sweeping along the graceful curves of the highway as it followed the river, Judy felt herself mellow into a warm, comforting feeling of security. Martin was a swell guy and she felt completely safe in his company. And he was smart, handsome and charming. The full package! Pretty soon she could see herself going steady with him ...

"Martin, look out!" she felt the cry escape her lips almost before she registered the danger on the road. A man had lurched out of the trees that screened the river and ran out onto the road, his face as pale as his shirt in the headlights. He hailed them, waving frantically as he stood in the path of the oncoming car, refusing to budge an inch.

Martin slammed on the brakes and the tires screeched. He steered left to dodge the crazed man, the sudden movement making the hamburger and cherry coke in Judy's stomach lurch sickeningly. The car threatened to flip but Martin held it steady, spinning the wheel to the right again as the tires rumbled across rough ground. He veered back onto the asphalt and pulled the car to a stop by some bushes.

"My God, we nearly killed him!" Judy exclaimed.

"Crazy fool!" Martin hissed as he opened his door and got out.

Judy remained in her seat and peered over her shoulder as Martin approached the man who was clearly terrified. She realized it wasn't a man at all, but a kid, not much older than they were. She didn't recognize him from school. Perhaps he came from Stockton or Turlock. Through the open door, she could hear snippets of their conversation.

"Please!" the boy begged. "You gotta help me get away! It's coming for me!"

"Take it easy, pal," Martin said. "What's coming for you?"

"A ... an awful thing, it's chased me every step of the way! We must go! Take me to Ralston, please! I need to be around light and people! I've been running all night, hiding in bushes and ditches but it'll find me! We're not safe here!"

Judy felt a rising panic, not at whatever the kid was so desperately afraid of, but at the notion that they had been pulled off the road by a disturbed and potentially dangerous maniac. She got out of the car. "Martin, let's go!" she called.

Martin waved a hand to acknowledge her, but he was insistent on persevering with the crazed boy. "*What's been chasing you?*" he asked him.

The whites of the kid's eyes were livid in the darkness. "One moment it seems far off, the next moment I can feel it breathing down my neck! I can hear its footsteps, always, can't you?"

Judy hugged herself despite the warm night air and glanced around at the moonlit fields that surrounded them on all sides. Long grass wavered in the breeze.

"But what *is* it?" Martin demanded.

The man glanced fearfully over his shoulder as if the thing were creeping up on them even as they spoke. "A thing made of shadow and its eyes! Oh, God, its eyes!"

Martin and Judy followed his gaze and, sure enough, there was some movement out there in the dark fields. The beams of torches wavered about in the distance and several dark figures could be seen moving through the crops. The lights wavered in their direction and suddenly froze. Judy knew that whoever was out there, they could see them. *A single car on a lonely highway.*

"Oh, God!" the man exclaimed. "It's found me! We have to go! Please!"

"All right," Martin said. "Let's get out of here. Get in the back seat. We'll take you into Ralston."

"Martin!" Judy hissed as he approached the car with their new passenger. "What if he's dangerous?"

"He's frightened out of his mind, is what he is," Martin replied. "Whatever trouble he's mixed up in, I can't leave him out here in the middle of nowhere. We'll take him directly to the police station. They'll figure this whole thing out."

Judy felt helpless and cursed Martin's good nature which she had so cherished earlier in the evening. But it was his car and therefore his call. She got back in and the terrified man scrambled into the back seat. Martin slammed his door shut and turned the ignition. Soon they were speeding towards the distant lights of Ralston.

They drove straight to the police station and ex-plained the situation to the sheriff. The boy, who revealed his name to be Frank Cherkovski, became even more er-ratic upon questioning, constantly looking towards the door and the street outside.

"Now listen, Mr. Cherkovski," Sheriff Benson said pa-tiently. "I can't help you if you don't tell me who's after you and why. You're perfectly safe here, believe me."

"Oh, I wish I could believe you," Frank Cherkovski said. "But the truth is that I don't know what to believe anymore. What's real and what's dream? What's night-mare?"

"He said something about something following him," Martin said. "But all we saw were some people out there with torches like they were looking for him."

"Why were they looking for you, Frank?" the sheriff asked.

"Oh, my colleagues," Frank replied. "They don't like that I left them. They want me to be part of it and I won't! I won't!"

"Won't what? And who are these colleagues of yours?"

Frank seemed about to say something but was sud-denly overcome by an even worse bout of terror than he had displayed so far. He threw himself on the ground and tried to crawl behind a potted plant, covering his head with his hands and all the while screaming; "It's here! It's found me! I knew it would come! Oh, God, please don't let it get me!"

Judy and Martin stood back, appalled at the display. The kid was clearly mad and Judy's stomach churned to think of what might have happened had this fit come over him while he had been in the back seat of the car.

Sheriff Benson summoned two officers and they hauled the wretch away to a cell.

"Can't let a mad dog like him run around town in the middle of the night," he said as the screams echoed down the hall. "I'll send for the doc. He knows a psychiatrist but we probably can't get him down here until morning."

"Sheriff, we'd better get going," said Martin. "I'm supposed to have Judy home by midnight."

They glanced at the clock. It was a quarter past twelve and Judy groaned.

"Now, you kids don't worry," said Sheriff Benson. "This was police business and I'm grateful for your help tonight. Give the young lady's folks a call from my office and then get going. If either of you catch it for being late, you just tell Mom and Pop to come talk to me."

"That's very good of you, Sheriff," said Martin. "Thank you."

They stepped out of the station and saw that it was raining hard. Thunder rumbled in the distance. They ran to Martin's car and he opened the door for Judy. "Boy, what a night," he said as he got in on his side, running his hands through his soaking hair. "I hope this date hasn't been ruined for you?"

"No," said Judy. "I had a lovely time, bar the last hour and then this thunderstorm. But I'd really like to get home now. That whole business back there gave me the creeps."

The truck stop was a neon oasis in the rain-streaked night. Trucks thundered past, sending up curling waves of water from the long, deep puddle that seeped across the edge of the highway. Mark Harris stood under the overhang of the service station, sheltered from the downpour, and watched customers come and go from the small, greasy diner. He glanced at the payphone on the wall of the service station. He could call Mom and Dad.

Just let them know he was all right. He had some quarters in his pocket. Just one call to put their minds at ease ...

No. They'd only try to come pick him up and he couldn't have that. It was best that he was long gone before they realized he was missing. He could call them from wherever he ended up and tell them he was sorry for running away.

The truck stop was about five miles south of Ralston. The kind man who had given him a lift had offered to take him all the way to Turlock but Mark knew that his best bet at getting a long-distance ride was with the truckers. He didn't care where he went as long as it was far away from Ralston.

It wanted his parents, he knew that much. Well, he wasn't going to let it have them. The fact that he had no idea what *it* was exactly, was beside the point. He didn't even remember how he had come under its power. It was like something half-remembered, in a dream or something. He remembered something about ... *water*?

Another truck splashed through the puddle, sending a mini tidal wave crashing across the concrete base of the truck stop's tall neon sign. Mark's thoughts drifted away along with the receding wash of dirty, oily water, bubbles vanishing as they popped soundlessly.

Mark shuddered as another one of his turns gripped his body. They had become more frequent now, worsening with every step he took away from Ralston. He knew now that he couldn't run from it. It wasn't Ralston that was the problem; the problem was in him. *Inside* of him. He had to flee so his parents would be safe.

That awful, itching, crawling sensation rippled through his flesh like the very worst case of goosepimples ever. But he knew it wasn't goosepimples. He looked down at his arm, rolling the sleeve of his jacket back to gaze upon the naked flesh. There, slight at first, but

increasing the longer he looked at it, came the small bubbles.

The skin rose and fell as several small objects moved
about beneath it, forcing their way up and down his arm.
He could feel it happening all over his body. It tickled. It
itched and it made him feel violently sick.

Bugs. He knew it was bugs moving about underneath
his skin. But how could that be possible? It had to be a
trick of his mind, a trick intended to make him stay, keep
him in Ralston, make sure his parents also became, like
him, a slave.

That was how it felt. *A slave.* That thing, whatever it
was, needed slaves and lots of them. Well, Mark decided,
his parents sure as hell weren't going to become its slaves.
For over a day now, a little voice in the back of his mind
had been telling him to take his parents to the water so
that they could be converted as he had been. And every
hour it got harder and harder to resist. Mark was determined to stay strong, to defy it to the end. He loved his
folks and he'd rather die than let any harm come to them.

That was when the hallucinations had started. The
bugs crawling under his skin. It had been a small sensation at first, a mild tickle. But when he actually began to
see them moving about along his arms and legs, he knew
he had to get away. If it meant running away, so be it, for
he knew that it would only get worse and he couldn't
fight it forever.

The door to the diner swung open and a trucker
emerged, zipping up his jacket and adjusting the cap on
his head.

"Hey, mister," Mark said. "You heading south?"

The trucker looked him up and down, taking in his
small backpack and tired, downtrodden appearance.
"Sure am. You heading anywhere in particular?"

"No, just away from here."

The trucker smirked. "Running away from your folks, huh? Well, I did the same when I was your age. Ran away and didn't look back. Sure, I'll give you a lift. I'm heading for San Bernadino myself. You're welcome to ride with me. C'mon, follow me."

Mark pulled his jacket up over his head and gratefully followed the man out into the rain. They headed towards a powder blue cab hauling an unmarked silver trailer. Mark clambered up into the passenger's seat. The trucker started the engine, flipped on the radio and soon they were rumbling out onto the highway and pushing through the night, windscreen wipers battling against the rain.

"So, you finally got sick of your folks, huh?" the trucker said. "I know how it is. My pop was a bastard of a drunk and I couldn't get out of there quick enough. The open road is the only home for free spirits."

Mark said nothing as he gazed out the window at the trucks and cars flitting past in the opposite direction, heading towards Ralston. *Keep driving*, folks, he thought. *Keep driving and don't stop.*

He felt the crawling sensation all over his skin again. *Stop! Please stop!* He didn't want to freak out now, not now he'd scored a ride all the way to San Bernadino. If he could just keep it together for a few more hours …

It didn't go away. The itching, crawling sensation was relentless as if it was trying to drive him madder and madder the farther he drifted from Ralston. *It wants me to go back, but I mustn't!*

They plunged on into the night. The itching and scrabbling got worse and worse. Eventually, Mark couldn't help himself. He rolled up his jacket sleeve to inspect a particular spot of activity on his left forearm. There was a bulge there, almost the size of an egg that stretched the skin painfully tight. It moved and seemed to push itself upwards. The agony was excruciating.

The skin split and the black head of a large beetle emerged, wet and shiny with blood. It clicked its pincers together and used its stubby little legs to pull itself out of the wound. Mark screamed.

The trucker glanced suddenly at him, startled by his outburst. "Something up with your arm, Pal?"

He can't see it! Mark realized as he looked down at the beetle scuttling along his arm, dragging a tendril of loose flesh from the hole it had ripped open. He could feel more swellings rising like beestings all over his body. The pain was agonizing as, one by one, they began to burst and release their vile occupants. Mark writhed and squirmed in his seat, feeling warm patches of blood seep through his clothes.

The alarmed trucker had begun to slow down, probably thinking his passenger was having some sort of heart attack. Mark couldn't take it anymore and flung the passenger's door open.

He tumbled down onto the slick asphalt. He could hear the trucker's cries of warning as he got to his feet and began to run across the highway. He had no thought in his mind except the primal desire to flee, to outrun that which could not be outrun.

He didn't realize the danger until he was fully bathed in its light. A horn blared somewhere in the distance. He turned to face the light which was growing steadily closer through the pounding rain and suddenly comprehended. He was glad when the truck slammed into him; ten tons of steel and its cargo wiping him off the road and out of existence, ending his pain forever.

Chapter 9

Donnie, Burt and Tommy headed out of town on Sunday morning in the pickup truck, dressed in jeans and tee-shirts. The sky was clear after the previous night's thunderstorm and the hot sun made the heat waver above the road.

The farmhouse Johnny had directed them to was a derelict old place next to a tangled orchard a little off the road that led north to Del Rio. It had been white once, but its paint was peeling, leaving its boards a pale grey. They drove the truck into the orchard where it would be hidden from view and approached the house on foot.

Several tumbledown outbuildings surrounded the main house and the rusted hulk of an old Ford truck stood like an island amid the weeds on its southern side. Donnie, Burt and Tommy crept over to it and squatted behind its rear fender to get a good look at the layout of the place. In the shade of the porch that faced the road, they could see the dim outline of two figures sitting at a table playing cards, cigarette smoke in a fug above their heads.

"They look like they're wearing jackets to you?" Donnie asked.

"Can't see from here," said Tommy

"We need to get closer," said Donnie. "Can't see shit from here."

"Let's go around the back way."

They kept low as they crept through the weeds, conscious of the black windows on the house's northern face that looked out over the fields for trespassers. Junk littered the yard at the rear of the house; rusted bed frames, old sofas and busted up furniture was piled all around, providing them with ample cover to make their way closer to the house.

Gunshots rang out and the three boys threw themselves flat on the ground. Whoops and yells could be heard in the orchard beyond. There was another gunshot followed by the smash of glass and another cry of satisfaction. Donnie poked his head up.

"Shit, they're just playing target practice."

"But those aren't air rifles they're playing with," said Tommy.

Three men were taking potshots at some improvised targets set up in the orchard. Their backs were to the house and the emblem on their jackets could be seen clearly; a tiger wearing a crown. The emblem of the Jungle Dukes.

"Well, Johnny's tip was at least half right," said Burt. "This is a Dukes hangout all right."

"But we need to make sure the girl is here," said Donnie. "One of us needs to sneak inside the house while the other two stand guard. Tommy, you go in."

"Me?" Tommy exclaimed. "Why me?"

"Because Johnny said to make sure you got your hands dirty. Think of it as an initiation test."

"And then can I join?"

"Not so fast. You wouldn't believe the stuff I had to do to become a Camelot. Go on, get going! Burt and I'll keep an eye on those trigger-happy boys in the orchard."

Tommy wasn't sure what help his two friends would be if those 'trigger-happy boys' should tire of their game and head back to the house when he was still inside it but there was nothing else to be done. He was *not* going to chicken out. If he did, then he could kiss his hopes of ever becoming a Camelot goodbye.

Still keeping low, he crept towards the house. The porch ran around the whole house and three warped steps let up to the screen door at the back which hung open. Willing the steps not to creak under his weight, Tommy made his way slowly up onto the porch and crouched by the open door. He could hear voices from within but had no way of telling how many were in the house. Peeping around the edge of the doorframe, he could see a dim hallway and some carpeted stairs. If that girl was here, she would probably be in an upstairs bedroom.

A doorway at the end of the hallway led to a kitchen where, silhouetted by the light from the windows on the other side, he could make out two figures; one sitting at the kitchen table, the other leaning against the counter, a beer bottle in his hand. There was no way he could sneak in and reach the staircase without one of them spotting him.

As he pondered this conundrum, he spotted a door at the foot of the stairs that led to some side room. If he could sneak in that way, he could get upstairs without being spotted from the kitchen. He crept around to the side of the house and found a glassless window looking in on what had once been a dining room. He rose and gingerly lifted his leg over the sill and climbed into the room. He made his way over to the door and slowly opened it.

In the hallway beyond, he could hear the voices of the two men in the kitchen. Leaving the door ajar for ease of escape, he crept into the hall and made for the stairs. It was only then, as he softly climbed the carpeted stairs that the madness of what he was doing sunk in. The realization that he had broken into a house infested with gun-toting gang members was almost enough to make him lose his nerve, but he had already crossed the threshold. He was on the landing and he might as well try and complete his mission before he bolted.

There were four rooms that faced the landing. One of them had no door and Tommy could see the wrecked bathroom beyond, light streaming in from its broken window. Two of the others were ajar and, by creeping across the landing, he was able to peep in. They were bare but for dirty mattresses on the floor, a few men's magazines and crushed beer cans were scattered between them and Tommy figured these were the crash pads of the Jungle Dukes currently guarding the girl.

But where was she?

There was one door left, this one closed. *Of course* it was closed. Tommy would have to open it, having no idea what was waiting for him on the other side. He put his ear to the door and listened hard.

Nothing.

He tried the door handle, slowly. It was unlocked. He opened the door a little and peered through the small gap. He could see a pair of bare legs on a dirty mattress. *Female* legs.

He opened the door wider. The room's sole occupant was a girl in a silk nightie slumbering soundly on the mattress. It was her all right. Johnny had shown them the pornographic photograph before they had set out and Tommy had tried not to ogle those creamy breasts, instead taking in the girl's tired-eyed face, storing it for future reference. There was no mistaking it. This was Marie Giorgino.

He briefly flirted with the idea of waking her and getting her downstairs, through the window and into Donnie's car. To sneak off with the girl under the Jungle Dukes' noses would be a coup that would surely see him initiated as a club member. But that was a hopeless idea. The girl was clearly hopped up. The joints in her elbows were bruised and dotted with needle pricks. Drug paraphernalia littered the floor next to the mattress; matches, a scorched teaspoon, a needle and tourniquet. There was no moving this girl.

He had done what he had come for and now it was time to get the hell out of there. He left the room, closing the door softly behind him, and made for the stairs. He froze at the top of them. There was movement from below. One of the thugs from the kitchen was in the hallway, heading for the stairs. Tommy backed away and looked around frantically. The stairs groaned under the man's heavy tread. He was trapped!

He made for one of the spare rooms and closed the door behind him. It wouldn't do. With one man upstairs and another downstairs, he didn't dare try to escape the way he'd come. There had to be another way.

He looked out the window. He was facing the orchard where the three guys were still working on their target practice. He looked down at the junk-strewn yard and could make out the top of Donnie's head. Directly below him was the shingled roof of the porch that circled the house. He tried the window. It was jammed but, with some shoving, he was able to unfreeze it and slide it open. Swinging his leg over, he climbed out and lowered himself down onto the shingled roof. He crouched, catlike, as the weathered old shingles bent and groaned under his weight.

Donnie and Burt had spotted him and rose from their hiding place, their faces shocked. Tommy eased himself towards the edge of the roof. A bush grew on the corner of the porch and he dived into it, rolling as it enveloped him and then spat him out in a shower of leaves and twigs. Then he was up on his feet and running towards his friends.

"That was a hell of a chance you took!" hissed Burt.

"I had no choice!" said Tommy. "One of those cats came upstairs."

"She there?" Donnie asked.

"She's there. They keep her in a back bedroom, out of her skull on hop."

"Okay, nice work. C'mon, we gotta get back into town and tell Johnny."

They crept away from the house and its surrounding wreckage, keeping as low as they could. The last thing they needed was to get spotted now and end up with a bullet in their backs for their troubles. As soon as they judged the distance safe enough, they were up and running like jackrabbits towards Donnie's pickup truck.

Ray and Claire's romantic Saturday night had been spoiled somewhat when Judy didn't make it home by midnight. Ray instantly found himself on the offensive, uttering his previously unspoken suspicions that this Martin Landers was no good. Claire saw through his sham and pointed out that the kid had seemed all right, polite, well-spoken. Maybe they had had a blow-out? Or, God forbid, an accident in this atrocious downpour?

Claire was right, of course and, after he had realized this, Ray felt ashamed of his rush to place the blame on Martin. It was this town that gave him such knee-jerk reactions. Oh, it was a nice enough place but pleasant facades could hide dark secrets. Who knew what went on in the mind of a nice-looking kid like Martin? They had spoken to him for all of five minutes. He could be a maniac or a pervert or something like that. And as for the rest of the town with its greaser gangs and hot rodders, well, Tommy was already gravitating towards them. When you let your kids out into the night, you just didn't know what sort of people they might run into.

It was a quarter past midnight when Judy phoned, from the police station, no less, the very mention of which had them in a flap. But, Judy insisted, nothing was wrong and Martin was going to drive her home right away.

When she got home, they had the whole story from her. Martin, Ray agreed, had acted admirably but the thought of their daughter in the company of a deranged drifter who might have done anything to them on that lonely stretch of highway, put the frights on him. Madness was something you couldn't account for or predict. He found himself thinking of Nick Short's wife and her imaginary son again.

He had been thinking about poor Nick's situation a lot recently. Perhaps that was why he was so quick to suspect everybody of being up to no good. Although Claire and the kids seemed content enough here in Ralston, he just couldn't get over the feeling that there was something wrong with this town, something rotten at its core, and he hated himself for being such a pessimist.

His mood wasn't improved by the events of the following Monday. He and Rose drove over to the hardware store to pick up some guttering to replace a section that had been damaged during the storm on Saturday night. He left the store with the guttering under one arm, his other hand holding Rose's.

He had parked his car by the entrance to a narrow alley between the hardware store and an Italian restaurant. As he popped the trunk and tossed the guttering in, he caught sight of somebody rummaging through the garbage cans in the alleyway. *Strange*, he thought. You didn't often see hobos in Ralston. The person was young, just a kid and, as he turned his face towards them, Ray suddenly recognized him. It was Donnie somebody or other. One of the greaser kids Tommy had become chums with.

Now why would a high school kid be rummaging through garbage cans like a hobo? He decided to approach Donnie and find out what was the matter. It felt a strange decision on his part and later he put it down to his intentions of being better at giving this town and its residents the benefit of the doubt. Donnie seemed to be a tough kid but the sight of him with his hand in the garbage, looking for a scrap to eat, tugged at Ray's conscience.

"You all right, Kid?" Ray called out as he and Rose entered the alley. "Donnie isn't it? You hungry?"

"Leave me alone!" Donnie hissed back, his eyes livid, not with aggression, but a deathly fear that gripped his whole body, making it shake erratically as he backed off.

"Just trying to help you out, Donnie," Ray said. "Are you out on the streets? Trouble with your folks?"

"I said leave me alone, dammit! You can't help me! Nobody can and if you don't want to get hurt, then you'd better stay out of my way!"

"Now, listen here, Buster," said Ray, feeling his anger rising. "That's no way to talk."

There was something bestial about Donnie's mannerisms, like he was regressing to a more primitive form. Or, that he was battling something deep within himself. The confrontation proved too much for the kid and he bolted from the alley, nearly knocking Ray and Rose over as he passed them on his way out onto the road.

"Wait! Stop!" Ray yelled but it was too late. Tires screeched and he heard a sickening thud as the delivery truck slammed into Donnie, knocking him down. It had only clipped him, but the force of it sent the boy rolling across the asphalt.

Somewhere a woman screamed. People all around froze. Ray tugged Rose along as he hurried to the boy's side. The delivery man was climbing down from his cab, face as white as a sheet.

"I didn't see him!" he cried. "Crazy kid came running out of nowhere!"

"It wasn't your fault," Ray said, kneeling at Donnie's side, checking for a pulse. Rose watched with saucer eyes, her lollipop clutched in her hand, forgotten for the time being. "He's alive," Ray confirmed.

"Somebody call an ambulance!" the driver said.

Donnie murmured something and his eyes fluttered open. He tried to sit up.

"Take it easy, son," said Ray. "You've had a lucky break. You could have been flattened."

"I ... I'm okay," Donnie said in a weak voice. Blood trickled from a scrape on his forehead where he had hit the asphalt but otherwise he seemed to be in once piece.

"Well, let me take you to the doctor anyway," said Ray. "You need to be looked over."

"No! I gotta get away! You people aren't safe around me! I don't want anyone to get hurt!"

"Easy!" Ray said, but the kid was getting up. He was in some desperate hurry and Ray wondered what trouble he was in. "You might have a concussion. Have a sit down."

Donnie didn't resist as Ray helped him over to his car. He eased him into the passenger seat and then saw to Rose. He got in the car, started the engine and left the crowd of gawkers standing on the curb as he made his way to the police station.

"You're handing me in?" Donnie asked, sensing where they were going.

"If you won't let me take you to the doctor, then at least I can take you to the police who'll bring the doctor to you. I don't know what trouble you're in, kid, but you need help."

"The police station ..." Donnie murmured. "Yeah, that might not be such a bad idea."

Having no clue what he meant by that, Ray took him in and informed the desk sergeant of what had happened.

"Where's your gang jacket, Donnie?" the sergeant said. "I thought you guys had to wear them at all times. Like a gang rule."

"I tossed it," Donnie admitted. "I ain't in no gang no more. I can't be around people."

"So you ran away, is that it?" the sergeant said.

"Yes. But you can't make me go back to my folks. They're not ... not right!"

"What did they do?"

"I ... I can't tell you. But something's wrong with them. And something's wrong with me too!"

"What's wrong?"

"It wants me to ... get more people ..."

Ray frowned as some sort of physical change seemed to come over Donnie. He was sweating profusely and his body jerked as if wracked by spasms. It was as if he was trying to get the words out but something was stopping him.

"More people? What for?"

"I can't tell you!" Donnie screamed. "Just lock me up, please! I don't wanna hurt people! I just want it all to stop! Put me in a cell, lock me up, just don't send me back to them!"

The ruckus roused Sheriff Benson and he emerged from his office, placing his hat on his head. "What's the hubbub?"

"This kid is falling apart, Sheriff," the desk sergeant said.

Donnie had curled up on the ground and was weeping, his head in his hands.

"Jesus, not another one," Sheriff Benson said. "All right, get him in a cell and call for the doctor. But eyes on him at all times!" He turned and spotted Ray. "Well, now, Mr. Weldon. "Did your little lady get home all right on Saturday?"

"Yes, Sir, she did. Thank you for letting her call us. We were starting to worry."

"Nothing to worry about with a kid like Martin Landers taking care of her. He's a swell fellow."

"Yes, I mean to thank him. Say, what became of the crazy fellow they brought in? Did the psychiatrist figure it all out?"

Sheriff Benson sucked the air in between his teeth and shifted his hat to the back of his head. "Well, that's an unfortunate business altogether. The doc came and gave him a sedative. We put him in one of the cells for the night. The sergeant on night duty heard some loud banging coming from his cell and by the time he got there, the poor fool had slammed his own head against the wall enough times to cave his skull in. He was dead before the ambulance got here."

"Jesus, that's awful!"

"I've seen criminals take their own lives in the solitude of their cells before, when the quiet of the night gets to them and the enormity of their crimes sinks in, but to do it like that ... he must have been running from some pretty awful demons."

"Any idea who he was?"

"Yeah, he was a kid from Stockton. He was an apprentice irrigation worker over at the plant. Only been there a year after finishing high school."

"Did you find out who was chasing him that night?"

"Sure, I sent a couple of deputies over to the irrigation plant to see if they knew anything. They said he had some sort of breakdown Saturday night and went running out into the fields. He'd been acting erratically the last few days. They went off after him with torches, thinking he might come to harm. Guess they spooked him pretty bad. And now this Donnie kid ..."

"Sheriff, have you had any other reports of madness or delusions recently?"

"Well, it's funny you should say that, but yes. There was a lady in here just the other day, saying that her teenaged son was pretending his father was back. He'd run off with his secretary two years ago, you see, and the kid was pretty cut up about it all. Well, now he's as happy as a spring lamb, talking to his dad at the dinner table and acting like he never went away. The mother's worried sick."

"And what did you do?"

The Sheriff shrugged. "Not much I could do except tell her to get the boy a doctor. No crime has been committed so it's not a job for the police."

"I heard a similar story," Ray said, "of a woman under the delusion that her dead son was back with her. And another story about a girl whose dog was run over, now thinking it's following her around everywhere."

"There's been other reports," said the sheriff. "People not acting right, acting happy, sure, but having delusions. Then there's the other side of the coin; this ugly business on Saturday. A man so terrified of something that wasn't there that he bashed his own head in."

"And now Donnie, raving like a loon," Ray added. "Do you think something might be going around? To have so many incidents in one town is surely unusual."

"Sure is. I don't know what's got into folks. Maybe some kind of mass hysteria. Or it could just be another one of those summers. The heat does something to people, you understand. If I told you half of what I've experienced in the hottest of my twenty-seven summers as a law enforcement officer, you wouldn't sleep at night. Hell, I barely do."

"Will Donnie be charged with anything?"

"Nothing that I can think of. But we can keep him here for his own good until the doc comes and then we'll have his folks come to pick him up. Might be a case for the shrink but I'm guessing that whatever it is, it's got something to do with that gang of his. Bunch of kids are half crazy to begin with."

Ray nodded. "Those kids and their hot rods put the wind up me. I wouldn't mind so much if it wasn't that my son is pally with them, Donnie especially. I don't want him hurt in some dumb game of chicken."

"You'd best watch him close, then. These kids have some stupid initiation rites. And the rods they drive are more than most of them can handle. Especially that Chevy Johnny Packer hurtles around in."

"I've seen it down at Nick's Garage. Where does a kid like Johnny Packer get the dough for all those speed parts? Sure, his uncle owns an auto repair shop, but the kid's father has split and his mom takes in laundry. It doesn't add up."

"It adds up," said Sheriff Benson with a grim smile. "There's a lot of money to be made in dealing hard drugs."

"Drugs?" Ray asked, appalled. "Is that what that greaser gang is into?"

The sheriff nodded. "We've had our eye on them for some time but haven't been able to pin it on them. We've rousted their clubhouse once or twice, picked up one or two of them on traffic violations, put the squeeze on them here at the station but they're as tight-lipped as a bunch of clams. But we'll get them, don't you worry about that. One of these days, I'll nail that Johnny Packer but good and bust up his whole gang. And you might have delivered a small piece of the puzzle to me today."

"Donnie?"

"He's small fry but an initiated gang member all the same. And in whatever desperate state he's in now, he may spill just enough for me to get to Packer."

Ray felt sick as he drove home. The thought that Tommy was getting involved with a gang that liked to tear around town in souped-up hot rods was bad enough, but drugs? Well, that was it. He was going to have to put his foot down. No son of his was going to join a gang of criminals. That was probably why poor Donnie had been out of his mind today. His brain was probably frazzled on hop and marijuana. Well, that wouldn't happen to Tommy, he would make damn sure about that.

That evening, when Tommy got home, Ray summoned him into the living room. He lay down the law right from the get-go. "I don't want you hanging out with that gang anymore, do you understand me?"

Tommy's face was dumbstruck. "What do you mean?"

"I picked up your friend Donnie today and took him down to the police station. He's run away from his folks, did you know that?"

"No. Nobody's heard from him since yesterday but ..."

"Well, he's half out of his mind on whatever that Johnny Packer is dealing."

Tommy was silent, his face blank.

"Don't play dumb, Tommy, I'm sure you know what I'm talking about."

"I really don't, Pop."

"Drugs, Tommy. Hard stuff. Sheriff Benson has had his eye on that little gang for a while now. It's only a matter of time before he cracks down on them hard and I don't want you to go down with them. I also don't want you to end up like your friend Donnie. You should have seen him today, he was a gibbering wreck! Sheriff Benson and his officers were measuring him up for a straight jacket. I don't know if he'll ever recover."

"But Dad, nobody does drugs in the club. I never seen Donnie or anybody ..."

"I don't care what you've seen or what you think, your association with those hoodlums is over."

"That's not fair! They're my only friends!"

"Find yourself some new ones."

"I don't want new ones! You and Mom dragged us here and now you won't let me hang out with the only kids who like me! This town stinks without the Black Camelots!"

"That's enough! I'm doing this for your own protection!"

"No, you're doing it because you want me to be as lame and lonely as you are! You can't stand it that I have some friends and you don't!"

Ray could have struck him for that but he forced his hand to remain at his side. Tommy was storming off anyway. He thumped upstairs and the slam of his bedroom door reverberated throughout the house.

Claire came in from the dining room. "What happened?"

"I feel like an ogre, Claire," Ray said. "But I just want him to be safe, can't he see that?"

"He's sixteen, Ray. He's just venting his frustrations."

"But he's got no right to talk to me like that."

"No. But it's been tough for him. It's been tough for all of you, and I'm sorry."

"Hey, it's not your fault."

"Every town has its troublemakers. Tommy just needs to find the right crowd."

"It's not just that, Claire. There's something going on in this town. Sheriff Benson agrees with me. They've had several reports of people losing their minds. I don't know if its drugs or what, but I don't like it."

There was even worse news to follow that shook the town to its core. The day after Donnie had been taken in, his parents came to pick him up and take him home. The following morning, the police were summoned to their farm by reports of gunshots. Donnie had murdered his parents in their bed and then committed suicide.

Chapter 10

Judy didn't want to stop kissing Martin. She didn't want to leave his embrace or the back seat of his car where the orange glow of the setting sun made their skin seem aflame with warmth. But she had to. Connie and the other girls were waiting and, as this was to be the prom committee's first official meeting, she didn't want to be late.

"I have to go," she said, drawing her lips away from Martin's.

"Pick you up later?" he asked.

"Sure. We should be finished by nine o'clock."

"Nine? You can't have that much to discuss. The prom isn't for another two months."

She sighed. "You have no idea what goes into the planning of a prom. We have tons to prepare. Connie wants it to be perfect."

"Of course she does."

She kissed him again and grabbed her purse. She got out of the car walked across the parking lot towards the school building, its outline a silhouette against the sinking sun.

Connie, Heather, Karen and Trudy were in the auditorium, sitting at a trestle table that was spread with sheets of paper; designs for theme ideas, invitation designs and seating plans, all in Connie's neat hand.

"I'm not late, am I?" Judy asked as she hurried over to them.

The four girls looked up in one synchronized movement. "Not at all," said Connie. "Take a seat."

Judy did so. "Is this it?" she asked. "I thought there would be more members on the committee."

"We are the executive committee," Connie replied. "We make the decisions and then we recruit volunteers to help with the labor such as making decorations."

"Under our strict supervision, of course," said Heather.

"Of course," Connie said. "Not everybody is artistically inclined, but some are good with their hands and just need to be told what to do."

"Lord, could you imagine if we let everybody else in on the decision-making process?" snorted Heather. "It would have no class at all!"

"Now, let's talk about our dates," said Connie. "Naturally, Heather and I will be going with Ross and Steve."

"Ricky Douglas has asked me," said Trudy, beaming with pride.

"Well done, you," said Connie approvingly. "His father sold daddy his current Jaguar. And what about you, Karen?"

The four girls looked at Karen who was silent, her face flushing somewhat.

"You *do* have a date, don't you?" There was an implied threat in Connie's voice that seemed to bring Karen close to the edge of tears.

"Not yet, but I will!" Karen said quickly.

"Do you mean that nobody has asked you?" Heather demanded in an appalled voice.

"Oh, sure! Several have, but none of them are suitable."

"Who?" Connie asked.

Karen cleared her throat. "Well ... Sean Brooke asked me last Thursday, but he's a whole head shorter than me ..."

"Definitely not," said Connie.

"... and Peter Cunningham told a friend that he was thinking about asking me ..."

"Peter Cunningham?" said Connie. "He buys his schoolbooks second hand, doesn't he? Hardly suitable. You'd best hurry up, Karen. There aren't many men of quality to be had in this school. You can't very well remain part of this committee if you don't find somebody to bring."

"Lord, Karen, imagine if *you* ended up having to ask somebody!" said Heather and she broke into a giggle at her own remark. The other girls smiled, all except Karen.

"I'm sure you'll find somebody, Karen," Judy said, feeling a little bad for her. "We still have two months. Most people haven't even started asking yet."

"*Most* people can afford to wait," said Connie. "But, as members of the committee, we have to set a good example and the quality of our dates are paramount to the whole tone of the evening."

"Who are you bringing?" Heather asked Judy.

Judy felt the sudden interest of the four girls, including Karen, bore into her as if they were police officers interrogating a suspect. "Well ... we haven't actually discussed it yet, but I suppose it will be Martin Landers."

The girls looked at one another their expressions communicating silent signals and, as always in such situations, it was left to Connie to do the explaining. "Judy, Martin Landers is far from suitable. You'll have to find somebody else."

"But we're going steady ..."

"Yes, we know all about that and we really think it would be best if you broke it off with him and found somebody better."

"Better? I don't understand what you mean."

Connie smiled, shifted in her seat, and spoke in the kind of voice one uses to explain something important to a child. "Martin Landers is from a poor family, Judy. We've all seen him carrying boxes about in that stationary store all nights of the week. His father is a janitor for God's sake."

"Well, why does that matter?" Judy felt hurt and a little angry.

"He has no prospects and if you stay with him, *you'll* have no prospects. And most of all, no reputation. We are trying to maintain a high standard. The whole school looks to us for inspiration. Our boyfriends must be as good as we are."

Judy felt at a loss. Martin was the only boy who had so much as looked at her since she had walked into Ralston High. Where could she find another boyfriend or even a prom date that would meet Connie's satisfaction? But Connie's unspoken orders were clear. She would have to break it off with Martin.

The rest of the meeting passed in a blur and she hardly paid any attention to what was being discussed. Soon, it was nine o'clock and the girls left the auditorium and went out into the parking lot. It was dark and only a few cars were in the lot. Connie and Heather were being picked up by their boyfriends and Trudy was giving Karen a ride home. Judy looked across the lot and saw Martin sitting behind the wheel of his Ford. As she approached, he started the engine and she was bathed in the yellow of his headlights.

"Where shall we go?" Martin asked her as she got in. "Feel like a hamburger? Or maybe a movie?"

"I'd like it if you just drove me home," she heard herself say in a mousy voice.

"Huh? It's early still. We could ..."

"Martin, please! I'm not feeling very well and I just want to go home."

"All right, home it is. How did the meeting go?"

"Fine."

They drove through town in silence, him staring at the road and her out the window at the neon-lit storefronts as they flashed past. *He knows something is wrong but he's giving me the time and space to tell him. He's such a great guy, how can I ...?*

But she had to. She knew what it would mean if she didn't ditch him. She would be off the committee and probably out of Connie's clique. She really liked Martin but if she stayed with him, she would be throwing away everything she had gained over the past few weeks. She would be back to being a nobody and eating lunch with Susanne Crane in the cafeteria. It was more than she could bear.

They didn't talk until Martin rolled to a stop outside her house. They sat in the dark shade of the mimosas for a while, both of them waiting for Judy to work up the courage to say what she had to say.

"Martin, I don't think we should see each other any-more."

"Why not? What's wrong?"

"Nothing's wrong, I just think that we're not right for each other, that's all."

"*You* think? Or is that what Connie and her friends think?"

"Don't make this about them. I know you don't like them."

"All I know is that we're crazy about each other and now all of a sudden, after your prom committee meeting, you're giving me the cold shoulder. Have they put you up to this?"

"Martin, please! You're making this harder than it is already."

"Well, is it true? What's the matter, my daddy's not rich enough? We're not members of the country club, is that it?"

"I'm not going to listen to any more of this." She opened the passenger door.

His hand grabbed her arm. "You're making a mistake," he said. "You're letting them push you around, deciding your life for you."

"It's *my* life," she replied. "And I'll do what I want with it." She pulled her arm away and he let her go. She walked up to the house, not looking back. When she closed the door behind her, he was still sitting in his car, its engine idling. As she heard him pull away, she broke down in heavy sobs.

The following day, news had got around that she and Martin had split. Susanne approached her at her locker, her eyes wide. "I heard you and Martin are finished," she said in a hushed voice as if half the school didn't already know. "What happened? You guys were real cute together."

"It just wasn't working out."

"Did he ditch you?"

"No, I ditched him."

"But why? I thought you were mad about him?"

Judy sighed. "I just need to set my sights a little higher, that's all."

"What does that mean?"

"It means that I need to be going steady with a boy who has better prospects."

"Prospects? This wouldn't have anything to do with Connie Lund, would it?"

Judy slammed her locker door shut in irritation. "What if it does?" The words slipped out without her meaning to. She found that she was angry at Connie for all that she desperately wanted to remain her friend. Ditching Martin had hurt and the worst of it was that she couldn't tell anybody the real reason.

"Did she make you?" Susanne asked. "Is it because he's poor?"

Judy sighed. "No, she didn't make me. I made the decision. And yes, it's because he's dirt poor and Connie and her friends have rich and popular boyfriends and I would be embarrassed to turn up to the prom with a date who works in a stationary store, all right?"

Susanne looked a little shocked at her sudden, angry outburst. Then she said "Judy, do *I* embarrass you?"

"Why would you say that?"

"Is that why you don't sit with me at lunch anymore? Or want to meet up after school? Or even call me? Am I not good enough for Connie Lund?"

"Don't be silly."

"You've changed Judy. Since you became Connie's friend, you've really changed."

"That's baloney."

"The old Judy liked smart, well-dressed boys, not just rich, popular ones. The old Judy wouldn't have ditched a swell guy like Martin Landers just because he wasn't good enough for her snooty friends."

"If you like Martin so much, then why don't *you* ask him to the prom?" She turned her back on Susanne and walked away, regretting her harsh words but not knowing how to take them back. She didn't know how to fix any of this. It was done and there was no undoing it. But secretly she knew Susanne had been right about everything. And she felt like a real heel.

CHAPTER 11

Donnie's death had hit Tommy like a sledgehammer. The whole club was reeling but for Tommy, who had been introduced by Donnie and looked to him as a role model, the news was devastating. The worst of it was not knowing why. Why had Donnie picked up his father's Colt and shot his parents in their beds before putting the barrel to his temple and blowing his own brains out? It made no sense. Donnie had no mental issues that Tommy had been aware of. He was a straight kid with good friends and a bright future in the club.

The breakdown in the police station Tommy's dad had described seemed entirely out of character for Donnie. What the hell had happened Sunday night? How had Donnie gone from the cheerful youth buzzing with excitement after their successful recon mission to a nervous wreck on Monday to a murderer and suicide on Tuesday? Tommy didn't believe drugs were to blame, no way. Donnie wasn't mixed up in that hard stuff. Nobody in the club was. Johnny was strictly against hop and came down hard on dealers in Ralston. Something else had happened and it had happened suddenly.

Tommy couldn't forget the image of Donnie's mother, dripping wet from her fall in the canal, bringing them lemonade at six in the evening, begging them to stay in that night. He didn't know why but he was sure that strange episode had something to do with it all. He should probably tell the police but how? Even if they listened to him, all he could say was that Donnie's mom was acting pretty strange Saturday night. Not exactly a helpful clue.

After his dad had forbidden him from hanging out with the club coupled with Donnie's death, Tommy had begun to worry that his connection to the club was over.

And without wheels of his own, he had no way of even meeting up with them anyway. But Dad couldn't stop him from hanging out with Burt. They were in the same grade, after all and when Burt turned up in the school parking lot in a battered but souped-up '49 Mercury, Tommy felt overwhelmed with relief.

"Nice wheels, Man," he said as they sped through the school gates after school.

"Thanks. My brother left them to me when he went off to college."

They headed to the strip to see who was out and about. It didn't feel the same without Donnie.

"There's another meet tonight," said Burt. "Johnny wants to go over our next move against the Jungle Dukes."

"My old man doesn't want me hanging out with the club anymore," said Tommy. "Thinks you're a bad influence and, after what happened with Donnie, he's convinced you're all hopheads."

"That's too bad," said Burt. "But what he don't know can't hurt him. The meet's at six o'clock. Tell your old man that you're grabbing a malt at the drive-in and studying with your bible circle or whatever. You can be home in time for dinner."

Tommy grinned. "That might just work. Why is the meeting so early?"

"Johnny wants to get this business with the Jungle Dukes seen to pronto. We're gonna raid that old farmhouse and get Marie out of there."

"Tonight?"

"Could be. That might be tricky to swing with your old man, but you might not be asked to participate anyway. It's pretty heavy stuff for a prospect."

They did a few circuits of the strip to kill time and then rolled into the lot behind Nick's garage a little before six. The place was jumping. There was an eager tension in the air. Everybody knew what was about to go down and they were thirsty for action. Johnny immediately called them inside.

"We lost a brother this week," he began, eyes roving the room to make sure everybody was displaying the appropriate level of solemnity. "And that stings. Donnie was a good kid and he would have gone far in this club. But we can't let anything distract us from our path. This beef with the Jungle Dukes is coming to a head and we're going to act on the information Donnie brought to me. We know where Chuck's sister is and tomorrow night we bust in and take her from them."

"How many jungle cats guarding her?" somebody asked.

Johnny looked over to Tommy and Burt.

"We saw two on the front porch," Burt said, "and three on the shooting range out back. Tommy saw another two in the kitchen."

"So that's seven," said Johnny. "At least."

"And at least one of them has a piece," Burt added. "Possibly more."

"Don't worry, Burt," said Johnny with a smile. "We won't exactly be walking in with lollipops in our hands. I want the prospect to come with us. He can stand as lookout on the road to make sure we don't have any bother from the cops or anybody else."

Tommy nodded despite the sinking feeling in his gut. How could he tell Johnny that his old man had put the brakes on his running around with the club?

"How come we're waiting until tomorrow?" somebody asked. "Why not snatch the girl now?"

"The mayor has called a meeting at the town hall tomorrow night," said Johnny. "Every square will be there, including the sheriff who's been getting too nosey lately. If he saw us all heading out of town in our rods, he'd have every radio car in the county on our asses. We wait until the meeting is in session and we don't let on that something is brewing. Then, we hit the Dukes and bring Marie back here before the town meeting has adjourned."

Tommy frowned. He had forgotten about the town meeting. Mom had said something about it the other day. Johnny was a smart cookie and his careful planning might enable him to save face. As Johnny had said, all the squares would be at the meeting, including Tommy's parents. That would give him just enough time to join in on the rumble and be home before his folks got back.

On the night of the town meeting, they ate dinner early and Judy slumped off to her bedroom to listen to her records and mope about. Ever since she had broken it off with that dork Martin, thought Tommy, she was as miserable as a wet Monday.

Mom and Dad got ready for their meeting and came downstairs in smart clothes accompanied by the scent of mom's rarely used perfume. They really were pulling out the stops to impress tonight.

"We'll be back around ten o'clock," said Mom.

"As long as this doesn't take too long," said Dad. "You know how these small-town types like to gossip."

"Well, it sounded as if Mayor Garland had an important announcement to make." Mom and Dad shared a look that indicated to Tommy that they had some idea of what all the noise was that night, but they weren't telling.

As soon as they had left, Tommy bolted upstairs to get his boots and jacket. Burt would be waiting farther down the street, his engine off, until Tommy's folks had left. No time could be wasted if they were to get down to the clubhouse in time to join the rumble.

"Where do you think you're going?" Judy asked as she emerged from her room and caught him on the landing while he was shoving his arms into the sleeves of his leather jacket.

"Out," he replied.

"You didn't say you were going out at dinner."

"I don't have to tell you everything."

There was the sound of a car with a powerful engine drawing up outside.

"Is that one of your scruffy friends?" Judy asked, her hand on her hip.

"None of your business."

"Mom and Dad are going to flip their wigs if they find out you've gone out with that gang."

"What Mom and Dad don't know won't kill them. I'll be back before they get home."

"I don't know why you hang out with that dumb crowd anyway. They'll only get you into trouble."

"Bull."

"I've heard what they get up to, all those races and initiation rites. It's pathetic and you're pathetic for being so desperate to be one of them."

"You know, you're a real hypocrite, Judy," he snapped at her.

"What do you mean?"

"Everybody knows you dumped lover-boy Martin because Connie Lund said so. You're so eager to please her that you'll do anything so don't give me a hard time about trying to fit in."

Judy's face colored, either with embarrassment or rage, Tommy couldn't decide. "Go on, then!" she screamed. "Go and get into trouble with your dumb friends! You'll be in worse trouble when I tell Mom and Dad you sneaked out while they were gone!"

Tommy ignored her and flung open the front door. Maybe she would tell on him, maybe she wouldn't. He couldn't worry about that now. Burt was waiting on the curb, the engine of his Mercury idling.

"C'mon, get in!" he cried. "We're gonna be late!"

They weren't late, not with Burt behind the wheel and the streets unusually quiet. Tommy guessed it was because everybody was at the town hall. They roared up to Nick's garage and swung around to the back where a large crowd of Black Camelots were assembled around their vehicles. They all seemed to be armed to the teeth; chains, knives, bricks in socks and bits of lead pipe were hefted from hand to hand and concealed under jackets and in pockets. Johnny stood with Mack and his girl, a black pistol in his hand which he was loading.

"I want an ass in every seat," he told the crowd. "We take as few cars as possible. The girls stay here. We're gonna have a party when we get back. Bill, you're riding with me. Burt, Tommy, you both ride in the back."

Tommy and Burt glanced at each other, both awed at being allowed to ride with the boss in his monster Chevy.

They set out immediately and, even though every car was filled and a good many had been left behind, it was still an impressive convoy of hot rods that rolled out of the lot behind Nick's garage. There was no peeling out, this was a covert mission designed to not attract attention. Even when they got onto the highway, Johnny in his black Chevy leading, they kept below the speed limit.

They met almost no cars on the road and pulled off a few yards from their destination. They reversed so the rear of each car was pointed at the house. When the time came for it, they would have a quick, clean getaway. Nobody spoke as they all got out and crowded around Johnny.

"All right," he said in a low voice. "I want half of you to go with Mack and cause a disturbance at the front of the house. Don't go rushing in but make like you're going to and that should draw those Jungle creeps out. Meanwhile, I'll lead the other half around the back. We'll bust in while their attention is focused on Mack and his boys. Our prospect here will watch the road and come running if he sees the cops. Everybody clear?"

Heads nodded in the dimming light of dusk.

"Crazy. Let's move out."

As Johnny's crew crept off through the orchard towards the junk-strewn yard, Mack thumped Tommy on the arm.

"Eyes peeled, Prospect," he said. "If you screw this up, I'll bury you myself."

Tommy nodded and watched them head off. He got the feeling Mack didn't like him very much. Feeling suddenly all alone, he wandered towards the road and took up position behind some bushes that afforded him a view north and south. The night air was still. He bit his thumbnail. It was all in motion. No turning back now. He tried to still his jumping nerves. All he had to do was what he had been told. Easy. They'd be out of here in a few moments.

The first time a car's headlights appeared in the distance, he found his heart hammering in his chest. All he could see were two pinpricks of yellow light. What kind of car was it? A cop car? He realized that he wouldn't know until it was almost upon him and then it would be too late. This was a dumb job! He found himself wishing he was with the rest of the gang, not stuck out here on a lonely highway.

The car roared past. It was a convertible on its way north. No big deal. Of course there were other cars on the road, normal people driving home from a late shift or on their way to a date in some other town. But he hoped the gang hurried up all the same.

Nearly ten minutes passed before he spotted another pair of approaching headlights, this time from the north. As they came closer, he could make out the oncoming car by its outline It was a hot rod of some sort but limned by another set of headlights behind it. Two cars. No, more! They were slowing down as they approached the house. Had Johnny called in a favor? Were these more Camelots coming to help out?

No. Far more likely that they were Jungle Dukes. They had pulled up on the driveway leading up to the house. Doors opened. Figures spilled out. Tommy didn't wait to count them. All he knew was that he had to warn Johnny and the others that enemy reinforcements had arrived.

He took off like a jackrabbit through the orchard, keeping clear of the track. As he approached the house, he could hear Mack and his boys hurling out catcalls and tempting those within to come out and play. He ran around to the back and could see a scuffle in progress. Johnny and his squad outnumbered the Dukes who were taking a beating in the back yard.

He found Johnny laying into a Duke who was crumpled at his feet, his face bloodied. "The Dukes have reinforcements!" Tommy gasped, struggling for breath.

Johnny whirled to face him. "What?"

"Some rods just turned up and spilled a bunch of Dukes. They'll be heading over towards Mack and the others."

"Shit! I just sent three guys in to get Marie and these apes came on us from that shack over there."

The house's screen door banged open and three figures emerged, two of them carrying the girl between them. She was barely conscious.

"All right, they got her!" Johnny whooped. "Get her back to the cars. Everybody else, round the front! Mack needs help!"

The Dukes who had already taken a beating remained on the ground, not eager to renew hostilities. Tommy found Burt and they followed Johnny and the others around the house to where a rumble was already in progress.

About ten Jungle Dukes had joined the scene and were laying into Mack's crew but they were quickly blind-sided by Johnny and the rest of the Camelots.

It was a hard fight. Tommy took a blow to the eye that opened up a cut in his brow which streamed blood. He slammed his fist into his attacker's guts, doubling him over. Two more Dukes came to their friend's rescue and he found himself hemmed in.

The Camelots were outnumbered. Either they had picked a very unfortunate time to raid the house or the Dukes had been tipped off and had sent in reinforcements. Tommy didn't have time to consider that now. He was about to take a brutal beating. In fact they all were. The Dukes surrounded the Camelots and the situation looked grim.

Johnny pulled the gun from his jacket pocket and aimed it at the Duke who seemed to be shouting the orders. "All right, cool it!" he yelled. "Or I blow your fucking head off!"

The Duke leader grinned and a gun seemed to materialize in his hand before they saw him reach for one. Everybody backed away. The two gang leaders faced off, each pointing a gun at the other.

"Too late, Martinez," Johnny said. "We got the girl. And if you don't tell your creeps to back off, the Dukes'll need to vote in a new VP."

"You ain't got what it takes, Packer," said the one called Martinez. "Even if you shoot me, my boys'll rip you all to shreds before you get off another round. You're over! The Black Camelots are over! Pretty soon whatever is left of your outfit will be trading their jackets for new ones with a tiger on them. We're opening a new chapter, you see, and we like the look of Ralston."

"Over my dead body," said Johnny.

Martinez grinned. "Sure. If you like."

It was a stalemate and if it broke, the Dukes would win for sure. The outnumbered Camelots nursed their wounds and watched their leader hold off their destruction with the only card they had. The gun in Johnny's hands was the only thing stopping the Dukes from murdering them all.

Sirens could be heard coming from the south.

"Shit, the cops!" somebody yelled.

Panic set in but nobody moved. Nobody dared without a signal from their leader. To make a break for it now might cause either one of them to pull the trigger.

"Everybody head back to the cars," Johnny ordered. Still, nobody moved. "Now, dammit!"

"What about you, Boss?" Mack said.

"I'll keep Martinez from shooting any of you in the back. Now get going!"

"You heard the boss!" Mack yelled. "Back to the rods!"

They didn't need telling twice and the Dukes looked on helplessly as their prey sprinted off through the orchard.

Tommy found himself rooted to the spot. He wanted more than anything to run but Johnny was left all alone, surrounded by Dukes, with a pistol aimed at him.

"Your turn," Johnny said to Martinez. "Tell your creeps to scram before the cops get here."

Without taking his eyes off Johnny, Martinez said; "Move!"

The sirens were close now and they had little time to get away. Johnny and Martinez continued their standoff. "Another time, Martinez," said Johnny, and he lowered his gun.

Martinez kept his gun trained on Johnny and, for a moment, Tommy thought he was going to shoot him in cold blood. Then, a smile crossed his lips. "Sure, Packer. Another time. And sooner than you think."

Johnny turned around and almost bumped into Tommy. "What the hell are you still doing here, Prospect?" he demanded. "I told you all to scram."

"Looked like a Mexican standoff," Tommy said. "Didn't seem right to leave you on your own."

"Get running."

They ran as fast as they could through the trees towards the cars which hadn't yet started their engines. The cop cars screamed past their position in a flashing blue blur just as Johnny and Tommy reached the Chevy. The trees screened them well enough that the cops were oblivious to the ten cars hiding in the orchard and instead bore down on the Jungle Dukes who were at the front of the house.

Tommy scrambled into the passenger's seat. Burt and Bill were already in their seats. Johnny turned the ignition and gunned the engine. Nine other cars followed suit and the orchard was bathed in light, making the withered old trees silver skeletons in the night. Then, they were off, rolling back onto the highway and heading back south to Ralston while the cops chased Martinez and his gang north.

Tommy leaned back in his seat and let out a great sigh of relief. "We made it!" he said.

"You did good back there, Prospect," said Johnny, his heavy brow furrowed and his dark eyes on the road ahead. "Those Dukes might have taken Mack and his boys apart without us knowing about it until it was too late."

"How'd they show up just on time anyway?" Burt asked from the back seat. "It was like they knew about the raid."

"They knew," said Johnny. "Ain't no way that was just bad luck. They knew 'cause somebody ratted us out."

CHAPTER 12

The mayor and the city councilors sat at the head of the hall along with Sheriff Benson and a couple of suited strangers. It was the strangers who earned most of the townsfolk's attention. Curious eyes and nods were cast in their direction as the public filed in and found their seats. One of the strangers was an elderly gentleman with thick glasses and a plaid jacket. The other was rather more sharply dressed, in his mid-thirties, handsome with a slick side parting. He sat observing the town's constituents with a cool gaze, taking in every detail.

Claire and Ray spotted the Robertsons waving at them, indicating the two available seats they had saved.

"I'd rather sit closer to the door to avoid the stampede once all this is over," Ray said.

"Oh, come on," Claire said. "We can't let Jerry and Ann down. They saved us some seats."

"Hi, Claire!" said Jerry as they approached. "Ray? How are you?"

"Just fine, thank you," said Ray.

"Have you met Pastor Mathews?" Ann said, indicating a middle-aged man in a black suit in the row in front. At the mention of his name he turned around and nodded in a friendly way that belied his grizzled face.

"No, I don't believe we've had the pleasure," said Ray, extending his hand.

"Nice to meet you," said the pastor.

His voice was gravelly and his grip strong. He was a well-liked member of the community although their paths hadn't crossed before, Ray's own folks being Jewish of the non-practicing sort and he dreaded to think what Claire's parents' views on religion had been.

Once most people had sat down, the mayor rose and called for quiet. "Folks, please, your attention, please!"

The chattering and murmuring died down and the mayor continued. "I think you all know why we have called this meeting. There isn't one of us here who doesn't know or know *of* some poor soul who has been affected by some contagion in the past few days, afflicted by some sort of delusions. There's been a lot of questions and a lot of theories going around. We care about each other here in Ralston and that's why we must turn to outside help. I therefore would like to introduce to you, Special Agent Michael Ashcroft of the Federal Bureau of Investigation and Dr. Hank Johnson, a psychiatrist from San Francisco."

This provoked a bout of murmuring. *The FBI, here in Ralston? And a head shrinker too?*

Claire gazed at the suited man with apprehension. Outside help or not, the FBI had been no friend to her father.

"Please, folks, let's show some decorum," the mayor pleaded. "Agent Ashcroft, you have the floor."

The sharp-suited man smiled and raised his hand slightly. "Mayor, I would rather Dr. Johnson had a chance to speak first, explain what we're up against. Then I will present my own findings."

The mayor motioned to the shrink in the plaid jacket who coughed nervously and stood up. "Ladies and gentlemen, I'd like to thank you for having me here. I am, as Mayor Garland said, a psychiatrist. I often work with our friends in the federal bureau, profiling criminals and helping with cases where some insight into the fascinating secrets of the human mind is needed. I was called in by Agent Ashcroft here due to concerns that a mental affliction was affecting large numbers of people in a concentrated area with some displaying outright psychotic behavior. Such an idea has few precedents; mental illness is not contagious like measles or the common cold.

"I have been in Ralston for a week now, seeing patients who suffer from this new illness. Most of them were brought to me by concerned family members and had no desire to see me themselves. This is because, for the most part, their delusions were entirely positive. Some believed that deceased family members had returned to them. Others were under the impression that they were working in their dream jobs or had received a promotion. More still felt that they had won large sums of money in lotteries or numbers games.

"It might be tempting to see these as harmless delusions that only lead to more tranquil and better-quality lives. But believe me when I say that any form of mental illness can be dangerous if left untreated. They may mask more serious problems and a few of these have indeed revealed themselves. Several cases have resulted in violence and suicide. Clearly these individuals were not experiencing pleasant delusions and the most unsettling thing is that they were predominantly adolescents. Kids, in effect."

"Well, who's to say these kids were affected by the same contagion as the others?" spoke up one of the council members, "They're crazy enough as it is. This isn't the first time we've had trouble in this town."

"And even if they were affected by ... *whatever* this thing is," said a man in the audience, "maybe their delusions weren't good enough for them to be content with. Everybody else affected remained productive members of society."

"That's nothing new," agreed somebody else. "The kids in this town are spoilt rotten. They have everything they want and still they make trouble."

"They're out of control," another spoke up. "Hot rods tearing up and down on Saturday nights, fistfights, drugs. As a fellow parent in this town, we need to take charge of our children and stop mollycoddling them. They need discipline, not leniency."

The psychiatrist smiled. "Gentlemen, you spout the theories of my Neo-Freudian peers who tend to lay the blame of all society's ills at the doors of parents. I've heard it all before; excessive leniency produces juvenile delinquents while overprotective smothering leads to homosexuality. Not a school of thought I personally subscribe to. But we are straying from the point. The danger here is not parenting, but some foreign influence."

Now it was the special agent Ashcroft's turn to speak up. "Nevertheless," the agent began, "the anti-social behavior of American youth is rapidly becoming a matter of national security. The communists would like nothing more than a generation of Americans who are dysfunctional, resistant to authority and eager for anarchy. Their impressionable minds are ripe for foreign influence seeking to corrupt and undermine and it is for that reason that the FBI expresses a strong interest in getting to the bottom of this mystery. It is not, and I do not wish to cause you good people undue alarm, it is *not* out of the bounds of possibility that whatever it is that is influencing this town's populace, is some sort of Soviet plot."

There was uproar at this with many frightened voices chattering over one another. Mayor Garland called for order and addressed Agent Ashcroft directly. "I wonder, Agent Ashcroft, as you have spent several days in this town investigating these occurrences, would you be able to share some of your findings with us?"

"Certainly." Agent Ashcroft stood up and walked over to a chalkboard that had been wheeled in for the occasion. He picked up a piece of chalk and wrote the name 'Cherkovski' on it.

"Frank Cherkovski," he began, "was a nineteen-year-old irrigation worker at a plant near the Ralston Reservoir. Believing he was being pursued by some entity, he went mad and killed himself in his jail cell."

He turned back to the board and wrote another name.

"Mark Harris. A teenager who worked at Al's Deli down on Orangetree Road. Went mad and fled town. He hitchhiked south and was picked up by a truckdriver who said that he had some kind of seizure and acted as if there was something crawling all over his skin. When he slowed down, the kid bolted from the truck and was run down trying to cross the highway. It may have been an accident but I haven't ruled suicide out."

He then wrote 'Kowalski Family' underneath the previous two names. Claire felt herself tense. That had been the family of Tommy's friend.

"The most shocking incident happened this week. The Kowalskis owned a farm west of the highway. Donnie Kowalski was brought into the sheriff's department on Monday, raving about his parents trying to do something bad. Drug use was suspected, and his parents came to pick him up. That evening he murdered them both and then committed suicide. Can anybody tell me what these three cases have in common? Besides suicide, I mean. Something about the victims."

"Farming?" one of the council members offered.

"Not farming, per se," said Agent Ashcroft. "But in the case of Cherkovski and Kowalski, farmland does figure." He waited for another answer. None was forthcoming. "Water," he said, writing the word on the chalkboard. "Specifically, the water in the irrigation canals. These canals run through this town and feed the farmland to the east and west of Ralston including the farm owned by the Kowalski family and, of course the plant where Cherkovski worked. The Root Lateral canal runs past the back of Al's Deli where Mark Harris worked."

"Are you saying it's something in the water?" Mayor Garland demanded.

"Yes, not Ralston's drinking water fortunately, but something in the irrigation canals."

Claire felt a chill to the very heart of her soul. *Something in the irrigation canals.* She suddenly felt complicit in something so awful she could barely contemplate it.

"I understand your skepticism," said Agent Ashcroft, surveying the room that barely comprehended what he was telling them. "But there is further evidence. I have studied the stories of every one of Dr. Johnson's delusional subjects and it checks out. In every case, the individual either lived near to one of these canals or passed by one on their way to work."

"But what is it?" somebody asked. "What's in the water?"

"We don't know," Agent Ashcroft admitted. "Some sort of gas was my first guess. I have called in some specialists from the bureau who will check the water for contaminants. They will be here in a couple of days but for now I have a very strong warning to everybody in this town. *Stay away from the canals.* Tell your children and your friends. Under no circumstances go near the water."

When the meeting was over, Claire made her apologies to the Robertsons and hurried to the payphone in the lobby, leaving Ray staring after her in bewilderment. Yesterday she had procured a map of Ralston's entire irrigation system from the irrigation office and given it to Andy so he could continue his investigations. He might be poking around in the canals right that minute and, as he lived in that RV of his, she had no way of contacting him.

She dialed Fred's home number. When he answered, it sounded like he was a couple of martinis into his evening and Claire heard the unmistakable giggle of a girl in the background being commanded to silence.

"Fred?"

"Claire! What's up?"

"Have you heard from Andy?"

"Sure, he called me a couple of hours ago. He's been snooping around the canals all day looking for more signs of our tentacled friend."

"He's home now?"

"Sure, it's late."

"Did he sound ... *different* to you?"

"How do you mean?"

"I don't know, happy, elated, *delusional*?"

"Um, no. Same old Andy."

"What about depressed or frightened?"

"Nope. Say, what's this all about, Claire?"

"We just had a town meeting. The FBI are looking into these cases of insanity here in Ralston. They think that something in the water has been causing it, something in the irrigation canals."

"That's crazy!"

"Is it? Admit it, Ray, we have no idea what we're dealing with. I think it's time we went to the authorities."

"What are you going to do?"

"That FBI agent is here in the building. I'm going to tell him what we know."

"Okay, Claire. You're the boss. I just hope he believes you, that's all."

"I have a feeling he will."

She hung up and pushed her way back into the hall. There was a secondary and far less formal meeting in progress. This time it was Pastor Mathews who was fielding questions from frightened parishioners.

"Why has this thing descended on Ralston?" a middle-aged man was saying. "What have we done to deserve it? Is this a punishment from God?"

"Be brave, man!" Pastor Mathews said. "Courage and faith must walk hand in hand! Else what good is our faith if we let it be destroyed by fear? Do you think this is the first time God has tested us? Is this the first time our world has known destruction, earthquakes, floods, famines and wars?"

"Is that what it is?" the man asked. "A test?"

"All our battles are tests of our faith. I know you're all frightened and I can't give you any answers the FBI or our people of science have already given us save one; only with courage can we emerge victorious."

Claire found Ray standing nervously to one side with the Robertsons.

"Claire, what happened to you?" Ray asked.

"I had to make an urgent call. Have you seen that FBI agent?"

"Sure, he went into a back room with the mayor and the sheriff."

"Wait here for me. I have to speak with them."

"What's going on?"

"No time! I'll tell you later!"

She hurried down the corridor that led from the hall to a series of offices in the rear of the building. She found Agent Ashcroft, Sheriff Benson and Mayor Garland in an office with the door half open. She rapped on it. Mayor Garland peered out.

"Mayor, I have some information Agent Ashcroft might find useful."

"Well, I'm sure he'll talk to you down at the police station tomorrow. We're kind of in a meeting here."

"I'm afraid it's urgent"

"Let the lady in," came Ashcroft's voice over the mayor's shoulder.

Mayor Garland stood aside and let Claire enter the room. The far wall was dotted with framed black and white photographs of the 1904 jubilee held to celebrate the completion of the Ralston irrigation system. In those frozen black and white images, the city was decked out in flags while women in bonnets and wide dresses waved from an excursion train as they toured the canals. A framed article clipped from the *San Francisco Chronicle* had the headline; "The Wedding of the Land and the Water".

"Now who might you be and what information do you have for me, Ma'am?" Agent Ashcroft said. He was leaning on the edge of a desk, a cigarette in his hand.

"Gentlemen, I am Dr. Claire Weldon of the National Advisory Committee for Aeronautics."

"I remember you," said Sheriff Benson. "You're the lady doc who was investigating that meteorite. Isn't your husband the fellow who brought in Donnie Kowalski?"

"Yes, he is. Donnie was a friend of my son."

"Meteorite, huh?" Agent Ashcroft said. "That got something to do with what you're about to tell me?"

"Yes. I'm a meteoriticist and we found something very unusual with that meteorite. A piece of it broke off and rolled down into the reservoir. It had an exposed cavity marked by many round impressions, as if it had been holding a cargo of small spheres that had since fallen out into the reservoir."

"Spheres?" Agent Ashcroft asked.

"Yes. At first we thought they could have been fossilized eggs which is a remarkable discovery in itself. But we met a marine biologist by the name of Andy Willard who was alerted to the existence of some undiscovered squid or octopus in the irrigation system."

"An octopus?" Sheriff Benson exclaimed. "Aren't they saltwater creatures."

"Yes, that is why such a creature in Ralston's canals is so unusual."

"And what makes this marine biologist think there's a creature like that in the canals?" Agent Ashcroft asked.

"He found an egg casing similar to those of cephalopods, only much bigger. My assistant and I looked at it ourselves. It exactly fits the round depressions found inside the meteorite."

The three men were silent for a time as they digested this. Agent Ashcroft took a drag of his cigarette and blew out the smoke towards the light fixture. "And you believe that this cephalopod came from ... *outer space*?"

Sheriff Benson slapped his thigh and guffawed loudly. "Squids from Mars! Is this the important information you have for Agent Ashcroft? You think some Martian with tentacles is floating around our canals and controlling peoples' minds?"

"I said nothing about Mars," Claire replied testily. "I don't know where it's from, but those eggs would have to have been incredibly old and resilient to still contain life after such a journey. Look, I didn't want to believe it at first either. But there are just too many coincidences. And now Agent Ashcroft here tells us to stay away from the canals because there is something in them, something dangerous that we don't understand, something that is influencing peoples' minds. I don't know if it's this creature and if it is then I certainly don't know how it's doing it but I felt it was my duty to tell you what I know."

"Thank you, Dr. Weldon," said Agent Ashcroft. "You did right to inform me. This potentially changes everything. I would like very much to speak with you further."

"You're not taking all this seriously?" Sheriff Benson cried.

"Sheriff," said Mayor Garland. "I find this as hard to believe as you do but I think it would be best if we let our friends in the bureau make whatever investigations they deem necessary."

"Thank you, Mayor," said Agent Ashcroft. "Dr. Weldon, could I please have your telephone number. I will call you in a day or so."

"Of course." She gave him her number and, feeling as though she was being dismissed, took the opportunity to leave the office.

She felt the eyes of the three men on her as she left. Sheriff Benson had acted as she had been worried they might all act; treating her with derision and mockery. Mayor Garland had been more restrained although his face did not suggest that he took the matter any more seriously than the sheriff did. It had been Agent Ashcroft who had surprised her. There had been no mirth or incredulity on his handsome features, only patient acceptance. She wouldn't go so far as to think that he believed her theory, but he had taken it into polite consideration nonetheless and that was something. Of all the people in the room it had been the FBI agent she had been most apprehensive about.

He called her the following afternoon and asked her to discuss her findings over a meal. The thought of having dinner with an agent of the bureau made her skin crawl. Ray already had a chicken pot pie in the oven and was about as pleased by the prospect as she was.

"I have to, Honey," she told him. "He's the only person taking my suspicions seriously."

"*I'm* taking them seriously," said Ray, a little petulantly.

"And I appreciate it." She put her arms around his neck and kissed him. "But you're not the government."

"I don't like the look of that guy," said Ray, still unable to let go of his jealousy. "He's a slick one and no mistake."

"When it comes to the FBI, they all are."

She met Agent Ashcroft at a little Italian restaurant – his choice – tucked away off 9th street. The waiter led them over to a quiet booth and brought them their menus. They had wine and bread and ordered their food; him the grilled calamari and her the veal cutlets with parmesan.

"I've passed on what you told me to the military," said Agent Ashcroft as their waited for their food.

"Colonel Baskin is coming to Ralston and he wants to put together a task force to deal with the situation. I have forwarded you as a member of the team."

"Thank you. And thank you for taking me seriously."

"The safety of the public is a serious issue, Dr. Weldon. May I call you Claire?"

"I guess so. If we're to be working together."

"Please, call me Michael."

"All right. *Michael.*"

"I have to say, Claire, I don't quite know what to make of this alien story of yours but putting several minds to the job seems to be the best place to start."

"And this colonel? Does he take the alien story seriously?"

"Let's just say Colonel Baskin has an open mind when it comes to the unexplained. I have scheduled the task force's first meeting for tomorrow morning. Is this a problem for you?"

"Not at all. That's short notice. The military must really be taking an interest."

"They are. Colonel Baskin is arriving tonight. I'm meeting him after our meal."

They sipped their wine in silence for a moment.

"Tell me, Claire," said Agent Ashcroft setting his glass down. "How did you come to work for the NACE?"

"The chief of the high-speed research division at the Ames laboratory hired me. He felt that solving the problem of aerothermal overheating of rockets during atmospheric entry could be solved if we looked to the shape of meteorites rather than pursue the traditional aerodynamic shape of rockets."

He smiled. "I knew all that, Claire. I'm well aware of Harry Allen's research. I meant, what motivated you to study meteorites in the first place?"

"A childhood fascination, I suppose."

"Inspired by your father, perhaps?"

Claire toyed with the stem of her wine glass. "By that, I assume you know who my father was."

Ashcroft smiled. "John MacReady, a rocket engineer and chemist who worked for the Jet Propulsion Laboratory. Known for his pioneering work with solid-state rockets and jet-assisted takeoff."

Claire waited for the punchline.

"Killed in an explosion in his Pasadena laboratory in 1952."

"Under suspicious circumstances."

"Ruled an accident by the Pasadena police department."

"After you boys hounded him on trumped up charges of espionage."

Ashcroft smiled. "That was all before my time."

"The FBI's methods haven't changed."

"In that, I'm inclined to agree with you. But you don't seriously believe the bureau had anything to do with your father's death, do you?"

"I don't know what to believe. FBI, CIA or some other agency I've never heard of. Even the shadows have shadows these days."

"Mmm. Your father was involved with some very shady types himself. That limey coot, Aleister Crowley, for one. Do you not think they might have had something to do with it? Some old grudge finally settled?"

"My father resigned as head of the OTO's American chapter shortly before Crowley's death in '47. The lodge more or less fizzled after that. It was all silly nonsense anyway. I'm surprised the FBI took such an interest in bunch of horny eccentrics."

"Well, these *horny eccentrics* were considered a potential risk to national security for a long time," said Ashcroft. "As all subversive individuals are."

"Subversive? I can't see that they harmed anybody but their own families."

"A report was filed that a sixteen-year-old boy had been raped at one of their orgies."

Claire swallowed, her face coloring. "I hardly think this is fitting dinner conversation."

"No, I suppose not. I'm sorry. I've read your father's file, you see and ..."

"Was that relevant reading for your work or just a personal interest?"

"Sometimes it's difficult to differentiate between the two. I am interested in my work and, when I learned that I was to be working with the daughter of John MacReady, I educated myself."

"Delightful reading, I'm sure."

"Claire, the bureau's opinion on your father's death is that it was the result of some sort of power struggle within the lodge. Rivals squabbling for the throne, that sort of thing. Were you aware of anything of the sort?"

"No," she answered truthfully. "I knew very little of the lodge's goings on. Is that what his file says? That he was murdered by someone in the OTO?"

"Not in so many words. It was all a bit inconclusive. And ultimately irrelevant as far as the bureau was concerned. Accident or murder. He was no longer a person of interest."

Claire was silent as she digested this new angle on her father's death.

"What was your relationship with him like?" Ashcroft said, interrupting her thoughts.

Claire cleared her throat as the image of her father's comb mustache and unruly black hair slightly streaked with gray returned to her. "He was a kind father but a conflicted man," she said slowly. "His scientific mind had always been tempered with a colorful imagination and a wild romantic streak."

She well remembered the scientific tomes on his shelves, interspersed with esoteric antiques from Egypt and Peru. A bronze statue of Pan stood by the door to his study. He wrote poetry as well as science fiction stories which he kept in the bottom drawer of his desk. He never submitted them to the pulps; an act of restraint for which Claire had always been grateful. Even he didn't go *that* far in ruining his reputation.

"He certainly was an enigma from the bureau's point of view," said Ashcroft. "But I don't believe he was a spy. For what it's worth."

"Thank you," Claire said.

The waiter arrived with their meals and their talk turned to the formation of the task force.

The arrival of the military caused a great stir in Ralston. As if an FBI agent poking about wasn't serious enough, now they felt uncomfortably like they were under martial law. No such thing had been declared of course. The military were here solely to determine what this creature was and how best to defeat it. To that end, a whole platoon had been dispatched and, as the jeeps and army trucks rolled into town, Ralston's situation suddenly felt a whole lot more serious.

The colonel was a tall man, broad in the shoulders and without any sign of hair on his head. He was pushing sixty but still cut an imposing figure with muscles not yet run to seed filling out his uniform jacket.

Claire looked around the table at the other members of the task force. Agent Ashcroft sat beside the colonel, a cool drink of water next to the military man's bluster. Dr. Johnson was also quietly contemplative.

They were sitting in one of the back offices in the town hall which had been largely given over to Colonel Baskin and his platoon as their headquarters. G.I.s carried gear in and out of offices, communications equipment was being set up in the main room and jeeps and army trucks were parked in the lot outside.

Introductions were made and, when it was Claire's turn, Colonel Baskin regarded her quizzically. "Meteor scientist, hmm? I suppose you've been studying this space rock since day one."

"Well, yes as a matter of fact," said Claire, not liking the colonel's tone.

"And it never occurred to you to notify the military as soon as you discovered that there was something fishy about it all?"

"Colonel, we had no idea the meteorite contained alien eggs. At first we thought it may have been fossils until we met Dr. Andrew Willard."

"Ah yes, the marine biologist Agent Ashcroft told me about," said the colonel. "And where is he today?"

"Until recently he was investigating the canals, looking for signs of the creature. I haven't spoken to him in the last few days."

"Well, you both could have saved a lot of time, not to mention lives, if you had spoken up sooner," said Colonel Baskin.

"Now, wait just a minute, Colonel," said Agent Ashcroft. "Claire ... *Dr. Weldon*, I mean, came to me right after the town meeting to convey her concerns. We don't know what we're dealing with here, none of us do. And I should make it plain that Dr. Weldon is on loan to us from the NACE where she is part of an important research project. Chasing after aliens is not her job."

"Don't worry," said the colonel. "The U.S. Army will see that she's not penalized while she's working for us."

Claire said nothing. She did not like Colonel Baskin one bit but refused to get drawn into an argument with him.

"What I can't understand," Colonel Baskin said, apparently changing the subject, "is what that critter has been eating." He glanced at Claire. "Now if what your marine biologist friend claims is correct, then it has to be a big sucker."

"Yes," said Claire "the egg casing he found suggested something much larger than a giant Pacific octopus although really, as we don't know what it is, it's very difficult to estimate its growth rate."

"There's plenty of fish in the canals," said Mayor Garland. "It could have been eating those."

"I'm in mind of something bigger," said the colonel. "Sheriff, have you had any reports of cattle going missing?"

A few people at the table sniggered but stopped when the sheriff didn't join in. "Why, yes," Sheriff Benson replied. "As a matter of fact there have been one or two cows that have vanished from the farms on the outskirts of town."

"Farms that have irrigation canals running through them?" the colonel probed.

"Well, those canals are for crops, not livestock, but some cattle farmers have land that edges on the canals."

"Jesus help us," said Mayor Garland after a short silence. "The thing has been eating cows? How big is it?"

"Huge by the sound of it," said Colonel Baskin.

"What do you propose we do, Colonel," asked Agent Ashcroft.

"I have enough men to plant detonation charges in the canals at strategic points," said the colonel. "My intention is to drive the creature into a section of canal where we can cut off its escape and kill it."

"Kill it?" Claire exclaimed. "Colonel, this is the first contact humanity has had with an extraterrestrial. We have so much to learn from it ..."

"Ma'am," said the colonel with a simpering smile. "I appreciate your scientific interest in this creature, but you need to appreciate my interest in protecting the citizens of the United States. This thing is too dangerous to try and capture and put into an aquarium or what have you. I promise you that you will be first in line to study its corpse once we have killed it but make no mistake, my aim *is* to kill it."

"What about the people of this town who have already been affected by it?" Mayor Garland asked, turning to Dr. Johnson. "Is there any indication that they might return to normal?"

Dr. Johnson, coughed and used his knuckle to push his glasses up onto the bridge of his nose. "Well, psychosis is a tricky thing to treat as the cure depends very much on the cause. And as we have so very little understanding of its cause, I can't say for sure how they should be treated."

"Killing the creature might not stop the delusions," said Agent Ashcroft.

"Precisely. We need to determine exactly how this creature is causing these delusions in my patients."

"And these patients of yours," said the colonel. "Where are they?"

"Well, the most serious ones, the ones I classified as dangerous, have been sent to a sanitarium in Los Angeles."

"And the others?"

"Are at home."

"Do you mean to say," the colonel grumbled, "that delusional people that have been influenced by some alien agency are wandering around Ralston unsupervised?"

"They're free Americans, Colonel," said Dr. Johnson. "They've committed no crimes."

"*Yet.* Who knows what they're cooking up? They should be watched, closely. Am I not right, Agent Ashcroft?"

"Ideally, yes," said Agent Ashcroft. "But Sheriff Benson doesn't have the manpower to stake out the homes of everybody exhibiting delusional behavior. And we have a bigger problem than that."

"Which is?"

"While most of this town's residents are taking every precaution, some people aren't taking the warnings seriously enough. Even though they've been told to stay away from the water, there have been reports of people near the canals and the reservoir."

"We've caught people fishing, even whole families swimming up at the reservoir," said Sheriff Benson. "Right beneath the signs we put up. We've moved them on and most of them are cooperative, but we've encountered some resistance."

"Resistance?" said the colonel.

"There are folks who think it's all a lot of fuss about nothing and that these suicides and delusions are the problems of delinquents and the mentally unstable. They don't believe it has anything to do with the meteorite. A local paper labeled it as mass hysteria over a small number of unconnected events and an independently published magazine went one step further and claimed it was being used by the government as a scare tactic to control people."

"Then there's that Pastor Mathews," said Sheriff Benson. "He's telling his congregation that this creature is one of God's children, just as we are and, as such, it's like a brother to us. I pointed out to him that it ain't showing us much brotherly love and do you know what he said? He said that it might be that the Lord has put two of his creations in opposition to each other so that we might learn to be brothers instead of enemies! How do you like that?"

"Well, damn them, they should all be rounded up and detained!" the colonel snapped. "Folks like that are part of the problem and must not be allowed to sabotage our efforts."

Mayor Garland shifted uncomfortably in his seat. "Colonel, we can't just round up anybody who has their doubts or alternative theories. We are all in uncertain waters here. The people of this town have every right to question, just as we do."

"And how do we know that these 'questioning types' aren't all under the influence of this alien? Or communist sympathizers if this whole thing turns out to be a Soviet plot? We surely are in uncertain waters, I'll agree with you there, Mayor. But we need to do all that we can to ensure the safety of this town and that includes worming out the bad apples who might wish us harm. Agent Ashcroft, I would think you might have something to say on that matter."

"I agree with the colonel," Ashcroft replied. "But only so far as to say that precautionary measures should be implemented. The names and address of those in question have been recorded."

"Recorded?" said Claire, alarmed and disappointed by Agent Ashcroft's support of the colonel's rather ruthless stance. "Their names have been recorded by the FBI just because they voiced their opinions about something that we don't understand ourselves?"

"As the colonel said, these people may be in league with something insidious and should be watched closely."

"Just because a person does not side with one theory does it automatically follow that they are the enemy? Keep people away from the water by all means, put up signs, fences, arrest those who defy these measures but for God's sake let people have their opinions in open discussion!"

"Claire," said Agent Ashcroft. "I know where your concern is rooted. But these are exceptional circumstances. We must use exceptional measures to combat them."

"What good is it all if we lose sight of who we are in the process?" Claire asked but nobody was listening. The conversation had moved on to battle tactics and she realized with a sinking feeling that the task force had become a war council.

CHAPTER 13

The house was called 'Dusty Creek Farm' because its one-hundred-and-thirty feet of frontage looked down on a creek that, once upon a time, had been as dry as a bone. Now, water flowed through it in a sweeping U-bend, which, shaded by trees, provided serene fishing and boating activities for the affluent residents of Dusty Creek Drive.

Farm in name only, the house itself was a newly built ranch house; one of Arthur Lund's luxury projects. Nestled on a one-acre bluff, it boasted a garage with ample room for Arthur's three sports cars, a pool with a cocktail bar, patio cabana and a boathouse.

Judy tried not to look too wide-eyed as Connie showed her around. Heather, Karen and Trudy were regular guests and made themselves more than at home lounging in the steel and vinyl chairs by the brick fireplace. A lime green carpet covered the floor from wall to wall and floor to ceiling windows looked out onto a wraparound balcony with a view of the surrounding farmlands.

A maid bustled about, dusting and polishing surfaces and Connie's mom came out from the pastel pink kitchen bearing iced tea and a glass dish of cashew nuts. She was a blonde bombshell in pink checkered cigarette pants and a matching blouse. Judy thought she looked a lot like Jayne Mansfield which was probably the look Mrs. Lund was going for, even around the house.

"So, Karen," said Mrs. Lund. "I understand you have a date for the prom."

Karen blushed. "Yes, Mrs. Lund."

"Oh, call me Abby, please," said Mrs. Lund. "Well, tell me all about him!"

"Well, His name is Joe and his father is a banker in Turlock. They have a yacht at Newport Beach."

"Lovely!" crooned Mrs. Lund. "And what about you, Judy? Has anybody asked you yet?"

"No, Mrs. ..., I mean, Abby. Not yet."

"But she's working on it," said Connie. "Aren't you, Judy? The girls and I have been giving her some pointers on how to dress."

"Oh, I'm sure there'll be a legion of boys queuing up before long," said Mrs. Lund, flashing Judy a smile. "You have such lovely eyes, and those curls! I'm positively jealous!"

They talked some more, filling in Mrs. Lund on their prom plans and a few snippets of high school gossip. Then, Mrs. Lund turned to Connie. "Isn't it time you took Judy down to the boathouse and showed her daddy's motorboat?"

Connie looked up at her mother with a hint of surprise on her face which quickly turned to understanding. She looked to Heather, Judy and Karen who smiled at her expectantly. "Yes, definitely," she said.

"Artie just bought it last weekend," said Mrs. Lund proudly. "He's not much of a fishing man or a water man at all, for that matter, but Artie, I said, we live next to a creek. We simply cannot continue to live next to a creek without a boat. *All* the neighbors have one and think of the picnics we could have!"

"Come on," said Connie, rising. "I'll show you."

The other girls stood up and followed them out. Judy had no idea what interest Mrs. Lund thought she might have in Mr. Lund's new boat, but she supposed that, having seen the rest of the house, it would be a shame to not show off another expensive possession.

They went out through the sliding patio doors and crossed the crazy paving surrounding the pool. Green lawns crept down to the creek where the boathouse stood, overhanging the still water. The air was balmy and there was no breeze. Judy was glad of the cool dampness of the boathouse. A narrow jetty ringed the interior and there, gently bumping its rubber fenders against the far jetty, was a wooden motorboat. Its vinyl seats were beige with red piping and its varnished surface was glossy and reflective as a mirror.

"Very nice," said Judy, still at a loss as to what they were doing in the boathouse.

"Forget the boat," said Connie. "Just look into the water."

Judy looked at her quizzically. All four girls were staring at her with serious intent.

"Don't worry," said Connie. "It doesn't hurt. And then, you will be one of us."

"One of us?" said Judy. "What is this, some sort of initiation ceremony? What do I have to do? Jump in?"

"No, nothing like that," said Connie with a smile. "Just stand still and it will come to you."

"What will come to me?"

"The most wonderful thing you'll ever experience," said Karen. "Your dreams are about to come true."

This had to be some kind of joke or hazing ceremony, Judy was convinced of it. She had done what they had asked and dumped Martin. What else did they want from her? Why else bring her out to the boathouse to look at some dumb old tub if it weren't a final trial, one last hurdle before she became, in Connie's words, *one of them*?

"Look into the water," Connie repeated.

Judy did as she was told. Whatever it was, she just had to get through it. She only hoped she wasn't going to get wet. This dress was new.

She stared at her reflection, and the reflections of her four friends, that floated below them on the skim of water so dark it could have been oil. Their reflections began to shimmer as if disturbed by the breeze. But there was no breeze inside the boathouse. It was some underwater current. The surface of the water was broken as something rose from those inky depths. At first, Judy thought it was some long-submerged branch or root finally breaking free from the slime at the bottom of the creek but it too flexible for that. The water parted around it as it uncurled and stretched, showing such flexibility and elasticity that it was almost *shapeless*.

That it was alive was known to Judy in the most primal depths of her soul. What it was, she didn't quite know, but if she had to put it into words then 'tentacle' would be the only word she could think of to describe it. It was pinkish but translucent and she could see throbbing veins within its milky, tubular form. It wasn't the tentacle of an octopus but something *other*, something that didn't seem to conform to the limitations of nature. She got the impression that it could stretch for great distances and squeeze its way past any obstacle, so fluid was its form.

All this was known to her in the second and a half she spent staring at its long, glistening length but all she could vocalize was a long, howling scream from the bottom of her gut. She backed away but felt the hands of Connie and the other girls grab her shoulders and hold her steady.

"It's fine, Judy," Connie crooned in her ear. "It's fine. One kiss and it's all over."

Kiss? As Judy tried to fathom what that meant, the bulbous head of the tentacle retracted, sliding back on itself to reveal a large sucker-shaped nodule that unfolded, dripping long strings of goo from its mucous membrane. A thin syphon-like tube emerged beneath the sucker. Something hard and shiny caught the light there and Judy realized that it was some sort of dart. She writhed with revulsion at the wavering thing and Connie and the girls tightened their grip. The sucker leant forward, blindly seeking out her face, somehow knowing it was there to find.

"It's best not to resist," said Heather. "I didn't want to either, but it is necessary."

"Just let it embrace you," added Karen, "and it will be over in a heartbeat."

The thought of that thing 'embracing' her face made Judy's stomach turn and she twisted violently in the girls' grip. They struggled to hold her, and she jerked away from the approaching tentacle, swinging Karen towards it. Karen screamed and tumbled into the water. Trudy made a grab for Judy's neck but Judy ducked and shoved her into Connie and Heather, bowling them over. Then she made a break for the door.

She ran out into the hot sunshine, feeling like she was in some sort of nightmare. She ran back to the house and in through the open patio doors. Mrs. Lund was in the kitchen discussing dinner plans with the maid.

"Mrs. Lund!" Judy gasped. "The boathouse ..."

"Yes, dear?" Mrs. Lund's face was concerned. "Did you come back alone?"

Judy couldn't get the words out. Her body was racked with terror. Mrs. Lund seemed to comprehend the situation.

"You mean, it isn't done yet? Oh, my dear, you simply *must*. I know it's frightening but we've all done it."

"You ... you mean ...?"

"Yes, I have too. And Doreen here. Haven't you Doreen?" She turned to the maid who nodded sagely. Mrs. Lund turned back to Judy, her face full of sympathy. "You don't want to be the one left out, do you now?"

Judy walked backwards through the patio door, keeping Mrs. Lund and the maid in her sight. They just stood there, smiling at her.

"Sooner or later, it just has to be done," said Mrs. Lund. "Like ripping of a band aid."

Judy could see Connie and the other girls running across the lawn from the boathouse. She turned and ran around the house to the drive where her Chevy was parked and thanked goodness she had left her purse with her keys in it on the passenger's seat. She slid in behind the wheel and fumbled for the keys. Glancing up at the rear-view mirror, she could see Connie's face, red with rage as she came around the corner of the house.

Turning the ignition, Judy slammed her foot down on the accelerator, sending up a spray of gravel as the wheels spun. Then she was off, tearing down the drive towards the road.

A white Corvette Roadster lurched into view, having come up from the highway. Judy caught a glimpse of Mr. Lund's shocked face as he slammed on the brakes to avoid colliding with her as she careened towards him. *He's one of them too*, she thought. *They all are!*

She shot off the dusty country road and onto the highway in a squeal of rubber on asphalt. She didn't stop sobbing until she reached Ralston.

Ray and Claire listened to Judy's story with ever deepening horror. She had come home that afternoon, parked the car haphazardly on the drive and spilled out of it, her face streaked with tears. They took her in and sat her down. She was almost hysterical, and Ray was concerned that some kid had tried to rape her. Eventually she calmed herself enough to tell them the whole story.

"Well, I think Judy has found your elusive alien," Ray said to Claire at last.

Claire frowned. "I just don't believe it. The size of the thing Judy is describing! How has somebody not found it already?"

"By the sound of it, it's been finding people all over," said Ray. "Travelling up and down the irrigation canals and even slipping up the creek to old Arthur Lund's place."

"Tell me again what the girls and Connie's mom said to you," Claire said to Judy. "About becoming 'one of them'."

"They said I just needed to let it kiss me," Judy sobbed. "And that it was like ripping off a band aid. One moment and then it would all be over. Even the maid was one of them."

"I need to call Agent Ashcroft," said Claire, heading for the phone in the hallway.

"Judy, I want you to go and lie down," said Ray. "You've had an awful fright but you're safe now."

"I can't sleep," said Judy. "I don't know if I ever want to sleep again. What if I dream of that ... that *thing*?"

"All right just take it easy. Mom's calling that FBI friend of hers and then we'll send for the doctor. He'll give you something for your nerves."

"No! I don't want the doctor here! What if he's one of them?"

"One of them?"

"One of the people who've had their minds messed with by that creature!"

Ray frowned. Paranoia was understandable, of course, but he couldn't help but agree with her. He liked this town even less now knowing that a good deal of its residents may have had their minds altered by some tentacled monstrosity. "Okay, no doctor. But let me fix you a brandy. For medicinal purposes only."

As he was pouring her a small dose of brandy at the drinks trolley, Claire came in.

"I can't get hold of Agent Ashcroft," she said.

"Never around when you need one, these FBI types," said Ray sardonically.

"I called Andy and Fred. Fred is over at the lab, but Andy will drop by. He wants to hear all about this tentacle."

"I don't want Judy worked into a state again," said Ray, handing Judy the tumbler of brandy. "She's already told us everything."

"I know, but Andy will have some questions for her."

"She needs rest, not an interrogation."

"It's not an interrogation! I know Judy has had a fright, but the safety of this town is at stake! Now, Andy will be here in a few minutes. Drink up that brandy, Judy, and Ray, pour me one."

"Brandy all round," said Ray, pouring out two more measures. "I think we need it."

Andy arrived promptly, squeezing his RV onto their drive next to Judy's Chevy which Ray had gone out to straighten up. He came hurrying in, eager to see Judy, pausing briefly to be introduced to Ray and to accept a drink from him.

Judy, feeling a little better, gave him the same story she had given Ray and Claire. Andy nodded thoughtfully throughout and was particularly interested in the tubular syphon beneath the tentacle's single sucker.

"A dart, you say?"

"What could that be?" Ray asked.

Andy rubbed his shaggy beard. "Well, some land snails reproduce using a gypsobelum, that is to say a calcareous 'love dart' which they insert into their prospective partner before mating."

"Mating ..." Judy mumbled. "I'm going to be sick!"

Claire rushed to fetch her a bucket while Andy continued his ruminations. "This 'love dart' doesn't contain sperm – that comes later – no, the dart injects a hormone-like substance that allows more of its sperm to survive once the mating begins."

They watched Judy dry heave over the bucket Claire had brought.

"Oh, my dear," said Andy, "I don't think the thing was really trying to mate with you. You're hardly its type. And I've never seen a cephalopod use a gypsobelum so its purpose remains unknown."

"Could it not have something to do with mind control?" asked Ray.

"Hmm?"

"Instead of injecting a hormone, perhaps it injects some other substance that causes these delusions."

"Like a hallucinogen? Yes, that could very well be it! Tell me, Judy, if this sucker thing did manage to ... *kiss* your face, then its dart would be positioned under your chin, correct?"

Judy shuddered at the mental image this conjured but she nodded.

"What does that tell us?" asked Ray.

"Well, not a lot," Andy admitted. "Wherever this thing came from, it probably isn't used to using its tricks on humans. Who knows what shape or size its usual prey is? But if this dart or whatever it is, is inserted under the chin, then we surely must be able to find some wound or sign of entry on some of the people now suffering from delusions."

"It boggles the mind," said Ray. "All those people who think they've won the lottery or their dead dog has come back to life, all of them have been face-hugged by this monstrosity and haven't said a word! Just carried on with their lives as if everything was fine!"

"It's a fascinating evolutionary defense mechanism," said Andy. "It's not unknown for some species to use other species for defensive purposes. There is a crab in the Indian Ocean which carries a poisonous urchin around on its carapace to deter predators."

"You think this alien is using people as a defense?"

"Could be. It seems pretty clear that it has been attacking people at random, those who happen to go near the canals, and messing with their minds. It makes them bring more victims to it, just as Judy's friends tried to do, fresh recruits, as it were."

"But to what end?"

"Well, concealment of its existence seems to be a main priority. As you said, none of those who have encountered this creature have ever mentioned it. Not one! Except Judy here, who had a lucky escape. Those who were not so lucky seem to be unwilling to talk about it. This could be part and parcel of the delusionary effect its darts have on them. Maybe they don't remember or maybe they don't want to remember. That's why they are given pleasant delusions in place of the horrid truth."

Ray remembered poor Donnie Kowalski and his seizure at the police station. He had been desperate to tell them something but had been unable to get the words out. "Even those who want to speak out may be physically unable to," he said. "What of those who have been plagued by waking terrors? Like Donnie Kowalski and that young irrigation worker?"

"Yes," said Andy. "The drug may be so powerful that it causes a psychological inhibition when its subjects try to speak out. Even when the delusions take a nasty turn, the sufferers are still unable to tell anybody that there is a creature out there preying on the town's populace. They just can't physically put it into words. It's incredible!"

"A carrot and stick method," said Andy. "The drug produces pleasant delusions in those who accept its commands while giving frightening visions to those who reject them. That way it is able to raise an army of willing servants who are *compelled* to do its bidding."

"And those who resist are driven mad and eventually to suicide," said Claire. "But why is that young people seem to be the ones who resist the most?"

"Something to do with the immaturity of the mind?" Andy suggested. "Perhaps the drug doesn't work very well on the young."

"Children have been affected also," said Ray, remembering little Nancy and her imaginary dog. "It seems to be adolescents who present the biggest challenge to the drug."

"I'm sure our friend Dr. Johnson would have something to say about phases of development and the adolescent mind but my guess is that the natural rebelliousness of the teenage years creates a tendency to reject the drug or at least try to overcome it. After all, doesn't everybody say that teenagers have no respect for authority these days? Why should it be any different with an alien authority?"

"But Connie and her friends succumbed," said Judy, looking up from her bucket. "They're kids and they don't seem to have suffered any delusions, good or bad."

"From what you've told me about Connie and her friends, they are a far cry from rebellious," said Claire. "In fact, they seem desperate to conform at all costs. What's more, they live relatively comfortable lives anyway. No carrot is needed for them and no stick either. In that way they are the perfect servants for the alien."

"Yes, I'm guessing the creature's true obstacles are the rough, tough kids who hate being made to conform and follow orders," said Andy. "But we must get Dr. Johnson in on this, I'm sure he will have some fascinating theories. Have you had any luck with Agent Ashcroft?"

"No, I've tried the motel he's staying at and the mayor's office. Nobody seems to be able to place his whereabouts."

"Well, he'd better check in sooner rather than later. This news will require an emergency meeting."

"You know, I think I will have that lie down," said Judy, rising from the sofa.

Claire helped her upstairs, leaving Ray and Andy alone. Ray poured them another drink.

"You know, it's funny," Ray said, handing a scotch to Andy. "Us adults have been giving these kids a pretty hard time. Criticizing their music, their clothes, their friends and all the rest of it. We don't like their rebelliousness or individuality. It's ironic that those very things could end up being their saving grace. Though what that means for the rest of us, I daren't think."

CHAPTER 14

Tommy flicked his lighter on and held the blueish flame to the cigarette in his mouth. He sucked a drag and put the lighter back in the pocket of his leather jacket, exhaling slowly, blowing the smoke out to add to the fug above the card table.

Burt was there, along with a couple of other club members called Lou and Ralph. They were playing pinochle. Burt shuffled the deck and dealt the cards. Some of the other club members were lounging around on the sofas behind them, smoking and reading copies of *Real Men* and *2-Gun Western*.

"C'mon, Burt, are you dealing or wiping the grease off your fingers with those cards?" Tommy said. "Hurry up and deal."

"Wiseguy," said Burt, grinning at the other two. "Just because the boss is pleased with him for standing lookout, he thinks he can bust our balls. Just remember, you're still a prospect."

Tommy grinned and picked up his hand.

There came a loud scream from the backroom followed by a bout of sobbing. A shudder went through the club members and they began to talk louder in an attempt to cover up the racket and pretend they didn't know what was going on back there.

A couple of days had passed since the rescue of Marie Giorgino from the Jungle Dukes. She was currently going cold turkey on a mattress in the backroom of the clubhouse, waited on and watched over twenty-four-seven by Johnny and his boys. They weren't going to risk losing what they had gained, and they weren't going to send her back to her parents a hophead. Her brother had been insistent on that. It would kill them, he said, and they had no dough for any fancy rehabilitation. They knew where she was and that she was being looked after and that was enough.

A couple of the boys had been through the mill themselves, mostly in reform school where, after the initial few mercy shots of morphine administered by the nurse trailed off, cold turkey was part of the whole vacation. You spent the first few weeks crawling the walls, but you got clean, there was no doubt about that.

There had been no sign of retribution from the Jungle Dukes. Sheriff Benson and his boys in blue had chased them back north but whether any of them had wound up in the clink was not known. The gang were on edge anyhow, armed to the teeth at all hours. And it wasn't just the Dukes they were prepared against. It took a town hall meeting and a speech from an FBI agent to convince the squares that something wasn't right in Ralston but for those who spent their nights cruising its neon-lit streets in search of fun, the weirdness was old news.

It wasn't just Donnie Kowalski murdering his parents and then killing himself that spooked them. There wasn't one member of the gang who didn't know of somebody who had gone missing or was currently suffering from delusions. Some people had even approached the gang showing an unusual interest in either joining them only to somehow separate members from the pack, asking them to follow them down storm drains or take moonlit walks along the canals. Initially dismissed as fags trying to score some teenage ass, it gradually became clear to them that something more sinister was trying to muscle in on their turf and turn their members and it sure as hell wasn't the Jungle Dukes.

Even old Nick – Johnny's uncle who owned the lot their very clubhouse sat on – had started acting funny, talking about throwing a party up by the creek. Nick Short was a good guy, generous too, letting them have their clubhouse and fix up their cars in garage but he was notoriously cheap when it came to money. Every bolt and nut, every drop of oil had to be paid for, that was the deal. The idea of him throwing a picnic party for them was just plain weird. It put them on their guard, made them paranoid and even more distrustful of outsiders.

Marie's screaming trailed off to sobbing and then silence. The mood in the clubhouse immediately improved but it was not long before another commotion secured their attention. They could hear excited talking and some whistles of admiration outside as if somebody had rolled up in an exceptionally tasty rod. When Tommy, Burt, Don and Lou abandoned their game to find out what the hubbub was, they discovered it wasn't a car causing the stir, but a man.

Archie Novak, the hopeless junkie had turned up and was barely recognizable. He'd washed, put on a clean shirt and looked like he'd had a couple of good meals. He wasn't even asking around for money but seemed to be purely there on a social visit.

"What gives, Archie?" somebody asked. "You look like a million bucks compared to what you used to!"

"Yeah, who's the broad?" said somebody else. "When a guy gets spruced up that good, you just know there's a broad involved."

"No broad but my lovely wife," said Archie.

"No kidding? I thought she kicked you out?"

"Since I turned over a new leaf, she took me back in," said Archie, his face beaming.

"You mean to say, you're clean?"

"Clean as a whistle and never looking back. This is the new me, boys!"

They were dumbstruck. "How'd you get clean in just a few days?" Burt asked him. "I saw you Tuesday and you were doped up to the eyeballs."

"Well, that's a little secret and I can't say too much, but let's just say, I found The Cure."

"The Cure?" said Lou, "Well, c'mon, Archie, tell us? What is it, some new pill?"

"No pills. No more drugs for me from here on out."

"Then what's the secret?"

"It's kind of psychological."

"Boy, that's a big word for you, Archie. What does it mean?"

"You dummy," said Burt. "It means he did it in his mind."

"That's pretty much it," said Archie. "Although I did have some help from a special friend."

"A doc, huh? What did he do, hypnosis?"

"Yeah, kind of."

"Boy, we could do with that special doctor here," said Burt. "We got a dame who's going cold turkey and it ain't pretty."

"Really?" said Archie. "Then I'm sure my friend could help."

"We'd have to put it to Johnny first. Nobody sees the girl without his say so."

"He's inside," said Lou. "Let's go ask him!"

One of the gang went inside and fetched Johnny. He came out wearing a frown at seeing Archie who he made no secret of disliking. "I thought I told you to beat it, Archie," said Johnny. "No hopheads around here."

"I ain't a hophead no more, Johnny," said Archie. "I'm clean. That's what I came here to tell you."

"Yeah, he ain't kidding," said Lou. "Look at him!"

"What gives?" asked Johnny.

"There is a doctor I know," said Archie, "who fixed me up, good as new. I don't crave, I don't get the panics, I am one hundred percent cured!"

"Maybe we could get this doc of his here to look at Marie," Lou said to Johnny.

"I am afraid that's impossible," said Archie. "He doesn't do house calls. But I can take the girl to see him."

"Where does he live?"

"Oh, I'd be happy to take you there right now."

"Another time. We got important business right now."

"All right then but let me know. I'd like for you all to meet my doctor."

"Come back later. Right now, I gotta talk to our prospect."

"Me?" Tommy asked as Archie headed off through the wrecked cars, a spring in his step.

"You're the only prospect we have at the moment," said Johnny. "Follow me."

He led them over to his car which was parked in pride of place beside the clubhouse. A few other club members were hanging about, inspecting their engines and talking shop. Johnny reached under the back fender of his car and pulled something off. As he rose, Tommy saw that it was a small metal box, presumably magnetized so it could be concealed underneath the car. Johnny opened it and took out what looked like a cigarette, fatter towards one end like a small carrot.

"Smoke?" Johnny asked, offering it to Tommy.

"Um, sure. What is it?"

"Grass. Tea. Mary Jane. All of the above."

Tommy took the reefer and held it delicately in his fingers as he contemplated the small thing that seemed to cause so much uproar among parents and teachers. "I thought you didn't ..." he trailed off, not knowing how to finish without insulting Johnny.

"Didn't deal drugs?" said Johnny with a grin. "I don't. This ain't drugs. This is just funky tobacco. Just natural leaves, you see? I don't deal hop, that's something else entirely. Trouble is, most squares can't tell the difference between a little tea and a life-ruiner like heroin. Don't ever end up like Archie Novak. I don't care how clean he says he is now, that boy's been to hell and back because of his addiction. Stick to booze, smokes and a little tea now and then and you'll be all right." He took his lighter out and flipped it on, offering the little flame to Tommy.

Tommy realized he still had a cigarette in his other hand. It was nearly down to the tip and had a good head of ash on it. He took one last drag and then tossed it, grinding it into the dirt with his heel. He put the reefer in his mouth and cupped his hand around it as Johnny lit it for him. He took a tentative drag and winced as the sickly-sweet smoke filled his lungs.

"First one's on me," said Johnny, grinning at Tommy's reaction. "Buck a stick from here on out."

"Thanks," Tommy wheezed, his eyes tearing up.

"You did good the other night. You stuck with us and warned me about those Jungle cats coming in."

Tommy shrugged. "Don't really feel like I helped much. They fell on Mack's crew just as I got to you. What's the difference?"

"The difference is, you didn't cut and run, not even when the cops showed up. That's good, we like that. You've been putting in the work around here and you know cars even if you ain't got one. And Donnie vouched for you, God rest his soul. That makes you all right with me. Tommy," he put his hand on Tommy's shoulder. "I want to make you a member of the Camelots."

"Gee, no kidding?" said Tommy, immediately hating the way his voice made him sound like an excitable schoolboy. "I mean, you do, huh?"

"Sure. You've got what it takes. There's just the initiation to do."

"What's the initiation?"

"You gotta race Mack. He's our best driver and if you go the distance with him without crapping out or getting wasted, then you're in."

Tommy nodded excitedly although his heart was sinking down to his boots. *Race Mack?* He hadn't been behind the wheel of a car since Judy freaked out over that pickup truck incident. That was the first and last time she had let him drive. He was no racer and Mack was a hardhead. He wouldn't go easy on him. "I thought you had to be twenty-one to race?"

"That's at the dragstrips," said Johnny with a laugh. "You ain't ready for Laguna Seca yet. Besides, the strips are for competing with other clubs. This is a private race."

By private, Tommy knew he meant 'illegal'.

"Sylvia Avenue has a nice stretch of blacktop perfect for racing," Johnny went on. "Saturday night, late. You dig?"

"Yeah, Saturday, sure." His curfew was midnight so he didn't know how he was going to swing that with Mom and Dad but he had more pressing concerns. Namely, he had to learn how to race.

If there was anybody he could come clean to then it was Burt. He spilled to him when they were driving home. Burt had been ecstatic to learn that Tommy was going to be initiated and told him he could use the Mercury as he didn't have a car of his own. He even told him that they would make some adjustments together to get it race ready.

"We've got bigger problems than that," said Tommy. "I've never raced anybody."

"Not even in your Coupster back in Virginia?"

Tommy sighed. "I wasn't exactly telling the complete truth when I said I had a Coupster."

"What *is* the complete truth?"

"I've never owned a car. I've only ever driven that old heap my sister uses."

Burt took his eyes off the road to goggle at him. "You're shitting me."

"I wish I was but honestly, my sister has spent more time behind a wheel than I have."

Burt whistled. "Boy, have we got our work cut out for us. Starting from tomorrow, you and I are gonna be working on the car and working on your driving. There's a dirt track at the back of my house but you need to get some blacktop experience in too, and I know just the place."

Susanne Crane closed her book and put it down on the coffee table. It was a Pam and Penny book by Rosamond du Jardin – one of her favorites – but she just couldn't concentrate. She didn't know what it was, but something felt wrong; *off* somehow, either with herself or her surroundings, she wasn't quite sure.

She gazed at the bookshelves and framed pictures that lined the walls of the Hurley's living room. Little Anthony was asleep, and she was left with her thoughts until Mr. and Mrs. Hurley came home. She often babysat for them. They were nice people and the money sure came in handy, especially now that she had a boyfriend.

Maybe I should call Marty? she thought to herself mischievously. She knew she wasn't supposed to use the Hurley's telephone for personal calls, but now that she had an honest-to-God boyfriend (and Martin Landers, no less), the temptation was almost too much.

She still could barely believe how her life had turned around in the last few days. Ever since Connie Lund and the gang had ditched that stuck-up Judy Weldon for reasons she still hadn't figured out, it was almost as if all the opportunities Judy had enjoyed had been suddenly turned over to Susanne. First, Connie Lund had asked her to start hanging out with her, then she had been put on the prom committee and now, out of the blue, Martin Landers had asked her out. Finally, it was her moment to show the world her true colors! No longer was she second fiddle to Judy. She had eclipsed her and now it was her turn to shine while Judy slipped away into obscurity (*and serves her right*).

So why then did she feel so apprehensive?

It was something to do with the voice in the back of her mind that called to her; not in words exactly, but the message was clear nevertheless.

Go get Anthony.

She didn't like that voice, even though it wasn't exactly a voice. It was as if her own mind was reminding her to do something she had forgotten and didn't want to remember.

Go get Anthony and take him down to the drain at the end of the street.

I don't want to, she thought. *It's wrong to wake him. It's wrong to take him out of the house.*

But you must.

She was feeling something slipping from her the more she questioned herself. *Why? Why must I?*

Do it!

No! You can't make me!

Oh, but I can ...

Who was that talking to her? Who was in her head, giving her orders? She was starting to feel scared now. Something was wrong. Something was very wrong.

I should call Marty. He would know what to do.

Wait. Call Marty? *Martin Landers?* He wasn't really her boyfriend, that was just a fantasy of hers, wasn't it? But she had almost phoned him just then, really, actually picked up the phone and called him. Was she losing her mind? Martin Landers wouldn't look twice at her! He'd laugh if she called him up!

But she was so sure a moment ago that they were going steady. That had felt so real. And Connie Lund ... *Connie Lund?* Had she really believed that they were best friends? That she was on the prom committee?

Memories began to resurface in her mind, ugly memories she didn't want. She remembered water, ripples, a slimy wet kiss. She remembered being scared and revolted and ... and then ... *bliss*. Happiness had flooded her being after that, a happiness that had banished all the sadness from her mind, all the rejection and humiliation she had felt all her life. Gone in a heartbeat. But it wasn't really gone, was it? It would never be gone. It would always be there just below the surface, no matter how hard she pretended, no matter how enjoyable the fantasy.

Go get Anthony. And you could use a top-up yourself. You're losing it, kid.

"No!" she said. "Get out of my head!"

Don't you want to be popular? Don't you want Martin Landers to date you?

"Shut up!"

Then, another voice spoke to her, or rather, sang, and she was pretty sure this one wasn't in her head, but an actual voice that her ears were picking up. It was a child-like voice that had a haunting echo.

"You'd better watch out ..."

It was the beginning of a song, a song that was instantly familiar but one she couldn't quite put her finger on.

"You'd better not cry ..."

She felt suddenly sick. It was definitely a child's voice, singing a popular Christmas song about ... *Santa Claus*. Ever since she had been four years old, she had loathed Santa Claus. The very sight of his overly jovial red cheeks and fat belly gave her a sick feeling of dread. She knew why. When she had been four years old, her mother had taken her Christmas shopping. There had been a costumed Santa in a flimsy grotto outside of Walgreens. Kids were lining up to sit on his knee and tell him their wishes for Christmas.

Her mother had left her in line while she ran into the store. Susanne hadn't wanted to be left alone. She hadn't wanted to sit on Santa's knee. She had wanted to stay with her mom but it was too late now. Her mom had vanished and the line was getting shorter. Soon enough, it was her turn and still, her mom had not come out of Walgreens.

Santa beckoned. Susanne held back, sucking her finger. One of Santa's elves scooped her up and placed her on Santa's knee. Up close, he was terrifying. The beard was fake, Susanne could see that even at age four. His real face was old and round but not at all like the happy Santa you saw on Coca-Cola advertisements. He was ugly and smelled funny and Susanne was struck by one thought and one thought only; *this is not a nice man.*

She had cried. She had wriggled. Santa's hard hand gripped her tightly around her middle, crushing her to him. His face leered in at hers, angry, his eyes demanding that she be quiet and play the game. But Susanne didn't want to play. She wanted her mommy. Eventually, Santa released her and she slid down from his knee and ran out of the grotto screaming for her mom.

Ever since then she had never been able to look at Santa Claus and not feel uneasy. And now, all alone in the Hurley's home with little Anthony slumbering upstairs, somebody was singing *Santa Claus is Comin' to Town* to her.

She looked around in a panic. The voice seemed to be coming from the far wall.

The fireplace. *The chimney.*

There was a scuttling noise. Soot trickled down in a black stream. A gloved hand gripped the edge of the fireplace, fat, sausage-like fingers grasping, pulling at its rim.

An upside-down face appeared, bloated and sweaty, ruddy-cheeked with a false beard hanging from it like old, gray seaweed. Its eyes were glowing coals set deep in the pudgy flesh. It opened its mouth and grinned a vile grin of broken, yellowed teeth.

"Hello, Susanne!" it hissed. "Have you been a good girl?"

Susanne screamed and clamped her hands over her eyes, willing the hideous vision to disappear. The noise of further scrabbling forced her to open her eyes. When she did, she saw the grotesque thing pulling itself down the chimney and out through the fireplace towards her.

She screamed again. The thing was on its feet now, soot crumbling off it and blackening the Hurley's good carpet. She pressed her back into her chair, unable to move as the thing towered over her. It seemed to be swelling, expanding like a balloon, folds upon folds of flabby flesh stretching its cheap red suit to bursting point. The hideous, grinning face sat atop a sphere that was rapidly filling the whole room.

Susanne gasped in terror as the balloon man enveloped her chair, flaccid flesh pushing against her frail form, suffocating her. She could smell its stink and it reminded her of that day outside of Walgreens when she had been four years old, terrified as Santa had held her in his grasp, the feeling of helplessness, of being unable to get away.

"All right!" she screamed. "All right! I'll do it! I'll do what you want!"

She had known what it was all along. She knew this was her mind playing one mean trick on her. She knew what she had to do. There was no other choice. She squeezed her eyes shut and told herself over and over again to do what was needed.

When she opened her eyes, the horrible vision was gone. The room was as it had been moments before, untouched.

She got up out of her chair, dizzy and shaking. She forced herself to fight her nerves. She forced herself to do what was necessary. She went upstairs and roused Anthony. She put his dressing gown on him and then made him step into his slippers.

"Come on, Anthony," she said softly. "We have to go outside for a bit."

"Why?" Anthony asked, sleepily.

"Only for a little it. Then you can go back to your nice warm bed."

Yes, once it was done, Anthony could go back to sleep. And then she would call Marty. She knew she wasn't supposed to, but she didn't care. She deserved to. As a reward to herself. Yes. A reward. Speak to Marty.

And just like that, the mask of make-believe slipped back over her head. Her small flirtation with the truth had been punished ruthlessly. The brief spark of rebellion that had been briefly kindled inside her had been snuffed before it had even had a chance to glow.

She led Anthony downstairs and over to the front door. Softly opening it, the two of them slipped out into the night and walked hand in hand down the silent street.

CHAPTER 15

The following morning, Ray went down to the police station to see if there had been any word on Agent Ashcroft. Claire had tried calling but found the line busy on repeated attempts. She also tried the motel and mayor's office again but there had been no sign of him.

At the station, Ray found Dr. McCarthy railing against the desk sergeant who was regarding him with patient eyes, his face as cool as a cucumber.

"I tell you, this is all highly irregular," Dr. McCarthy was nearly shouting. "And just when will the man's replacement arrive in Ralston?"

"We have called the bureau and they will send their agents as soon as they can," the desk sergeant replied. "They should be here as early as tomorrow morning."

"Good morning, fellas," said Ray, approaching the desk.

Dr. McCarthy regarded him irritably. "You heard the news?"

"What news, Doc?"

"That FBI fellow, Ashcroft, was murdered last night. I got the call to come and do the autopsy this morning, now here I am and they won't let me see the body!"

"The federal bureau have their own pathologists," said the desk sergeant. "As I said, they are sending their men as soon as possible."

"Then why am I here?" Dr. McCarthy exclaimed.

"Agent Ashcroft murdered!" Ray exclaimed. "My wife has been trying to get hold of him. What happened?"

"I'm not at liberty to discuss the details," said the desk sergeant.

"Officer Williams told me on the telephone last night," said Dr. McCarthy, "that Agent Ashcroft was found in the parking lot of the motel he was staying in. He'd been stabbed to death."

"That call was made in error," said the desk sergeant. "Officer Williams had no right to go over the sheriff's head."

"Who's going over my head?" said Sheriff Benson, emerging from his office. "Ah, what can I do for you boys?"

"Dr. McCarthy has come to see Agent Ashcroft's body," said the desk sergeant. "I told him the FBI have been called and that they'll send their own people."

"Oh, I'm sure we can let the good doctor take a peek if he wants to," said the sheriff with a smile.

"Well, if the FBI want to perform the autopsy themselves then it's no skin off my nose," said Dr. McCarthy. "But I don't like my time being wasted. I've got a list of patients as long as my arm."

"And you, Ray?" asked the sheriff. "What brings you here?"

"Well," said Ray. "I'm looking for Agent Ashcroft actually, but I guess I've found him too late. My wife has some important information to pass on, but she hasn't been able to get hold of him. Now I know why. Say, we've been calling you boys all morning but can't get through. Trouble with your line?"

"We've had a lot of calls," said the desk sergeant.

Ray glanced at the telephone behind the sergeant. It was quiet enough now. *Odd*, thought Ray. *And odd that the folks at the motel said nothing to Claire about a stabbing in their parking lot last night.*

"Well, we hate to be the bearers of bad news," said Sheriff Benson, "but poor old Agent Ashcroft is in our basement, dead as a doornail. Why don't you both come take a look?"

"Me?" asked Ray. "Well, I ..."

"Sure! Come on down while I put the good doc's mind at rest. Then we'll have some coffee in my office and you can call your wife and give her the bad news."

Ray and Dr. McCarthy exchanged a befuddled glance and then, shrugging their shoulders, followed Sheriff Benson over to the door that led down to the cells, feeling the eyes of the desk sergeant on them every step of the way.

Sheriff Benson heaved open the heavy door and at once, Ray was hit by a strong smell of dank moisture. Dr. McCarthy had noticed it too and wrinkled his nose with distaste.

"Trouble with damp, Sheriff?" he asked.

"We're getting someone in to look at it," said the sheriff dismissively.

Ray followed the doctor and Sheriff Benson down the steps that led into the basement. A light flickered and the smell of damp increased as they descended. Somewhere, he could hear gushing water. "Sounds like you got a bust pipe," he said.

"Ain't nothing to worry about," said the sheriff.

But Ray *was* worried. None of this was adding up. Not the call Dr. McCarthy got about Agent Ashcroft's murder, not the silent phone behind the desk. Why was it constantly engaged and yet it hadn't rung once since he had got there? And now this damp smell and the sound of rushing water in the station's basement.

He stopped dead in his tracks. Had Benson and his boys opened up a pipe that was connected to the canals or storm drains? Sheriff Benson looked back at him, the flickering light making the shadows on his face shift and change erratically.

"You with us, Ray?" he called.

"I just remembered," Ray replied, "I left my wallet on the desk. I'll just be a moment."

He turned his back and left the figures of the sheriff and Dr. McCarthy in the narrow corridor as he made his way back up the stairs. As he hurried through the reception area towards the double glass-paneled doors, the desk sergeant rose and came around the desk towards him.

"Where are you going, Sir?"

"I ... gotta be somewhere," said Ray.

"Can't let you do that, Sir."

The sergeant came to intercept him. *My god, he means to detain me by force!* Ray thought in a sudden panic.

He dodged the sergeant's outstretched arms and flung himself through the double doors, stumbling out into the sunlit parking lot. He didn't stop running until he got to his car.

When he got home, he told Claire of his suspicions. "I'm telling you, Claire, the police are in on it. The sheriff, the desk sergeant, the whole lot of them."

"And you think they tried to convert you down in the basement?"

"They've got a serious water problem down there, that's for sure. My guess is that they've opened up a pipe in the floor and the creature can pop one of its tentacles up in the police station's basement. God knows how many people they've converted! And I left Dr. McCarthy down there, God forgive me!"

"There wasn't anything you could have done," said Claire. "I'm just glad you got away safely."

"Now they'll know that we know," said Ray. "We need to be careful."

Claire stood up and went out into the hall.

"Where are you going?"

"To find that colonel. He's the only person I can go to now. While you were gone, I tried to call out of town. The switchboard sent me round in circles."

"Then those operator gals have been converted too," said Ray.

"And Ralston is effectively cut off. It wouldn't surprise me that the FBI have no clue that one of their agents has been killed."

"They'll send someone eventually, won't they? When Ashcroft doesn't check in?"

"By then it may be too late. We might all be under that creature's control."

"All right, go tell the colonel. But be careful, Claire! And for God's sake avoid the cops."

Claire had no desire to speak to Colonel Baskin but, with Agent Ashcroft dead and the police now under the control of the alien, she had nobody else to turn to. And, as leader of the task force, he needed to know what they were up against.

She drove down to the town hall and parked among the jeeps and army trucks. Uniformed men hurried in and out of the back offices which were spread with reports, maps and charts as if Ralston was the subject of a military campaign. She found the colonel in the largest office, bawling out somebody on the telephone.

"I don't care what you say, just get me a better connection! I've had one of my boys trying you all morning and you're giving us the runaround. What? Well how can *all* the circuits be busy? No, you can't call me back! Do you know who this is, Missy? This is Colonel Arthur Baskin of the United States Army ... hello? Hello?" He slammed the receiver down. "Damned woman hung up on me! There's something funny going on in this town. Milton! Where are you, Milton?"

A short G.I. came running past Claire, throwing up a salute to the colonel.

"Milton, get on the military frequencies. Contact Camp Roberts, tell them to get the FBI on the horn. Tell them we got one of their agents on a slab here in Ralston and a town that seems set against us."

As Milton hurried off to execute his orders, Claire stepped into the office. "I see you've heard the news."

Colonel Baskin glanced up at her and his already seething face took on a deeper red. "Get her out of here!" he commanded. Two G.I.s came forward to hustle her out of the office.

"Wait a minute!" Claire exclaimed. "I'm part of the task force!"

"Not anymore you're not!" snapped the colonel.

"What do you mean?"

"I mean I don't trust you. I had a word with Agent Ashcroft's superiors before this town's switchboard went haywire. They told me all about your family history and after your little performance in our last meeting, I can't say that I'm surprised."

Claire felt rage boiling inside her gut. "What my father was accused of has no bearing on me! You don't like me, Colonel Baskin, well that's fine. I'm not too crazy about you either. But this town is coming under the control of an alien influence and we need to work together if we're to have any chance of stopping it!"

"Aliens!" the colonel barked. "How do I know this alien story isn't something you cooked up as part of a commie plot to take over this town? After all, we only have your word for it that an alien is involved at all. Nobody's seen the damned thing!"

"My daughter has! Her school friends tried to convert her. She barely escaped!"

"Again, your words with no corroboration."

"Colonel, please! You must listen to me!"

"You don't give me orders! Agent Ashcroft may have been soft on you, but I'm not and his superiors sure as hell aren't. I told them about your views and they are considering listing you as a subversive individual. You'll be lucky to have your precious job at the NACA before the summer is out."

Claire reeled as if she had been slapped. Amid all the madness that the alien had visited on Ralston, she had been unprepared for good old-fashioned paranoia being their downfall. America's fear of communism had everybody so busy looking for reds in their breakfast cereal that they were blind to even greater dangers. Men like Colonel Baskin would turn on their fellow Americans over perceived 'subversive' behavior rather than cooperate with them. That was the real threat to their society. To even suggest otherwise made you a suspect, but they just couldn't see it.

"That's crazy ..." was all she could say, knowing that she had already lost.

"Well, pretty soon we'll have a few more of those FBI boys in Ralston," said the colonel with a smile. "We'll see what they think of you. But I run this task force and I say you're out!"

She turned and left the office, walked out of the building and got behind the wheel of her car. After giving herself a few moments to seethe and think about what to do next, she started the engine and drove east to the campground where Andy Willard was currently staying.

Hearing her approach as the wheels of her car crunched across the gravel, Andy opened the door to the RV and peered out.

"Claire!" he said in surprise. "I was going to call you. You gotta come in and see what I found!"

"Andy," said Claire, "we need to talk." She climbed up into the RV and took a seat at the kitchen table.

"Can I get you anything?" Andy asked her. "Coffee?"

"Do you have anything stronger?" she asked hopefully.

He grinned. "As a matter of fact, I do." He opened a small, refrigerated cupboard and brought out a bottle of syrupy cold Smirnoff vodka with ice crystalized on the glass. "Don't tell anyone, but I believe the Russians have got one thing on us." He flashed her a conspiratorial wink and poured a couple of tumblers. "I got some ginger beer mixers too. Rough day?"

"Well, if you consider finding out that the cops in Ralston are being controlled by an alien squid and then getting accused of being a subversive by the military a rough day, then sure. I've had a hell of a one."

"Jesus ...," said Andy as he topped up their tumblers with ginger beer and passed one to her. "The cops you say?"

Claire nodded and sipped the fizzy cocktail. "I couldn't get hold of Agent Ashcroft because he was murdered last night. When Ray turned up at the police station looking for him, they nearly talked him into a date with our tentacled friend. They've opened up a water pipe or something in their basement. Sheriff Benson, the lot of them are under the creature's sway."

"Oh my god," said Andy, his eyes wide behind his glasses.

"I went to the colonel and he damn near had me thrown in jail as a traitor. He's been in touch with the FBI. Threatened my job."

"That bastard."

"Andy, this town is under the control of that alien and it gets worse with every minute. You have to get out of here while you still can. Who knows how long before the whole town is converted?"

"Me? What about you?"

She drained the rest of her glass and set it down. "I have my family to think about. We have nowhere to go, besides, I can't just abandon this town to its fate. I don't know if Colonel Baskin will be able to halt the spread of this creature's influence. Have you found anything out about how it does what it does?"

Andy smiled at this, despite her distressing news. "As a matter of fact, I have. Come with me."

He got up and she followed him into the lab section of the RV. There, in a tray under an inspection lamp was the object of his excitement.

It was small, about an inch in length, and very thin. He brought a magnifying glass on a swing arm down in front of her so she could inspect it closely. It was slightly curved, tapering to one end and ending in a barbed tip.

"Is this what I think it is?" she asked.

"A gypsobelum? Yes."

"Where did you find it?"

"On the ground near one of the canals."

She glanced at him sidelong. "You've been back near the canals?"

"Yes. One of the victims must have plucked it out themselves and discarded it. This is fabulous, Claire! It's unlike anything I have ever encountered. It seems to be calciferous but without the proper testing I can't be sure."

He was talking too fast, rushing out information to cover his tracks. *He wasn't prepared for my sudden visit* she thought. "You'll be famous for its discovery, no doubt."

"Yes," he chuckled. "I telephoned some peers this morning. They're just as excited as I am."

Claire straightened from the magnifying glass. "You called them this morning, you say?"

"Hmm? Yes."

"Andy, where did you really find this dart?"

"What do you mean?"

"I mean, it seems remarkably lucky to simply come across one by one of Ralston's many canals. Considering its size. It would be like looking for a needle in ..., well, *Ralston*."

Andy looked at her and she looked at him. Sweat had started to bead on his forehead.

"You pulled it from your own flesh, didn't you?" she said at last. "After the creature suckered you. You haven't called anyone. The switchboard operators are blocking all calls out of town. But you didn't know that, did you?"

Andy bit his bottom lip. "I really wish you hadn't found me out. It rather complicates things."

"What things? What has it made you do?"

"It hasn't made me do anything. Yet."

The way he was talking made the alarm bell inside her head ring even shriller. He stood with his back to a counter upon which several tools of his trade were arranged. His hand reached for a scalpel. The bright light of the inspection lamp played along its short, razor edge.

"Andy ..." she said. "Whatever is going through your mind, you know it's the drug the alien injected you with, right?"

"Claire, you don't understand," said Andy. "*I* didn't understand. We saw this alien as a threat, something to be destroyed, but we were so wrong! Its coming is a miracle to be celebrated! It can give us so much, *teach* us so much!"

"Andy, you're under its influence! I don't know what it promised you or what it's showing you but remember all the others! Remember all those fools who think their lives are perfect now, remember the little girl with the invisible dog! It's lies, all of it!"

"Yes, lies to keep the public pacified. When has it ever been otherwise? The masses must always have their opiates; religion, patriotism and all the rest of it. How else are we to control the simpler members of society? But people like us, Claire, you and me, the scientists, the great thinkers, we do not need such lies. We are content to be in contact with a superior being! The answers to the great questions in the universe are at our fingertips! We stand on the brink of the void and all it takes is a little courage to put one foot out and enter a new plane of existence!”

“I’ll never take that step,” said Claire, shaking her head defiantly. “For to do so is to give up our independence, our free will, our very humanity! Your mind has been tampered with, Andy, do you not see that? These thoughts you are having are not really yours!”

He sighed. “I had a feeling it would be useless to try and persuade you. You’re bright, Claire, but you are also stubborn. It is such a shame. If it were otherwise, I would take you to it, but I have a feeling you would not come willingly.”

“No, I would not.”

“Then I am sorry.”

He lunged at her suddenly, seizing her arm and twisting her around so that her back was to him, pulling her close. He raised the scalpel to her neck and the terrifying thought passed through her mind that he meant to cut her throat.

She lashed back with the heel of her right pump and scraped Andy’s shin. In the same movement, she shoved his forearm away and then slammed her elbow into his stomach. He gasped in pain and she heard the clatter of the scalpel on the floor as she bolted from the lab.

As she made her way through the kitchenette towards the door, she felt his arms grab her around the waist and hurl her away from it. He threw her onto the vinyl seats and clambered on top of her. He no longer had the scalpel, thank God, but his hands worked their way around her throat as he tried to strangle her.

She gasped for air and clawed at his face but to no avail. He was as a man possessed in his mission to kill her, to silence her for his master’s protection. Her hands gave up their futile scratching and pummeling and floundered about for something else. The only thing to hand was the bottle of vodka on the folding table. Seizing it by its neck, she swung it down as hard as she could on the top of Andy's head.

It shattered on impact, dousing her with vodka and blood from the opened gash in Andy's scalp. His hands released their grip on her throat and went up to clutch his wounded head. Barely conscious, he fell flat on her with his pressing weight.

She squirmed out from under him and wiggled her way underneath the table, grasping for the door handle. Then, she spilled out of the RV and ran for her car, sobbing as she fled the awful scene.

It was the last straw for her. She wouldn't remain in this town a minute longer now she knew that nobody could be trusted. She would drop by the house, pick up Ray and the kids along with a few essentials and then they would hit the road and not stop driving until they found a motel far enough away from Ralston that she felt safe again. She was worried there wasn't enough gas in the world to take her that far.

As she headed back into town and wound her way through the late afternoon traffic, she grew conscious of a radio car in her rearview mirror that had been tailing her for two streets. It drew up close behind her and, sure enough, turned on its siren.

Its piercing wail tore at her already overworked nerves. There was no confusion. It was her it wanted to pull over; it was practically riding her rear fender. What could she do? What would *they* do? Take her in? Take her down to that basement of theirs? There was nothing for it, she *had* to pull over.

She slowed down and let her wheels ride the curb. She kept her engine running. The radio car parked immediately behind her. Its driver's door opened and Sheriff Benson climbed out, placing his hat upon his head.

Claire's heart hammered in her chest. He would try and convert her, she was sure of it and, when she resisted, he would kill her as Andy had tried to do. Those were the only two options offered by the monster that was slowly strangling this town; join or die.

Well, she wasn't going to let it come to that. She refused to choose. She had a family to think of and she was going to do everything she could to make damn sure they didn't have to choose either. She rolled down her window and let Sheriff Benson approach her door. In the tail of her eye she could see his well-worn belt buckle hover outside her window but before he could open his mouth, she slammed her foot down on the gas pedal and spun the wheel to the left, swinging out into the road.

Horns blared, drowning out Sheriff Benson's cries for her to halt. She kept going, weaving in and out of traffic with such speed it would put some of the town's young hot-rodders to shame. The siren of Sheriff Benson's car started up in the distance as she took a corner to the sound of squealing rubber.

She had to accelerate her plans. Benson was onto her. There would be no time to gather things from the house; they had to get out of there immediately. She took a few more turns to make sure she had lost her pursuer before heading for home.

The sunlight was fading as she turned onto Maple Street. She saw the radio cars as she approached the house and immediately slowed down and let the engine idle as she watched the scene from the end of the street. Two police cars were parked outside her house. *Damn them!* Of course Sheriff Benson had put out a call. She had to come home sometime, and they would be waiting to haul her in. Maybe they were hauling Ray and the kids in right now. And what could she do about it? Nothing!

She hammered the steering wheel with her palms in frustration. Everywhere she had turned today she had been thwarted. The alien had a tight grip on Ralston, and it was starting to squeeze. The cops were against her. The colonel was against her. The switchboard was useless. She had to get outside help. But how? Who would believe her?

There was always Clark Foreman, an old friend of her father's from the JPL; one of the few who had not turned on him. He had spoken up for her father when he had been accused of espionage and he had connections in Washington. Would he do the same favor for his daughter?

She was out of other options. Gritting her teeth and willing herself not to cry, she put the car into reverse and backed down the street. Turning the corner, she drove off in the direction of the Golden State Highway which would take her south to Bakersfield, and to her past.

CHAPTER 16

The cops said that somebody was after their mother. They said that her life was in danger and her whereabouts was unknown. They said she had made some enemies by poking around the current problem in Ralston and was now a woman marked for death and therefore required police protection. As Judy and Tommy sat on the top of the stairs and listened to their father argue with the two officers who had parked their radio cars in the street outside, Judy knew it was all lies. More lies. Lies within lies; that's what this town had become. They couldn't trust anyone, not even the police.

Their father knew it too but what could they do? The cops wouldn't let them leave. They were waiting for their mother to come home so they could ... what? Arrest her? *Murder* her? Judy wept at their predicament but, as the clock in the hall struck seven, it kindled a small flame of hope in her heart. Mom had been gone for a long time. The cops didn't know where she was. Had she been warned? Was she in hiding?

The small flame of hope was stifled slightly by the feeling of abandonment. Maybe Mom had run away or was hiding out at the NACE lab. If so, good for her. But what about them? What about Ralston?

Dad did his best to act like everything was normal. He clattered around the kitchen and made dinner; a meal none of them had much of an appetite for but they knew they had to carry on regardless.

They ate their corned beef hash on folding tables in the living room while *The Buccaneers* blared on the television set. None of them talked. As *The Jackie Gleason Show began*, Tommy headed upstairs, leaving Judy to help Dad clear away the dishes.

"Do you think Mom made a run for it?" she asked in a hushed voice as she picked up a towel and started drying. There was little point in whispering for the officers outside wouldn't be able to hear a conversation in the kitchen, but she felt like whispering anyway. She would do nothing to snuff that brave little flame of hope in her heart.

Dad sighed. "I hope so, sweetheart. It certainly looks that way."

"What will the cops do when they find out?"

"I don't think there's much they can do. Until the problem spreads to other counties, Sheriff Benson's boys are somewhat limited in their jurisdiction. Your mother has done nothing wrong and honest, law-abiding cops can't touch her. It's better that she's well away from here."

"But what will we do?"

Her dad put down the dish he was washing, peeled off his marigolds and hugged her close. "For the time being we must be patient. And brave. Your mom went to see that colonel today to tell her what happened to you out at Connie's house. Right now, he'll be coming up with a plan to blast this thing back to where it came from."

"Will everybody be all right after that?"

"I don't know, Judy. I just don't know."

She went upstairs to read and try and take her mind of the awfulness of the situation. Tommy's bedroom door was open and through it, she could see him standing in front of his mirror, combing his hair. He was wearing his leather jacket and boots.

"What do you think you're doing?" she asked him, pushing the door open wider.

"Going out."

"You're crazy. The cops have us under house arrest."

"Those cops ain't cops anymore," said Tommy. "They can't tell us what to do. Besides, I got a thing tonight. It's important."

"A thing? A *gang* thing?"

"We're a club, not a gang, and yeah, it's a club thing."

"Tommy, Mom is in danger, the town has gone crazy, we're under house arrest and all you can think about is your lousy greaser friends?"

"You think I don't know what's going on? But we gotta stick together, safety in numbers. The Camelots have been like a family to me and I gotta show tonight if I'm gonna be one of them."

"Wait, is it your initiation tonight? Is that what's so damned important?"

"Yeah, if you must know!"

"I don't believe it, I just don't believe it! I'm telling Dad."

She headed downstairs and found her dad on his knees organizing the magazines in the magazine rack. He always did this when he was troubled about something. *Tidying up*. Little jobs to keep his mind occupied. "Dad, there's something you should know."

He glanced up at her, a copy of *Harper's Bazaar* in his hand. "What is it, honey?"

"Tommy thinks he's going out. To meet that gang of his."

Dad blinked. "Well that's out of the question. And I've forbidden him from having anything to do with them. Wait a minute, has he been meeting them and lying about it?"

Judy bit her lip. "Maybe. I don't know."

Dad shoved the magazine roughly back into the rack and stood up. He marched towards the stairs, clearly intending to give Tommy a piece of his mind. Judy followed him, feeling guilty about dropping her brother in it but it was the only way she could think of to keep him home.

"Tommy!" Dad barked as he stomped up the stairs. He shoved open the door to his bedroom and stood in the doorway. Judy looked over his shoulder and gasped.

Tommy's room was empty. The window was open, and the curtains wavered in the warm night air.

Sneaking out hadn't been difficult. The cops had their eyes on the street out front, waiting for Mom to come home. They hadn't counted on anybody leaving through a back window and hopping the fence into the neighbor's yard.

Tommy cut through a couple more yards and made his way to the payphone at the end of Maple Street. He called Burt and told him he would need picking up an hour earlier than planned. Then, he lit a smoke and hung about on the curb until Burt showed.

It didn't take long for Burt to roll up to the curb in his newly souped-up Mercury. Tommy hopped in and they roared off to hit 10th street for an hour or so until the race began. They took a couple of rounds of the strip but saw none of the other Camelots.

"They'll be keeping their heads down," said Burt. "They always do before a race so as not to alert the cops that something's up. You ready for this, my man?"

"Born ready," lied Billy.

He and Burt had spent all last night tinkering with the engine, doing everything they could to squeeze more speed out of it. They swapped Burt's disc brakes for drums and adjusted them for zero drag, uncorked the exhaust system and tightened the intake-manifold bolts. The car might have been ready but Tommy sure didn't feel like he was. Once the car was fine-tuned to Burt's satisfaction, they had taken a few test runs on the deserted road on the edge of town.

The sheer power of the car frightened Tommy. It roared like a caged lion and had lurched forward as he pushed down on the accelerator with a sudden release of pent-up energy. Although the road was straight, the speed at which the car streaked down the blacktop made even the slightest movement a risky decision that could send him veering off into the scrub. There was no margin for error.

They headed over to Nick's garage to fill up on gas and check the tire pressure. They found most of the Camelots in the back lot, gearing up for a fun night.

"You racing Mack in Burt's old heap?" Lou marveled.

"Hey, it packs a punch," said Burt defensively. "I might not have the dough, but I know what I'm doing when it comes to engines."

"Ready to get your ass kicked?" said Mack, leaning against the hood of his black '55 Chevy, his arm around his girl, June.

"Are you?" Tommy retorted, drawing laughter from the crowd.

"Kid, I don't care what Burt's done to it, you'll never beat Mack's Chevy in that old rust bucket!" somebody yelled.

"He doesn't have to beat him," said Johnny, emerging from the clubhouse. "He just has to go the distance. If he reaches the finish line in one piece, he's made it. But Mack ain't gonna make it easy for him, are you Mack?" He threw a wink at the VP.

Mack flashed him a shark's grin and Tommy swallowed. He didn't know what the two of them had planned but it couldn't be good.

They hit the road as they had done the night of the raid on the old farmhouse, only this time there were more cars, more girls and a whole lot more noise. Windows rolled down, they whooped and cheered, sending catcalls between cars all the way out of town. The streets were deserted. The fear of what had infested the town kept everybody afraid and indoors. But not the Camelots. The night belonged to them and, Tommy got the feeling that they believed the town belonged to them too. They didn't care about the alien or the people under its control. Ralston's loss was their gain and, as they sped out into the night, they knew nobody would stop them, not their folks, not the cops, nobody.

They parked up on either side of Sylvia Avenue, hot rods lining the blacktop, a multitude of colored roofs under the warm, moonlit sky. Lines had been painted on the asphalt, measuring out a quarter mile. People spilled out of their cars and clustered around the starting line. Johnny sent Lou up to mark the finish line and June was selected as the starter girl. She walked out between the two cars, blowing pink bubbles with her gum, her hips swaying in her tight slacks. She held a scarlet handkerchief aloft.

"Good luck," Burt said to Tommy and he got out of the car, leaving the driver's seat vacant.

Tommy felt sick as he slid over into it. His hands shook which made him feel even more nervous because shaky hands could be the death of him now. He glanced over at Mack who was lounging in his Chevy, the window rolled down, a cigarette hanging from his lips. He grinned at Tommy and revved his engine. The noise was deafening.

"All right, everybody!" Johnny called. "This here is Tommy's initiation. If he goes the distance with Mack and comes out of it alive, he's made the club!"

There were some whoops and cheers at this, and Tommy tentatively took this as belief in his ability or, at the very least, sporting encouragement.

Tommy looked ahead at June, bathed in the headlights of the two cars. At a signal from Johnny, she brought the handkerchief down in a flutter of scarlet.

Tommy was barely aware that the race had started before his foot pressed down on the gas and he released the brake, his own body making the decisions his brain was too slow or scared to order. Tires squealed on the asphalt and both cars rocketed forward. The cheers of the crowd were drowned out in Tommy's ears; drowned out by adrenaline and the roar of the Mercury's engine.

"I just can't believe it," Dad was saying. "What's gotten into that boy? He knows what's going on, what the town is up against. Why take the risk just to meet up with his friends?"

He was sitting at the kitchen table staring into his coffee cup as if the answers were in that small, black mirror. Judy leaned against the countertop and watched him. He looked utterly out of his depth and she felt sorry for him. He was trying to keep it together but Mom was missing and now Tommy had deserted them.

"And the worst of it," Dad continued, "is that he's been lying to me for days. I explicitly told him to stay clear of that crazy gang but they've somehow turned him against me, poisoned his mind, just like that creature is doing to this town."

"I think he just wants to feel part of something," said Judy, not really understanding where her sudden sympathy for her brother was coming from. "He was lonely and they offered him a place, some relevance. He wanted it so bad that he's been blinded to what they really are; a bunch of hopeless dropouts who try to make up for their shortcomings with their fast cars and tough-guy attitudes."

She realized Dad was staring at her. "I guess everybody wants to belong, don't they?" he said wearily. "The innate need to fit in."

"I guess so."

"Perhaps I've been too hard on him. A boy needs friends after all. I just wish he'd picked better ones. Still, at least they aren't the types to have been converted by that monster. In fact, they might be the ones who are most resilient to its drug." His face brightened a little with this thought. "I mean, it's not like he's gone running to a bunch of kids like your Connie Lund who is recruiting kids for that alien."

"No," Judy said, slowly. "I suppose not."

"He might be safer than I thought. I'd rather have him here of course, but let's face it, at this moment he could be with a worse crowd."

Looking rather pleased with this revelation, he drank the rest of his coffee and stood up to put the cup in the sink. "I'm going to go and see if our boys in blue are still out front and then I think it might be time for bed."

Judy remained in the kitchen, biting her nail. She hadn't the heart to tell Dad the dangerous games Tommy would be playing in order to 'fit in' tonight. His sudden optimism was heartbreaking, and in that moment, she decided that it was up to her to stop Tommy from getting himself killed.

She could leave the house the same way Tommy had done, but there was no way she could get her car out of the drive without the two police officers noticing her. Nick's garage was where the gang would undoubtedly be hanging out before heading off to wherever this dumb race was supposed to happen and that was just about within walking distance, but she had to hurry.

While Dad was footling around upstairs, Judy silently opened the door that led from the kitchen to the back yard. She slipped out into the balmy night air and closed the door softly behind her.

She hurried over to the fence and scrambled up it, glad that she was wearing slacks and flats rather than a skirt and pumps. Dropping down into the neighbor's yard, she wondered which way Tommy had gone and ultimately decided it didn't matter. Once she reached the sidewalk, she hotfooted it in the direction of Nick's garage.

She got there just as they were setting out; a whole cavalcade of roaring engines and whooping kids leaning out of windows, smoking cigarettes. It was like a scene from the end of the world. Kids ruled the earth and there wasn't a damned thing any responsible adult could do about it.

Judy had no idea what sort of rod Tommy was tearing around in, but she was desperate not to be left behind in a cloud of dust. She threw herself in front of a car and involuntarily covered her eyes with her hands as it screeched to a stop a few feet from her.

"Hey, are you crazy!" cried out the driver; a greasy-haired kid with a bad case of acne.

Judy hurried around to his open window. "Do you know Tommy Weldon?"

"Sure, he's the prospect who's racing tonight!"

"I'm his sister, can you take me to the race?"

"His sister! Gee, I dunno ..."

"C'mon, let her in!" said another boy who was sitting with his girl on the back seat. "She's a bitchin' babe! The more the merrier!"

"Hey, remember me?" said the girl next to him, thumping his arm.

"I didn't mean nothing by it!" the boy said. "You can scoot over on to my lap and she can have your seat!"

"Hey, aren't you the girl who's going steady with Martin Landers?" asked the girl in the passenger seat. Judy recognized her as Bette Sommers from her grade.

"Not anymore," said Judy.

"Come on, get in, if you're getting in!" the driver said.

Judy gave him a grateful smile and hopped in the back seat as the frowning girl clambered onto her boyfriend's lap.

It was a circus at Sylvia Avenue. The cars were already lined up on either side of the road. A crowd of kids stood around two cars that were parked side by side on the asphalt. Judy clambered out of the car and ran up to the starting line. She could barely fight her way through to see Tommy in his car, his engine revving.

"Tommy!" she cried, but her voice was drowned out by the roaring engines and appreciative cheers of the crowd. She fought her way through the clamoring greasers and their girls and tried to run out in front of the two cars. Somebody grabbed her around the waist and pulled her back.

"Steady, Doll," said a voice in her ear. "You'll get run over flat."

She realized it was Johnny Packer who held her, and she shuddered. "Let me go, you ape! That's my brother in that car!"

"Oh boy, are you here to drag him home by his ear?"

Some of his nearby comrades laughed at this. Judy struggled free from his grip, but it was too late. The girl in the tight slacks and sweater at the starting line had dropped her handkerchief and the two cars leapt forward and a squeal of burning rubber.

The asphalt rushed beneath Tommy's eyes, his headlights making the road ahead a yellow and gray blur. The nose of his car was level with Mack's Chevy as they rocketed down the street. The needle on the speed dial hovered around 90 miles per hour. Any slipup now could be fatal.

Tommy knew Mack was going easy on him. His car could outrun his easily. *What's he waiting for?* Tommy knew something was coming but he didn't know what, or when.

And then it came. With a sudden lurch, Mack, slammed his car sideways into Tommy's. Hubcaps scraped briefly and the shock of the blow sent Tommy veering towards the edge of the road. His left tires rumbled on dirt and the steering wheel jerked frantically in his hands.

So that's it. He means to run me off the road!

Tommy frantically tried to regain control of the vehicle. He glanced over to Mack and saw his white teeth grinning manically. But he was giving him space. He was letting him get back on the road for another go.

Tommy eased all four wheels back up onto the asphalt but he knew it would only be a matter of time before Mack would slam him again.

He floored the gas pedal. The needle crept over 100 miles per hour. If he could somehow get in front of Mack, then he could maybe keep him from sidewinding him again. But Mack was on to him, matching him pace for pace. Tommy pressed down with all his weight on the pedal, willing his car to go just a little faster. The engine struggled. The needle wavered around 110. The nose of Mack's car was inches ahead of Tommy's. he cursed. He simply couldn't go any faster.

Then, came Mack's second attack.

If Tommy hadn't been ready for it, it would have sent him off the road and deep into the scrub at a dangerous speed. But Tommy was prepared. As soon as Mack's car swooped in for the kill, he closed the gap to meet it. The cars slammed together in the center of the road, hubcaps grinding, paintwork slithering as they fought for dominance.

Tommy and Mack glared at each other through dust-streaked windows. Mack broke off suddenly and Tommy's car lurched to the right. He fought the road as the back end of the car began to swing wildly from left to right. Just as he got it under control, Mack came in for another slam.

Tommy stamped on the brake pedal. He lurched forward and struck the bridge of his nose on the steering wheel as the tires screamed in protest. Mack's car shot across the road in front of him and sent up great clouds of dust as it rumbled off the road into the scrub. Tommy accelerated quickly, shooting past Mack who struggled through the dust and bushes to get back onto the road.

He couldn't believe it! He had outwitted and overtaken Mack! What's more, Lou's car was up ahead marking the finish line! He had done it! He had won!

Lou's face was the picture of surprise as Tommy whooshed past him, refusing to ease off the gas until he was absolutely sure he had made it. He gasped with relief and slowed down. It seemed to take an age for the car to come to a halt and when it did, he sat back in his seat and tried to stop his whole body from shaking.

He had just about managed it when Lou thumped on his window, making him jump and starting the shakes all over again. He rolled down the window.

"You crazy bastard, you did it!" Lou roared "Mack's eating your dust!"

Tommy leaned out the window and looked back. Mack had come to a stop and had got out of his car to kick its tires in frustration. The crowd at the starting line had piled into their cars and were coming down the road towards him in one great celebratory convoy.

"Get out and meet your fellow club members," said Lou.

With shaking knees, Tommy got out of the car and was swept up in the cheering crowd who were eager to slap him on the back and shake his hand.

"Looks like you cut the mustard," said Johnny, thumping him on the back.

"Yeah, while Mack cut the cheese!" somebody said, eliciting a chuckle from the crowd.

"Welcome to the Black Camelots," said Johnny. "We'll see about getting you your jacket on Monday."

"Let me through, you creeps!" screamed a female voice from the back of the crowd and Tommy cringed when he recognized Judy pushing her way through to him.

He heard somebody mutter "Hey, who's the square?" before the flat of Judy's hand struck him across the mouth.

There was an audible gasp from the onlookers along with a few chuckles.

"You inconsiderate bastard!" Judy cried. "You could have been killed!"

"Yeah, but I wasn't, Sis," said Tommy, rubbing his face which was red from more than just the blow. "So just cool it, huh?"

"Glad your sis could join us," said Johnny. "Bring her back to the clubhouse. We're gonna have the mother of all parties!"

Judy spun to face him. "I wouldn't set foot in your clubhouse if it was the last place on earth!"

"What's eating her?" Johnny asked Tommy. "Ah, forget it. Bring her or ditch her, it's your decision. Ordinarily I don't allow squares around the clubhouse, but this is your night so it's your call."

"Dad's worried sick!" Judy continued. "Mom is missing, the town has gone mad and you sneak out to race?"

"You just don't understand," said Tommy with a sigh. "Now, I'm going back to the clubhouse. You want a ride back into town, or do you want to stay out here and enjoy the night air?"

Chapter 17

It was after nine o'clock in the evening by the time Claire got to Bakersfield. She had seen little traffic on the highway; nobody seemed to be going in or out of Ralston and she wondered how long that had been the case.

Dr. Clark Foreman lived in one of the single-story modern ranch-style houses built after the '52 earthquake. Claire parked in the drive and could see through the high windows that the living room lights were on.

Dr. Foreman opened the door wearing a silk dressing gown and smoking his pipe. He was little different to Claire's memory of him, his hair a little whiter, his skin a little more wrinkled around his eyes which showed no recognition of the woman on his doorstep.

"Clark Foreman?" Claire asked, hoping to stir some memory in the old man.

"Yes?"

"It's Claire Weldon ... I mean, Claire MacReady as you might remember me."

"MacReady ..." Dr. Foreman mumbled, as if grasping at something in his mind that was trying to elude him.

"John MacReady's daughter."

The bristly white eyebrows lifted in sudden comprehension. "Good lord!"

He took her in and fixed her a drink. They sat in his book-lined living room and drank margaritas while Claire related what had occurred in Ralston since the meteorite hit. Clark listened attentively, interrupting only to refill Claire's glass from the cocktail shaker. Claire found the words spilling out of her in a cathartic release. It felt so good to be able to talk to somebody outside of Ralston who had been entirely unaffected by the frightening events of the past few weeks. When she was done, she sank back into the sofa and let her body relax as the numbing qualities of the two margaritas sank in.

Clark got up and went over to the telephone and made some calls. He tried three or four different numbers and wrangled with a pair of operators before giving up and returning to Claire and his drink.

"All circuits busy in Ralston," he said. "I tried the police, the mayor's office and a couple of small businesses for good measure. Zip on the lot of them."

"They've cut Ralston off," said Claire. "Colonel Baskin may have been able to contact military command by radio but I can't say for sure. If he should fall under the alien's powers then he will do whatever he can to cover it all up. He despises me and God knows what he's told the FBI about me. Whoever they send to investigate Agent Ashcroft's death will already see me as some sort of troublemaker."

"I understand why you ran away," said Clark. "But why did you come to me, Claire?"

Claire frowned. "You helped my father once. You stood up for him when nobody else did. I don't know anybody in Ralston, not really. Even Pasadena is ancient history to me. When I left, I made a life for myself in Virginia but I abandoned it because, well, because I was offered a job in California and it made me homesick. So I dragged my husband and our kids back west with me, but it was all for nothing. I'm still a stranger in a place like Ralston and I always will be. I came to you because I'm lost and I have nobody else to turn to. And no matter how far I have tried to distance myself from my father, when everything gets turned upside down, I just want to run to him. But he's gone, and so I am left with you and the memories of your kindness."

She was close to tears and hadn't realized so much of what she had just said was true until now.

Clark got up again. He went over to a piano in the corner of the room and riffled through a few photographs on the music stand. He brought one over, smiling at it fondly. He handed it to Claire. It was a picture of him and her father and a few other colleagues at some test site for one of their rockets. The reverse of the photograph was marked 'Arroyo Seco, Halloween, 1936'.

"This was our first test of a liquid-fuel motor. It was hardly a success; the oxygen line ignited and scorched your father's eyebrows off. But it was a start and that day, October 31st, 1936, really was the beginning of what would become the JPL. We were seen as suicidal eccentrics at the time, carting our model rockets out into the desert and nearly blowing ourselves up. Then, after it was discovered that the Nazis were building the V-2 Rocket, our little group – and your father in particular - was suddenly taken a lot more seriously. We received military funding, took on more members and christened ourselves The Jet Propulsion Laboratory. It was the start of something great, but your father had his dark side which, sadly, eclipsed his triumphs."

"The Ordo Templi Orientis," said Claire.

Clark frowned. "Yes. He was already involved with the Church of Thelema long before I met him at Caltech. In fact, it was your father who was instrumental in helping that Aleister Crowley character found the American chapter of his lodge. He didn't talk about it much back then, but he grew more and more vocal about it as the years passed."

"Do you believe he was a spy?"

"Not on your life! He was an American, through and through. He might have had some funny ideas but he was no traitor and as for being a communist? Well, we were all fairly hedonistic chaps back then, sympathetic to the suffering of our fellow scientists of Jewish extraction who had fled the ghastly goings on in Europe. Many of them had Marxist leanings and I think it rubbed off somewhat on your father. But whatever leftist feelings he had fell far short of communism.

"Still, that didn't help him in the end. You see, the authorities had an axe to grind and his flirtations with Marxism were a damned good excuse to strip him of his security clearance. By that time he was pretty open about his involvement in the O.T.O. and the other chaps at the JPL didn't like it. They saw him as a pervert and an occultist and very few of them stood up for him when the FBI wolves came sniffing."

"But you did."

"Yes, for all the good it did, and I nearly lost my own security clearance for defending him. Such are the FBI's tactics and they have only gotten worse since then. But I couldn't stand by and say nothing. Whatever your father's sins, I liked him and considered him a friend."

"The FBI agent who was murdered – Agent Ashcroft – said the bureau had a file on my father and not just for his alleged communist sympathies."

"Yes, well, the FBI take a similar view on demonic sex cults as they do on communism. But, with the public not knowing much about the former, it's easier to ruin a fellow's reputation by accusing him of being a red. Less embarrassing questions have to be asked, put it that way."

"Agent Ashcroft alluded to some sort of power struggle within the lodge. He thought it might have had something to do with my father's death."

"I'm sorry to say that your father was a ruined man towards the end of his life. You were off studying in Virginia. You didn't see what he had become after your mother died. He earned his living making pyrotechnics for the movie industry, fake gunshots and the like. He drank heavily and used drugs a lot. No, your father's death was a horrible accident, no more than that. The combination of your mother's death and being fired from the JPL brought him to the brink I believe. He had few friends towards the end. Just me, really. Everybody else distanced themselves after the accusations, and even his own lodge wanted nothing to do with him. There *was* a power struggle, you see, but it had nothing to do with your father's death."

"What was the struggle about? Did he ever talk about it?"

"Look, it's getting late. All of this is ancient history and has nothing to do with your current predicament. Let me put you up for the night. Things will look better to-morrow and we can attack this problem with clear heads."

He was nervous, Claire could tell. Something she had said had set him off and made him want to drop the subject of her father like a hot potato.

"Clark?" she asked. "What is it? What are you not telling me?"

Clark suddenly looked a lot older. His shoulders sagged as if suddenly unable to bear their burden any longer. He gave a deep sigh. "I'm sorry for any hurt caused by what I am about to tell you, but I suppose you're a grown woman now. You deserve to know the truth, what-ever good it will do you. You see, in the lodge's early days, there was another man who was in the running to be its leader, a man by the name of Jack Talbot. Talbot and your father were good friends, at least in those early days.

"They became fixated on one of Crowley's more ob-scure ideas; to manifest the 'Scarlet Woman'; an incarna-tion of a Thelemite goddess called Babalon. Talbot and your father spent night after night out in the Mojave De-sert performing their incantations, the nature of which I shudder to contemplate. Not long after they returned, a newcomer arrived at the lodge; a beautiful woman with red hair by the name of Maud Jennings. Both Talbot and your father were convinced that she was the result of their efforts – the so-called Scarlet Woman – and unfortunately, they both fell madly in love with her. Your father was already married to your mother of course but, as you might have heard, the lodge was pretty free in its attitude to sexual relationships."

Claire felt her stomach turn as the memory of what she had seen that night, at nine years old, peeping into the living room; her parents and their guests spread out across the furniture.

"Your mother, God rest her soul, tolerated it but I don't believe she ever really forgave your father for it. Sexual freedom was one thing but he was head over heels in love with Maud Jennings. Their relationship was very strained after that. Then there was the second part of Crowley's ritual. Even more distasteful than the first. If the Scarlet Woman could be impregnated during some rite or other, then she would become the 'Mother of Abominations' and give birth to the 'Moonchild'. The antichrist in other words. All this was Greek to me when I first heard of it but I have read up on it since. Apparently this child would usher in a new aeon. Well, Talbot and your father were both eager to bring this about, and they grew fiercely competitive for Maud's affection. It was Talbot who succeeded in winning her heart and that's not all he did. He and Maud utterly betrayed your father."

"How do you mean?"

"Well, I'm not sure of all the details but there was some scam involving the investment in some sailing yachts in Florida. Talbot and Maud, the pair of scoundrels, completely defrauded your father and made off with his money. He found out about this the same time he learned that Maud had chosen Talbot over him. Losing her to Talbot made your father bitterly resentful and their relationship never recovered.

"Later, Maud gave birth to a baby girl. No antichrist, no new aeon, just a healthy, normal baby girl which goes to show what a load of old rot those characters believed in. Still, it was enough to put the wind up even old Crowley who apparently wasn't too keen on others taking his scribblings literally. Anyway, Crowley wasn't long for this world and after his death and the increased interest of the FBI in the lodge, your father's days were numbered. Talbot, always jealous of your father's position, made his move and ousted him, succeeding him as master of the lodge. That was the power struggle your FBI agent was referring to and it was a struggle Talbot won. Your father spiraled into obscurity and depression before his eventual, *accidental* death. It was nothing to do with Talbot. He had already won, you see. Your father's death, I am sorry to say, was due to clumsiness brought on by alcoholism and a distracted mind."

Claire got up from the sofa and walked over to the tall windows and looked out at the desert beneath the night sky. Her own reflection in the glass partially obscured her view. None of it mattered. Her childhood memories, the sordid details of her father and his damnable lodge, his downfall brought about by his own lust and betrayal of her mother, none of it had anything to do with what was happening in Ralston. What was she doing here? Why had she run to her father's old friend instead of the authorities? The past offered no help. It couldn't. The past was dead.

"Another drink?" Clark asked.

"No, thank you. I have a long drive ahead of me."

"Surely you're not heading out at this hour? Stay here for the night. We can talk more in the morning."

"Talk about what? I know the truth now and it doesn't help me. I don't know why, but I thought that perhaps it would. Perhaps that's why I really came to you. Oh, I was running away, certainly, but I kept thinking about what that FBI agent told me and I suppose I just wanted some confirmation. I'm sorry for disturbing your evening, Clark. I came here looking for answers but all the answers are in Ralston, that's why I need to return."

"Ralston! But you said so yourself, the place has gone wild! Stay here, I beg you. We'll make some calls, get the press involved perhaps. You can't just wander back into the lion's den."

"I must. Ray and the kids are there. I was a fool and a coward for abandoning them. By the time we make some calls and try and convince the outside world of what is going on in Ralston, it may be too late. I have to go back and try and stop it myself."

"But what can you do about it all?"

"I don't know. Colonel Baskin is still there with his men. If they have not yet been turned then perhaps there is a chance. I *must* try!"

Ray parted the blind in the bedroom window and peered down at the two radio cars. The cops were leaning against the hood of one, smoking and talking in low voices.

They look so normal, Ray thought. *How can they be so normal when they have orders to kill on behalf of that creature?*

Were its orders subconscious commands? Did its subjects know nothing until something triggered a reflex in their brains? But that didn't add up, else why were they here at all? Did the drug then desensitize feelings of compassion, empathy, loyalty; all humanity? That way a subject could pass the time of day with you, share a joke, act as if nothing was wrong and then kill you the next minute should you stand in the path of their master's plans.

He gave up thinking about the hows and whys of it all. Now was the time for action, not contemplation. Judy had left too, gone out into the night, probably looking for

Tommy. It was too much for him. He might have been content to be a kept man, but to sit at home with Rose while everybody else was out taking all the risks was too much even for his broad idea of masculinity. He was a husband and a father God damn it! He might cook and clean for his family but he would also protect them if he needed to. And with them all out in the night somewhere, getting into God knew what sort of danger, he just couldn't sit at home doing nothing.

Rose had cried a little when he had woken her and got her dressed, but she soon nodded off again. He left her asleep on their bed and went downstairs to open the front door. The two cops peered at him from the drive. "Excuse me, fellas," he said. "It seems that my son has made a run for it. Snuck out the back window. Could you call it in? Get one of your boys to pick him up and bring him home? I don't want him getting into any trouble."

Both officers leapt up off the hood of the car and stubbed out their cigarettes. He had their attention now. "When did he slip out?" one of them asked.

"Can't have been more than a few minutes ago," Ray lied. "I told him to go to bed a little while ago and just now found his window open."

"Take a ride around the block, see if you can't pick him up," said one cop to the other. "If not, then we'll call it in."

The other cop got into his car, started the engine and rolled off. *Good*, thought Ray. *One down, one to go.* They had reacted just as he had hoped. But he didn't have much time.

He went back indoors and fetched a five iron from his golf bag in the closct. He used to play on the links back in Virginia, but since the move, he hadn't the time. He walked back outside. The remaining police officer stood with his back to him, staring down the street as the taillights of his colleague turned the corner.

As quietly as possible, Ray crept up behind the officer and swung the golf club at the back of his head. There was a sickening 'thwack!' and, with a groan, the officer slumped forward over the hood of his car and started to slide off it. Ray caught him and pulled him over to the lawn and arranged him in the recovery position.

"Sorry about that, Officer," he said, hoping he hadn't hit the man too hard.

The radio in the police car squawked into life and made Ray jump.

"This is Sheriff Benson, calling all cars. Now is the time for action. Tonight is the night we purge Ralston of all subversives. I have contacted our allies individually and they will work with us. The military have not yet been converted so we will just have to work around them. Do not engage unless otherwise instructed. You know your orders. Keep radio channels open. Over and out."

What the hell was that all about? Purge Ralston of all subversives? That couldn't be good. It sounded like some sort of coup! Well, the military weren't in on it, so that was something. But they had to be warned! Discarding the golf club, Ray dashed into the house and ran upstairs to fetch Rose.

CHAPTER 18

Despite Judy's initial refusal, she found herself in the Black Camelots' clubhouse nevertheless, a reluctant guest at the party. A beer keg stood on the card table and the record player bounced to Buddy Holly. Smoke hung in the air and Judy wrinkled her nose at what she knew wasn't just tobacco. She sat on a busted sofa, watching the celebrations, refusing beer and dances in equal measure.

Tommy was the toast of the party and Judy watched him being hauled around and having his hair ruffled and his back slapped by almost everybody in the room. A blonde in plaid slacks danced with him while everybody cheered. Judy rolled her eyes. Enough was enough. When the dance was over and another record was put on, she got up and went over to him.

"Time to go home, Tommy. Dad must be going out of his mind."

"No way! This party is really swinging!"

"Don't you care about anyone but yourself?" she snapped. "Don't you care that Mom's missing and Dad is under house arrest? How can you be so selfish?"

"Listen, Sis," the beer he had drunk made him slur his words, "This town has gone to hell. The only genuine cats are right here in this room. So why shouldn't I have a ball? We might all be dead tomorrow."

Disgusted, Judy went out to get some air and think about how she could convince Tommy that he had to come home. She refused to return without him.

As she stood by the door to the clubhouse, she saw Johnny Packer along with the one called Mack whom Tommy had raced, exit the clubhouse via a back door. They had another man with them; not one of the Camelots, but an older, scrawny fellow in a plaid shirt. Two girls walked behind them; one of them was June, the blonde who had started the race, and the other was a pale, ill-looking girl who seemed to need help walking. Mack and the girls got into his car while Johnny and the skinny man in the plaid shirt got into his. The cars rolled out of the lot and peeled out when they reached the road outside the auto shop.

"Where's your big chief going in such a hurry?" she asked one of the gang who was hanging by the door.

"That skinny cat you saw with them," the gang member said, "is Archie Novak. He's a hophead, or at least he used to be. He claims some doctor fixed him up and now he's not a junkie anymore. He's taking Johnny and Mack to see this doc and ask if he can't do the same to Marie."

"Marie?"

"Marie Giorgino. She's the sister of one of the club members. Hop head. Anyway, Archie thinks he and his doc can help. He calls it 'The Cure'."

"What kind of doctor takes patients after ten on a Saturday?" Judy asked.

The boy shrugged. "He's some sort of quack, not a real doc. They said something about an old house on Morton Avenue, down by Dusty Creek."

"Dusty Creek?"

"That's what old Archie said. I know the place he means. It's an old derelict, half falling into the creek. Archie probably used to score there after his old lady kicked him out. What this doc of his is doing in an abandoned house beats me."

Judy crept back inside, a deep feeling of unease gnawing at her gut. Why would this Archie character take Johnny Packer to an abandoned house by Dusty Creek? And what was this super effective 'cure' he was talking about? None of it added up and, as she thought about it, a feeling of panic set in.

"Do you know this Archie Novak character?" she asked Tommy.

"Sure, a little," Tommy replied. He's always hanging around here trying to get Johnny to take Marie to some witch doctor for her habit."

"They've just left. He's taking Johnny and Mack to some old house by Dusty Creek."

"So?"

"Tommy, we have to go now!" she insisted, grabbing her brother by the sleeve of his jacket.

"I already told you, I'm not going anywhere!" he snapped. "Now, go home and stop embarrassing me!"

"Archie is a convert! He's taking Johnny and Mack and those girls to get them suckered by the alien!"

"How do you know that?"

"How else do you think Archie dropped his habit so suddenly?"

Tommy and Burt looked at each other as they considered this.

"Say, she's got a point," Burt admitted.

"Even if he is, what can we do about it?" said Tommy. "I thought you just wanted to go home to Dad."

"We have to try and stop them! If Johnny becomes a convert, then he'll try to get the whole gang converted! And this gang might be the only clique left in Ralston who isn't under the alien's control."

Tommy and Burt looked at her, unsure.

"Old Archie sure did get that white monkey off his back quick," said Burt. "Whaddya say, Tommy? Is that how it goes?"

"Think about it!" said Judy. "The alien wants us to do what it wants and it does this by making our dreams come true. Isn't addiction all in the mind? What could a junkie want more than a cure for his addiction?"

"All right, Sis, you got me," said Tommy. "But as I said, what can we do?"

"We can go in my car," said Burt. "Where's this house he's taking Johnny to?"

"Somebody said it was an abandoned house on Morton Avenue," said Judy.

"That old pile? C'mon, let's get going!"

The three of them headed for the door. The party was in full swing and the rest of the gang was too drunk or doped to care where they were going. They got into Burt's Mercury and hit the road, heading to the eastern fringes of the town where Dusty Creek fed the Tuolumne River.

The house was a run-down old thing from the previous century with warped boards and a sagging roof. Its grounds were clogged with tangled weeds but a path had been formed through the foliage leading from the rusted iron gate to the sloping porch.

Johnny and Mack's cars were parked out front and Burt pulled in behind them. They got out and made their way up to the house. There could hear no sounds from within as they stepped up onto the porch and peered through the doorway into its dark recesses.

"Archie probably used this old place as his shooting gallery," said Burt, glancing at a needle and length of rubber hose on the bottom step of the curving staircase.

"Along with every other junkie in town," said Judy as she stepped over a broken bourbon bottle.

The place certainly looked like it had seen some tenants. The fireplace in the living room was full of white ash and the bare floor was littered with bean tins and other food containers.

They went into the kitchen which looked out over the overgrown grounds as they sloped down into the creek. Five figures stood down by the water.

Judy flung open the kitchen door and ran out into the tall grass. "Stop!" she cried. "Get away from the water!"

The heads of Johnny, Mack, June and Archie swiveled to gape at her and she realized she had reached them just in time. A pinkish tentacle had emerged from the water and was rising above their heads. "Look out!" she cried.

One by one, they turned and looked with a freezing horror at the thing that wavered above them; all except Archie who stood by, his eager face frantic. June screamed and held onto Mack, forcing him to take a few steps back, but it was not enough. The bulbous head of the tentacle slid back on itself and the glistening sucker unfurled. Judy felt sick as she recalled her last encounter with the vile creature in Connie's boathouse.

It struck with a savage force and lightening speed, attaching its sucker to Mack's face and Judy realized how lucky she had been to escape the boathouse. The tentacle held Mack in a terrifying grip that lifted him off his feet like some ghastly puppet.

June screamed again and seized Mack around the waist, pulling him back down to earth. Archie lunged for her and tried to tear her away, but Johnny intercepted him, slamming his fist into his jaw.

"Burt, Tommy!" Judy yelled.

The two boys came charging out of the kitchen and ran to help their leader. Another tentacle had risen from the water and was snaking its way towards June. Judy tried to cry out, but it was too late. The sucker grasped June's face and she let go of Mack and clawed at the horrible thing that had enveloped her head. The girl called Marie did nothing but sink to her knees in terror, not knowing what new horror this was.

Burt and Tommy grabbed hold of Johnny and pulled him back from the water before any more of the awful tentacles appeared. Archie got to his feet, rubbing away a smear of blood from his lip where Johnny had struck him.

"You don't understand, Man!" he cried. "Its coming is a miracle! I fought my addiction for years and now I've been given a fresh start! It can cure you of all your faults, all your weaknesses!"

"I'll pass," said Johnny.

Archie smiled weakly. "I'm afraid you have no choice. It's for your own good, after all."

Judy was aware that several figures had emerged from the house at their back and she spun to face them. They were ragged, wretched specimens of humanity; torn, dirty clothes and tangled hair and beards. Some were old and white-haired while others couldn't have been much more than thirty but looked a sight older. They were hobos, the lot of them, about ten in number and they crept towards them. There was something pantherish and predatory about their movements and Judy knew they intended to drive them back towards the water.

The tentacles had released Mack and June who were now on their hands and knees, choking and coughing up globs of slime. She could see a thin trickle of blood running down Mack's neck from a small wound under his chin. One of the tentacles snaked down and grasped Marie's face. It was her turn for the treatment and there wasn't a damn thing any of them could do about it.

"Tell your junkie buddies to back off, Archie," Johnny warned.

"Junkies?" Archie said. "You still don't get it, huh? These old boys and me might have been junkies before but that was back in the old world. The creature has built us anew! And now, it's your turn."

"The hell it is!" Johnny drew a pistol from under his jacket and pointed it at the advancing hobos.

It had no effect on them. They weren't frightened of the pistol any more than they would have been of a popgun.

"Johnny, look out!" Burt yelled.

One of the tentacles lunged and Johnny leapt out of its reach.

"Hold him steady!" Archie cried to his shabby friends.

Judy screamed as the group of hobos lurched towards them, grasping at them with hands and broken nails.

A gunshot cracked out in the stillness of the night and one of the men fell down with a shattered forehead. Johnny stared the smoke of his pistol with livid, terrified eyes as the converts, unphased by the death of one of their number, continued to manhandle them. He dropped the gun, not wanting to take another life, and relied on his fists to fend them off.

"Get your stinking hands off me!" Tommy yelled as one of them pulled him towards the water.

"Let's bust out of here!" Johnny cried.

Judy suddenly found herself being carried forward as the three boys pushed against their assailants with a sudden violence. The hobos might have been determined but they were weak and mostly old. Several of them were bowled over while others grabbed and clutched at them as they pushed through.

Judy screamed as one of them seized her by the hair. A right hook from Johnny felled him and he released her. She felt his powerful arm grab her around the middle and drag her with them as they raced towards the house.

They skirted the old ruin and made for the cars parked at the front. Their pursuers chased them and the long grass slowed them down, making Judy feel as if they were running slowly in a nightmare. Johnny's car was closest and they all piled into it, abandoning Burt's. Judy crawled into the back with Burt while Tommy slid over the hood and got in the passenger's side. Johnny turned the ignition and the headlamps illuminated the faces of the crazed hobos as they surrounded the car and yanked at its doors like ravenous fiends trying to get in at their prey.

Johnny put the car in reverse and stamped on the gas, spinning the wheel around. The powerful engine roared and the car swung around in a wide arc, hurling several men from it. Slamming the gearstick into drive, Johnny did the best attempt he could at peeling out in long grass and they rumbled off towards the broken old fence.

Judy looked back through the rear window and saw their pursuers bathed in the red of the taillights, growing ever smaller. As the car rocketed through the fence and onto the road in a shower of splintered wood, it picked up speed and only then, as the house receded into the night, did they all heave a sigh of relief.

"Jesus Christ," said Burt. "We left Mack and June and Marie back there!"

"Wasn't anything we could do for them," said Tommy.

"They are now converts, just like Archie and his friends," said Judy. "God help them."

"I shot one of them," said Johnny in a panicked voice. "I shot one of the lousy bastards! I'm on a real dime here!"

"Self-defense," said Burt. "Without a doubt."

"You don't understand, I ain't got a license for the piece. My family don't have the dough to get me out this! I'll be sent down for sure!"

"Johnny," said Judy, leaning forward to touch his shoulder. "Half this town is under the influence of an alien. The police too. I don't think anybody is going to come down on you too hard over this. Or even trace the gun to you."

"Yeah, these are special circumstances, for sure," added Burt.

"All right," said Johnny, sounding a little calmer now. "Let's get back to the clubhouse. And if that Archie shows up around there ever again, I'm gonna have two murders on my conscience."

They knew something terrible had happened as soon as Nick's Auto Shop came into view. The flames burned like a beacon in the dark, deserted streets. Both gas pumps had blown and half of the garage was burning, the flames reaching higher than the roofs of the nearby buildings.

"What the hell ..." Burt said as they all leaned forward in their seats to get a better look.

"What happened?" said Tommy.

Johnny drove around to the side and up to the clubhouse. Bodies littered the hard-packed dirt of the scrapyard; corpses wearing the satin jackets of the Black Camelots.

"Somebody hit us," said Johnny. "Somebody hit us bad."

They got out of the car and started poking around the wreckage of what looked to have been an almighty gang fight. Bloody bullet holes riddled the corpses. Blood collected in pools like water after a heavy rain.

"Hey, there's a cop over here!" cried Burt, standing over the body of a uniformed police officer. "Dead just like the rest of them. Caught in the crossfire?"

"There are no Jungle Dukes here," said Johnny. "Only our boys and that cop. This thing stinks."

Somebody moaned and they spun around, their nerves shredded raw. One of the corpses was moving; reaching out with a bloodied hand. It was Lou. Johnny ran to his side and eased him over onto his back. His face was scorched and blistered and there was a hole in his chest that pumped blood.

"Lou!" said Johnny. "What happened, Man? Talk to me!"

"The cops ..." Lou mumbled. "The cops hit us. It was that bastard Sheriff Benson and his boys. They came in swinging. At first we thought it was the Jungle Dukes and we rushed out to meet them but they brought firepower, man. They tore us apart! Fenced us in on all sides. Me and a couple of the other boys got some of those firebombs from the back room, you know, the Molotovs. Went through Nick's garage and tired to torch their asses but they were waiting for us. Opened up on us with shotguns. Micky had one of the Molotovs lit and he tried to throw it but they got him before he could. He went up in flames and that's when the gas pumps blew. We ran back and the cops kept shooting. I took a round in the chest and I think I passed out. Is anybody else ...?"

"No," said Johnny. "Nothing but corpses here. Did anybody escape?"

"How the hell should I know? I don't even remember it ending. Johnny, I'm getting' cold, Man!"

Johnny hurriedly took off his jacket and spread it over Lou. "Hang loose, Buddy, we're gonna get you some help." He stood up and looked at Tommy and Burt. "Stay with him. I'll bring the car closer and we'll put him in the back seat. I'll take him to the hospital."

"Johnny," said Burt, looking down at Lou with a grave face. "He's gone, man."

CHAPTER 19

When the gas pumps blew, it could be seen and heard across town. Ray slammed on his brakes and the car squealed to a halt as the flames rose in a mushroom cloud that briefly banished the night, casting the town in a mid-day glow.

Jesus! thought Ray. *That looked like Nick's place!*

Rose woke up in the back seat and began to whimper. Ray offered soothing words to her as he wheeled the car around and headed towards Nick's. If Tommy and Judy were hanging out with the Black Camelots in their clubhouse behind the garage ...

He saw the blue and red flashing lights as he turned down the street. Three cop cars were parked opposite the garage, the flames of the burning pumps and auto shop reflected in their windows. Ray pulled over by the side entrance that led to the junkyard and the Camelot's clubhouse. Two officers were guarding the entrance. He got out and approached them. Over their shoulders, he could make out several bodies lying on the ground in front of the clubhouse.

"What the hell happened?" he demanded.

"Stand back, sir!" cried one of the officers, drawing his gun.

"My kids might be in there!" Ray cried. "Now you tell me what happened!"

"These kids went wild and torched the gas station," the cop replied. "When we arrived, they attacked us. It's a full-on rebellion. They had to be put down."

Put down. Ray knew it was lies, all of it. Those kids had represented a threat to the creature's plans and Sheriff Benson had ordered a purge. The radio message he had heard made perfect sense now. There was a purge in effect and it was Ralston's kids who were to be 'put down'.

If he didn't have Rose in the car he might have tried to rush the two officers and get into the junkyard. He was desperate to see if Tommy and Judy were there, dead at the hands of the police, but he knew the cops would kill him and then who would look after Rose?

He backed away from them and headed towards the car. One of the officers followed him.

"Sir, you're going to have to come with us."

"Not on your life!" Ray snapped.

"I'm afraid I insist."

Ray fumbled with the door handle and got in. He slammed the door closed just as the cop grasped at it. Turning the ignition, he stamped on the gas and the car lurched forward, dragging the cop off his feet. His comrade drew his gun and opened fire. Bullets penetrated the bodywork with loud 'thunks' as Ray jerked on the steering wheel and the car squealed around the corner.

"Are you okay, Rose?" he asked over his shoulder.

Rose looked up at him with frightened eyes.

"Everything's all right. Daddy's got everything under control."

Like hell, he thought. This whole town had gone mad and he wanted to be on the highway heading away from it as fast as he could. But with Claire and the kids missing, he wasn't leaving Ralston. He had to get to the colonel. Only the military had any chance of stopping this.

It wasn't too hard to find the colonel. He spotted several army trucks passing along Robertson Avenue which ran parallel to the main canal that ran from east to west through Ralston. He found the colonel overseeing an operation at the easternmost end of the canal, just before it headed north-east out of the town at a forty-five-degree angle. A couple of jeeps and a truck were positioned near the water. The colonel and Pastor Mathews were standing by, watching a group of sappers drop explosives into the water.

Rose was awake and, as Ray lifted her out of the car and approached, there was a tremendous explosion that sent a fountain of water up in the air. G.I.s turned their heads as it rained down on the road, dousing them.

"Colonel!" Ray called. "What's going on?"

Heads turned. If Colonel Baskin recognized him, he didn't show it. "Don't you know the police put a curfew into effect?" he called. "Civilians are supposed to be indoors. First this Pastor comes along and now every Tom, Dick and Harry."

"Don't you know the police are under the command of the alien?" Ray said. "There was an explosion over at Nick's Auto shop. The police are going after the town's youths. My wife and children are missing ..."

"Yes, my men reported some sort of altercation," the colonel said. "The police are doing their job to keep this town under control. Kids have been running amuck here for too long and now they're trying to take advantage of the situation. If there was an explosion over at the garage, then I'm sure it was those little darlings who started it."

"Colonel, they mowed them down! There are bodies everywhere! I know for a fact that Sheriff Benson is a convert. He tried to convert me!"

The colonel wheeled on him. "How am I to believe a word you say? I don't know you from Adam. There's a thing in these canals that's infecting people's minds and turning them into anti-American liars. I have a job to flush it out and the police have a job to keep civilians from interfering."

"Ready to drop the next charges, Colonel," said a soldier.

"Drop them but wait for radio confirmation before detonation."

"Yes, Sir!"

As military radios squawked back and forth, Ray could see what they were trying to do. Colonel Baskin had teams of sappers set up at all the major points where water flowed into Ralston. They were detonating synchronized charges in an effort to force the creature into the center of town.

"What will you do when you have the thing cornered?" he asked.

The colonel nodded in the direction of a jeep with a machinegun attachment. "Blow the son of a bitch to pieces," he said.

"Do you even know how big this thing is?"

"Get him out of here," the colonel said to one of his men in irritation.

Two G.I.s came forward to escort Ray back to his car.

"Colonel, you have to listen to me!" Ray cried. "The police cannot be trusted! There's a massacre going on right under your very nose! They're killing our kids! Pastor Matthews, do you hear me? They're killing our ..."

The attention of the soldiers was suddenly taken up by a disturbance in the canal. A massive tentacle rose out of the water and made a swipe at one of the sappers. The man screamed as the sticky sucker of the tentacle fastened around his head, helmet and all, and lifted him off the ground.

"Oh, my God," said the colonel in a voice of disbelief.

G.I.s unslung their carbines and took aim at the tentacle.

"Don't shoot!" Colonel Baskin cried. "You'll hit Anderson!"

The soldiers kept their weapons trained on the tentacle, visibly shaking with terror. They watched as their comrade was held in a vice-like grip by the alien tentacle. It detached suddenly and the soldier called Anderson slumped to his knees, his face dripping with goo. The soldiers prepared to open fire but the colonel called them to halt once more.

"What the hell is he doing?" he demanded.

Pastor Matthews had walked out in front of the soldiers and was approaching the tentacle, bible in hand. He stood between the two soldiers; the stricken Anderson and his petrified comrade.

"Get back, Pastor!" Colonel Baskin shouted.

The Pastor was speaking to the tentacle and Ray realized that he was quoting scripture. Whether or not it was due to the words of the pastor, the tentacle did indeed seem to hesitate, its bulbous, sticky head sensing the presence of the man with its eyeless vision.

"It's going to strike him!" said Ray.

Sure enough, the tentacle reared up and prepared to attach itself to the pastor's face. Then, as if by a conjuring trick, Pastor Matthews reached underneath his jacket and pulled out, not a crucifix, but a .32 pistol and pointed it at the tentacle. The shot went off and the tentacle reeled back, struck through by the pastor's bullet. Blood spilled out of the hole as the tentacle swayed like a drunk man.

Pastor Mathews dropped to the ground and the soldiers opened fire, their bullets ripping through the snakelike arm. Chunks of flesh and gooey matter spattered the surface of the water and the wounded tentacle shot back down into the canal and retreated from sight.

Two G.I.'s hauled Pastor Mathews away from the water. He got to his feet, wiping slime and gore off his black suit.

"That was some trick, Pastor," said Ray. "They teach you that in theology school?"

"God helps those who help themselves," said Pastor Mathews as he slid his pistol back into the shoulder holster beneath his jacket.

"What happened to being brothers and not enemies?"

"I am as much a student of God's teachings as any man and I'm not ashamed to admit it when I have misinterpreted something. This thing's coming had a different meaning. As David triumphed over Goliath, so must we now triumph over our greatest enemy."

"Colonel!" a soldier at the radio in one of the jeeps called. "I'm getting no response from Beta team!"

"Try them again," said the colonel.

"I've tried all frequencies. I'm just getting static."

The streets were deathly silent as the black '47 Chevy prowled the tree-lined avenues of suburbia. Johnny slouched behind the wheel, peering through the slit of a windshield at the darkened houses. They had decided to head for Burt's home and lay low until the morning. Tommy and Judy would call their dad and let him know that they were safe for the time being. As they turned a corner, they could see a car's headlamps approaching from the other end of the street.

"Can you make out who that is?" Johnny asked the passengers.

Burt squinted through the back window as the car came up behind them, closing the gap quickly. "I think it's ..."

The blue light flashed and the siren started up.

"Shit, the cops!" said Burt.

Johnny floored the gas and the hot rod roared down the street. The cop car sped up, giving chase. They swooped around a corner with a squeal of tires as Johnny tried to lose them. They headed in the direction of 10th street but when they swung onto Ralston's main strip, they found it nearly deserted.

"What gives?" asked Burt. "Where is everybody? It's a Saturday night!"

"Something's up," said Judy.

"No kidding," said Tommy. "We need to ditch the car. The cops will have a bulletin out on us and we're easily spotted on these empty streets."

Johnny slammed his fist down on the steering wheel in frustration. He pulled into an alley and they all got out. The cops would find the car easily, but they would be long gone by then. The four of them headed down the street, keeping their eyes peeled for cop cars or motorcycles.

They had not gone far before they felt as if their footsteps had an echo. Glancing back, Tommy saw at least three figures following them, having apparently materialized from the shadows.

"Uh, we're being followed," he said.

"Oh, shit!" exclaimed Burt. "Up ahead, look!"

Two more figures had turned the corner ahead of them and were watching them with silent intent. They were normal, middle-aged men; the kind Ralston was full of, but their sudden appearance and their keen attention to the four youths gave Tommy a chill.

"Come on," said Johnny, as the two strangers walked towards them. "Follow me."

He stepped suddenly into the street and began making his way across to the other side. The other three followed suit and, by glancing over his shoulder, Tommy could see that the strangers were doing the same. There was no doubt about it now; they were being followed.

They hurried on past closed stores and brightly lit display windows. More people seemed to emerge from the shadows on both sides of the street. If there were few cars about, then there were certainly enough pedestrians. Some were men, some were women, some wore hats and ties while others wore the clothes of their profession; storekeepers, electricians, road sweepers. Tommy noticed there wasn't a single one of them under the age of twenty.

A cluster of them blocked the sidewalk up ahead and the four youths stopped short.

"They're fencing us in," said Burt, glancing back as more of them crossed the road.

"What gives?" Johnny called to them.

A man in a butcher's apron stepped forward. "This town has had enough of you kids and your gangs," he said.

"We're tired of your hot rods and your drugs," added an elderly woman in a purple felt hat. "Tearing around like you own the place, no respect for authority!"

"If you won't join us," said another, this one a mild-looking man in spectacles, "then it's time you were dealt with permanently!"

"Beat it!" said Johnny.

The others didn't need telling twice. They turned around and hot-footed it in the opposite direction. The mob gave chase and they pounded the asphalt, trying to put as much distance between them as possible.

Johnny led them around a corner and ducked into an alley. Tommy, who, for some reason, was at the back, almost didn't see where the others had gone before Burt's hand shot out of the alley and hauled him in.

The mob rounded the corner and kept on running, passing the entrance to the alley. In the darkness between two buildings, the four youths gasped and wheezed as they fought to get their breath back.

"The whole town is out after us kids," said Tommy.

"It's that bastard Benson," said Judy. "Why do you think the streets are almost deserted apart from his murder squads? It was always 'join or die' with that alien and now all the converts know that kids can't be turned as easily. I'll bet Benson has put out the order for everybody under the age of twenty to be killed."

"Jesus, you think so?" asked Burt.

"That mob wasn't kidding," said Johnny. "We need to find a place to lay low until the military gets control of this town."

"If the military have even been called in," said Judy. "Lord knows what's happened to that colonel."

"Somebody is sure to put the call in," said Burt, his voice panicked. "A whole town can't just go rogue and murder all its kids without somebody noticing!"

"It's doing a pretty good job so far," said Johnny bitterly. "Come on, follow me."

He led them down the alley which was blocked by a low wall. Scrambling up, he straddled it. "The supermarket's back lot is just over here," he said. "If we can bust in without being seen, we can hide out until morning."

He dropped down on the other side of the wall and Tommy and Burt helped Judy up before scrambling over themselves. Soon they were creeping between the garbage cans towards the blank brickwork of the supermarket's rear.

Johnny found a small window that looked in on the staff restrooms. He picked up a brick and, sending Tommy and Burt to make sure the coast was clear of anybody who might hear the noise, smashed the glass.

Clearing the wooden frame of all jagged pieces of glass, Johnny climbed up and wormed his way into the restroom headfirst. A few moments passed before his voice could be heard through the broken window.

"Hey, I'm in the ladies!"

"Well don't get too excited," said Judy.

"Ladies first," said Burt, winking at her.

Burt and Tommy lifted her up through the window and then climbed up after her.

The store was cast in gloom, the aisles like dark trenches. Tins of food and things pickled in glass jars caught the light of the street outside and winked in the blackness.

"At least we won't starve!" said Tommy, swiping a packet of Ritz Crackers and opening them.

"Tommy, that's stealing!" hissed Judy.

He shrugged. "The cops are after us anyway. What's the difference?"

"Yeah, he's right," said Burt grabbing a couple of candy bars. "We're on the lam. Finders keepers."

A flashlight from outside swept the storefront.

"Shit! Get down!" said Johnny.

They all ducked but Tommy was pretty sure the top of his head had been caught in the beam of light. As they crouched in the aisles, they could hear somebody trying the door. It was locked of course, but that didn't stop whoever was so intent on getting in. A window smashed and the four youths looked at each other, their eyes wide.

Hushed voices could be heard up at the front of the store. "Fan out," somebody said. "I saw one of the punks duck down. I'll bet they're all in here."

Johnny motioned to the others to head back to the restrooms but it was too late. Footsteps were echoing along the aisles to the left and right of them. They couldn't escape that way without being seen. Their only hope lay in moving to the front of the store and slipping out that way.

There were at least three pairs of footsteps moving through the store and it was difficult to tell which aisles they were in. Sneaking along on their haunches, they moved towards the end of their aisle which opened onto a wider aisle that crossed the breadth of the store. They kept out of sight as a man with a flashlight crossed it and disappeared down the aisle parallel to theirs. Johnny nodded to Tommy and Burt to cross over.

Still keeping low and moving as silently as possible, Tommy and Burt scurried across the aisle and hid behind a large display of canned peas. Johnny and Judy made to cross but another of their pursuers had appeared three aisles over and began to walk down the long aisle towards them.

Johnny and Judy would be seen if they remained where they were so they began to move back down the aisle and hide at its end as the man passed. Tommy watched them vanish into the shadows but the man had turned off the main aisle somewhere.

"Where is he?" he mouthed to Burt.

Burt shrugged his shoulders and then nodded towards the front of the store.

They were near the checkout now and they could see the smashed glass door. They could make it! *But what about Johnny and Judy?*

Burt urged Tommy on and, reluctantly, he began to make his way towards the checkout. There was nothing they could do but get out and wait for Johnny and Judy outside and hope they didn't get caught.

A flashlight shone down on them from the top of the aisle to their right. The face of a man who had climbed up on the shelves on the other side peered down at them. "Gotcha!" he hissed.

The game was up. Tommy and Burt were up on their feet and pelting down the aisle towards the checkouts. Flashlights shone in their direction and Tommy heard the unmistakable sound of a shotgun being pumped.

"Duck!" he yelled as they passed through the checkouts and they hurled themselves flat as the shotgun roared out in the stillness of the store.

The blast of pellets tore apart a display rack by the cash register. Tommy and Burt slid across the waxed floor and then were up and running for the door. A second blast shattered the window next to the door as Burt barreled into it and tumbled out onto the street with Tommy fast behind.

The street was deserted which was just as well but the men inside the store came hurrying out.

"Come on!" yelled Burt. "Don't stop now!"

Aware that they had left Johnny and Judy behind, Tommy and Burt knew there was nothing they could do but flee. They ran on into the night, taking sharp corners in an attempt to evade their murderous pursuers.

CHAPTER 20

Claire knew that something had drastically changed in Ralston as soon as she turned off the highway. There were a lot fewer people about for one thing. Saturday nights were usually buzzing with kids cruising up and down the strip. Now, the place resembled a ghost town with only the occasional car or frightened pedestrian hurrying on their way. There was also an orange glow in the west, suggesting a large fire.

As she drove past the steps of the Ralston Library, she saw a group of people chasing a young couple down the street. The boy and girl couldn't have been older than Judy and, when the girl stumbled in her high pumps and the boy turned to help her, the mob fell upon them, beating them with lengths of wood torn from some fence.

Claire stopped the car, appalled by the scene. No matter what the kids had done, to beat them so savagely with pieces of wood was an act she would have put past responsible adults.

She got out of the car and hailed the mob. "Hey! Stop that! What do you think you're doing?"

They looked up from their work and glared at her. "What's it to you, lady?" one of them demanded.

"They're kids!" Claire protested. "What have they done that you should beat them like that?"

She had the mob's full attention now and they turned on her, their juvenile prey temporarily forgotten. The boy and girl, beaten and bloodied, got to their feet and took the chance to make a run for it. One of the attackers noticed and yelled; "Don't let them get away!"

Three of the mob took off after them but the rest remained staring at Claire as if she were guilty of the same crime the kids were.

"You new in town?" asked the man who had first spoken to her.

"No, I live here," Claire replied.

"Then you must have had your head under a rock." He glanced at his comrades. "Fetch her along. We'll take her to be converted. If she's one of the resistant types, she'll get what we're giving those kids."

Suddenly understanding the situation, Claire feared for her life. She got back into her car and drove off. The mob gave chase for a block or so and then gave up as she left them in the distance.

So that was it! The converted were turning on those who had not yet been converted and kids were marked as dangerous obstacles to the alien's authority. *My God!* There was a full-blown pogrom going on in Ralston and kids were the target! Gripped by a desperate fear for Tommy and Judy's lives, she sped up and raced for home.

There was only one police car parked outside and when Claire saw the dead or unconscious cop on the lawn, she felt both hopeful and afraid. Something had happened. But what?

She left the motor running and rushed up to the house. The door was unlocked and, upon checking all the rooms and calling out for Ray and the kids, she learned that the place was empty. *Where are they?* Had Ray overcome the cops and taken the kids to a safer location? *But where?*

She reluctantly accepted that she had no way of finding them tonight. She just had to hope and pray that Ray had somehow got them to safety. All she could do was find the colonel. He had to be doing something to stop this madness.

As she headed back into the center of town, an army truck shot across the road in front of her, the helmeted heads of several soldiers bobbing about in the back. She accelerated and followed it, hoping that it would take her to the colonel.

The truck headed east and drew close to the main canal. Up ahead, Claire could see the lights of some sort of military post. Jeeps and trucks were parked and several soldiers could be seen milling around. She recognized the bulky frame of one man in particular; Colonel Baskin. The truck she was following halted and its soldiers spilled out of the back, guns at the ready.

Odd, Claire thought. The way they were running, keeping their heads low, taking up positions along the street resembled men entering combat. She realized what was happing too late. The crackle of gunfire lit up the street. The soldiers at the post flung themselves flat, a couple of them struck by bullets.

They returned fire with the immediacy of men with well-trained reflexes. Claire ducked as bullets whizzed and ricocheted down the street, smashing car windows and thudding into brickwork. Keeping her head low, she hurried back to her car, put it into reverse and backed up behind the truck, using it for cover.

From her position, she could see the attackers fanning out, covering each other as they advanced. Colonel Baskin's men did the same, taking up defensive positions while the *rat-a-tat-tat* of gunfire was a constant. Men fell on both sides, riddled with bullets as the two evenly matched forces battled it out in the street.

One of the attackers carried a bazooka and his comrade was fitting a rocket into it. Claire gritted her teeth. She didn't know much about warfare but she had a good idea that one hit from that thing could take out Colonel Baskin and his whole team.

She put the car into gear and pulled out from behind the truck. Then, flooring the gas, she roared down the street towards the soldier with the bazooka. The increase of covering fire as the man lined up his target drowned out the sound of Claire's approach.

The grille of the car slammed into the two kneeling men, crushing one under the wheels and bouncing the other off its hood. The bazooka misfired and the rocket went shooting down the street. It missed the colonel's position by ten feet, sailing over their heads and impacting above a storefront. The explosion lit up the night and the fire cloud rolled up the side of the building, scorching the brickwork. Claire stamped on the brake pedal and the car slithered to a halt a few feet from the colonel and his men.

Her heart hammering in her chest, Claire spilled out of the vehicle and scurried for cover as the comrades of the two men she had run over peppered her car with bullets. Colonel Baskin's men returned fire and used the surprise to their advantage, pressing the assault down the street. Soon enough, all the attackers had been taken care of.

"Well, Dr. Weldon," said Colonel Baskin, emerging from behind a jeep as he holstered his sidearm. "It seems I owe you my gratitude. If you hadn't run those two men down, we would be a smoking crater now. But what I want to know is what, in God's name happened here."

"It's Beta Team, sir," said a solider after checking one of the nearby corpses.

"The team we lost contact with," mused the colonel. "What happened to them?"

"I guess they got hit by the tentacle, sir. Just like Anderson."

"Just like half the town," Claire added. "It's a warzone out there. I just passed a group of grown adults trying to beat a young couple to death."

"Well what do you expect me to do about it?" the colonel demanded. "Declare martial law? I'm trying to do my job here. Where the hell are the police?"

"The police are converts too, you arrogant oaf!" called a voice from behind the trucks. "Now do you believe it?"

"Ray?" Claire exclaimed, covering her mouth and feeling tears of relief well up in her eyes as her husband emerged from his hiding place, their youngest daughter whimpering in his arms.

"Claire!" Ray called, hurrying over to her.

"Mommy!" Rose added, arms reaching out for her.

She ran to them and hugged them both tight. "Thank God, you're all right," she said. "But Judy and Tommy ...?"

"They snuck out," said Ray. "I was able to get out too and went looking for them. Claire, it's a massacre out there. The cops hit the Black Camelots. Slaughtered them. I don't know if Judy and Tommy were with them."

"Oh, my God," said Claire, tears falling from her eyes. "Our babies ..."

"The colonel has teams dropping explosives into the canals, trying to force the creature into a trap," said Ray. "He lost contact with one of his teams and I guess they were converted. It knows they are trying to destroy it now and will stop at nothing to halt us."

"It can try all it wants," snapped the colonel, "but we'll get the bastard and blow it back to Mars."

"Colonel, you just lost a whole team after they tried to kill you!" Ray bellowed. "One of its exits is now unguarded. That creature has free roam of the canals. It can escape back upriver if it wants."

"It wouldn't want to," said Claire. "It wants to be where people are. We are its prey. It wants converts. But I don't understand how it got so many in such a short time. It doesn't make any sense. People have been warned to stay away from the canals."

"It has plenty of recruiters who convince people into going near the water," said Ray. "You saw what happened with Judy. Everyone it converts can recruit ten or so more. It spreads like a virus."

"But in such a short time?" said Claire. Suddenly it occurred to her. "The storm drains!" she said.

"What?" said Colonel Baskin.

"The storm drains! That's how it converted so many people!" she hurried over to her car and popped the trunk. She still had the bundle of maps she had got from the irrigation office. She found the map she was looking for and spread it out on the car's hood. "We thought the creature would confine itself to the canals but we never considered the storm drains. They run under the city like a labyrinth, with drains on every street. Look here! She said, pointing at a junction of lines on the map. The sanitary sewage system has an overflow into the storm sewer. This thing might have been getting into peoples' plumbing, popping up inside their houses!"

"Yeesh!" exclaimed a young soldier. "Imagine sitting on the john and then suddenly ..."

"Can it, Greenbaum!" snapped Colonel Baskin. "The tentacle we saw was as thick as a tree. No way could that thing squeeze into somebody's pipes."

"Octopuses can squeeze themselves into remarkably tight spots," said Ray. "I saw one get inside a beer bottle once."

"And do any of us have any idea how long its tentacles are?" asked Claire. "Nobody has seen its body, have they? That thing could be sitting underneath the town, sending its cables out in all directions, reaching extraordinary distances."

"And you figure it's in the storm drains," said the colonel with a sigh of acceptance. "Very well, we'll just have to go in after it. My boys have flamethrowers. It ain't gonna be pretty but we can manage it."

"This town has a more immediate problem, colonel," said Ray. "Namely the murderous mobs running around killing kids."

"My husband is right," said Claire. "Killing the alien won't immediately set things to rights. It won't undo any of the damage it has already caused. This town will still be under mob rule while the drug remains in its subjects' systems."

"But killing the alien will stop it from turning more of the civilians against us," said the colonel. "And I'm not having more of my troops turn zombie on me. We go in and we kill it. Now."

Claire sighed. "Very well. But I'm going with you."

"Claire no!" said Ray.

"You're not serious," said the colonel.

"I have the schematics," Claire insisted. "I'm sure you boys can read maps but you might need every gun available once we're in those tunnels. I can be your pathfinder."

"Fine," said the colonel. "We head out as soon as we're suited up."

He stomped off to bark orders and Ray took Claire by the shoulders. "Claire, I know why you're doing this," he said.

"Really, Ray? Why is that?"

"You feel responsible. You were the first person to figure out that there was an alien in Ralston and now you want to see it through to the end. Or maybe you just want a look at an honest-to-God alien before these grunts blow it to smithereens, hell I don't know!"

Claire looked from him to Rose who was gazing up at her with those big, brown eyes of hers. She hugged and kissed them both. "You two look after each other. I'm going to end this."

They were led into a tent where Claire could get kitted out. They passed an army cot upon which a man was strapped, his arms and legs firmly restrained. Pastor Mathews sat by him, reading from the bible.

"Corporal Anderson," Ray explained. "The tentacle got him. Injected him with one of those darts. Colonel Baskin ordered him be restrained. The tentacle would have got another soldier had Pastor Mathews not intervened and blown the tip off it with a hidden handgun he apparently carries around with him."

Pastor Mathews glanced at Claire and gave her a friendly nod.

"It can be harmed, Claire," said Ray. "I saw it bleed. Make sure they don't take you in there without a weapon and promise me you'll use it if it comes to it."

"Promise, darling."

She was given a green combat uniform with no insignias, black boots, and a helmet all in the smallest size they had. When she emerged from the tent, Rose was sleeping in the crook of Ray's arm as he sat in the back of a jeep. He looked her up and down, his face grave with concern.

"This is all rather silly," she said. "I'm just going along as a map reader."

"What about a gun?" Ray asked the soldier who had kitted her out.

"She can take my pistol," said the colonel, overhearing him. He unholstered it and handed it to her. "Know how to use one?"

Claire took the gun from him and examined it. "I'll manage."

"Good. The team is assembled now. Come meet the boys."

They clustered around the colonel's jeep for the briefing. Claire was introduced to Sergeant Frost who would be leading the expedition.

"Where in this network do you think our alien would make its nest?" he asked her.

"Well, it would have to be somewhere fairly large to contain it," said Claire, spreading the map out on the hood of the jeep. "Although we don't know exactly how big the creature is. It could be using this recharge basin which was left over from Ralston's old storm drain system."

"Recharge basin? What's that?"

"Well, these days, the storm water runs straight into the river but back before the current system was built, all the water was diverted to a large concrete-lined cylinder which had a filter bed of stone and sand. The water then percolates through the filter and back into the water table deep underground. When the new system was built, the water was diverted to the river but it is still possible for overflow to enter the recharge basin."

Sergeant Frost nodded. "Seems as likely a spot as any."

The widest entrance to the storm drain system was a circular culvert about two meters across that opened into the Tuolumne River. At this time of year, the flow was just a trickle and promised not much more than a foot-wetting. The trucks were parked atop the bridge that spanned the river and the soldiers piled out of them and climbed down the riverbank to the culvert.

Colonel Baskin ordered a forward command post to be set up at the mouth of the tunnel and, as soldiers began stacking up sandbags and erecting communications tents, Claire kissed Ray and Rose goodbye.

"Lights on!" Sergeant Frost said and the soldiers flicked on their L-shaped flashlights that were strapped to their chests, illuminating the entrance of the drain.

There were twenty men in all, kitted out with flamethrowers, machine guns and explosive charges. They peered into the tunnel. The lights bounced off the curved walls, picking out every detail in the concrete but the blackness beyond was impenetrable. It was like staring down the throat of something.

"I want flame units up front," said Sergeant Frost. "Hiller, Rodriquez, if you see a tentacle, scorch it. Don't wait for my signal; we've all seen how fast these things move. Dr. Weldon, you're with me. Greenbaum, get a light on her!"

Greenbaum hurried over and held his flashlight over her shoulder so she could see the map she carried. Then, after Sergeant Frost had silenced the wisecracking and nervous horsing around, they set out.

The scummy water washed around their boots as they headed down the long tunnel. Claire followed it on the map with her finger. The first junction was up ahead but she couldn't see it. The tunnels were a lot longer than they appeared on the map. *The lair of the beast.* She tried to calm her nerves and appear as brave as the soldiers who laughed and joked around her as they went deeper and deeper into the tunnels. But they joked too much and laughed too loud. *They're frightened too*, she realized.

At last, the tunnel split off in two directions. "All right, Dr. Weldon," said Sergeant Frost. "Which way?"

"Left," Claire replied.

They pressed on, taking a few more turns, before the texture of the walls seemed to change to something much rougher and dirtier. Green slime caked the tunnels like cholesterol in unhealthy veins.

"What's happening to the walls?" Greenbaum asked.

"I think we're entering the old part of the system," said Claire.

"Then we should be close, right?" said Sergeant Frost.

"Yes. The recharge basin should be less than a quarter mile now."

The men fell silent, knowing they were close to their prey. It was here somewhere, lurking, *waiting*.

The tunnel they were in opened into a larger tunnel with several others leading off from it.

"The main storm drain that traverses the town," Claire explained. "We turn right here and follow it to the recharge basin."

They stepped down into deeper water and there was a definite feeling of current. Claire tried not to shudder as she felt things moving past her legs in the blackness. *Its only debris; sticks and garbage washed down from the streets above.*

The flashlights of the soldiers swept their beams along the walls, alert for any sign of danger. The circular tunnels leading off to other parts of the system gaped at them like lifeless eyes.

It was one of the flame units who saw it first. He gave out a cry and let loose a jet of flame that lit up the tunnel and reflected off the water. Before the streak of fire hit the far wall, Claire saw the tentacle illuminated in its glare. Fire engulfed it and it shrank back into the hole it had emerged from, its flesh bubbling and crispy.

"Watch it, boys!" Sergeant Frost said. "There are tunnels all around us. That thing could poke a tentacle out of any one of them."

The frightened soldiers swung their lights about, making their shadows dance along the length of the tunnel. Feet splashed about in the water making it impossible to hear if anything was approaching them.

"Steady, boys ..." warned Sergeant Frost.

"Hiller, watch it!" one of the soldiers yelled. Hiller, who was aiming his flame thrower at the opposite wall, was unaware of the thing snaking out of the tunnel at his back, its slimy sucker already unfolded, curling around to reach his face.

A machine gun opened fire as the sucker latched on, peppering the side of the tentacle with bullets, nearly severing it. With a savage jerk, the tentacle twisted Hiller around and there was an audible crack as his neck snapped. The tentacle released him and he landed in the water, his head at an unnatural angle. His comrade, Rodriquez unleashed a spurt of fire on the tentacle and it shrank back into its hole.

"Damn it!" one of the men cried. "Hiller is dead!"

"Apparently these things can kill when threatened," said Sergeant Frost.

"Up ahead!" said Greenbaum in a voice laced with terror.

They all followed his gaze, every light cast in that direction. Three tentacles had emerged from holes further along the tunnel and were snaking towards them, keeping close to the water.

"Open fire!" Sergeant Frost yelled and every weapon blazed in the direction of the approaching horrors.

The tentacles slipped down into the water and all that could be seen of them were their approaching ripples.

"Fall back!" cried Sergeant Frost. "Fall back!"

Rodriquez kept up steady bursts of fire from his flamethrower but it was useless. The things were submerged and he couldn't do much but warm the water for them.

"Rodriquez!" Sergeant Frost yelled. "Fall back!"

It was too late. One of the tentacles had reached him and, in the erratic light of gunfire, Claire saw him hoisted up into the air and slammed down into the water with terrific force.

"Get outta here!" Sergeant Frost yelled and all was sudden panic and confusion.

Somebody slammed into Claire and she fell backwards into the water. She choked on a mouthful of foul-tasting liquid and tried to rise, coughing and spluttering as boots splashed all around her. There was no gunfire now, the soldiers were fleeing for their lives and the flashlights they carried with them were quickly disappearing down the tunnel.

Claire tried to cry out for them to not leave her but her lungs were still choked with water and she couldn't make herself heard. By the time she had got to her feet, they were gone and she was alone in the blackness.

The dark was absolute. She couldn't see her hand in front of her face let alone the direction in which the soldiers had fled. She stood stock still, frozen with terror, willing herself not to cough even though her lungs screamed to.

Can the tentacles see me? She wondered. They seemed to possess some kind of vision despite lacking eyes but what about down here in perfect darkness? Maybe their vision was based on movement? If she could stay still, perhaps they would pass her by? Where were they anyway?

She heard something slip in and out of the water and couldn't help but clamp a hand over her mouth in terror. There was something in the tunnel with her. She could hear it slithering about, the moisture dripping off it.

Although she could see nothing, she could feel an object in front of her face. It had a coldness to it that seemed to suck the warmth from her head.

It's right there, in front of me!

And then it struck; a large, wet thing like an enormous pancake wrapping around her head. Her hand was still in front of her mouth and she ripped it free to grasp at the edges of the thing that smothered her.

She struggled and fought against it but its cable-like body was so strong. She felt herself being lifted and the pain in her neck was agonizing. She couldn't breathe. Something harder than the gelatinous consistency of the tentacle pressed against the skin under her chin. There was a sharp, agonizing pain and then everything faded from her mind.

CHAPTER 21

Finding herself suddenly alone with Johnny Packer in a supermarket at night was only slightly less terrifying to Judy than seeing her brother charging out into the night with three men chasing him with a shotgun. She had wanted to run out after them but Johnny had grabbed her around the middle and held her back. She had fought and beat at him to let her go but he wouldn't.

He was right, of course. She could see that now that she had calmed down a little. If the men had seen them, they would have turned their gun on them instead. And she had to admit, Johnny hadn't acted abominably so far. He had pulled her out of the grasp of those crazed hobos and he had been clearly upset when he had killed one of them. She had to wonder how much of his tough guy bravado was an act.

"Come on," she said to him after a while. "The coast is clear. Let's go find Tommy and Burt."

They crept out onto the sidewalk, glass from the shattered windows crunching under their feet. They looked up and down the street. There wasn't a soul in sight.

"Which way do you think they went?" Johnny said.

"I have no idea." She fought back tears. This whole nightmare seemed to be getting worse, not better.

"Let's head this way," said Johnny, seeming to sense her emotional state and wanting to avoid seeing her cry at all costs. "It's as good a direction as any."

Claire nodded in agreement and they set off.

"They couldn't have shot them," said Johnny, apparently in an attempt to raise her spirits. "We'd have heard it if they had. Tommy and Burt are probably lying low someplace."

"No thanks to you."

"Hey? What did I do?" he protested. "This town has it in for kids. Me included. It's not my fault."

"No, but if my brother hadn't been so desperate to impress you and your stupid gang, then we'd both be at home right now, not roving the streets getting shot at." She couldn't help her resentment bubbling up. Johnny might not have been the thug she had thought he was, but it was still his fault Tommy was in danger in the first place.

"Your brother knows what he's doing," Johnny snapped. "And don't call my club stupid. Ever."

"Oh, big deal! You guys cruise around looking for kicks and acting tough. Some club! If it wasn't for your hot rod races and your drug dealing, maybe the adults of this town wouldn't be so down on kids in the first place."

"Drug dealing? You don't know what you're talking about!"

"I might not be one of your trashy club girls but I know what a reefer smells like. The clubhouse stank of it."

"Reefers! Big deal! That's the trouble, people don't know the difference between a harmless bit of tea and the hard stuff. Now you take hop for instance. I don't let anyone in my club touch it. It's a life-ruiner."

"What about that girl at the clubhouse? Don't tell me she was in that sort of state over a little bit of 'tea'."

"That's Marie. She's been knocking around with the Jungle Dukes up in Stockton. They got her hooked on hop and made her do some other stuff besides. We busted her out of there and have been trying to get her clean. It's the Jungle Dukes who have been pushing hop in Ralston. I've been trying to keep it out for a couple of years now, but they've got some contacts here I don't know about. When I find out who they are, they'll be fishing their teeth out of their bellies. No one pushes hop on the Black Camelots' turf! We'll ..."

He tapered off as he realized that his club was no more and most of his friends were dead and fell into a brooding silence. Judy felt suddenly sorry for him. Tonight was the end for a lot of things and when it was all over, if any of them survived, who knew what the future might look like?

"There's a car coming," he said.

They broke into a run as its lights drew closer and ran into a used car lot, ducking between the cars marked with sale tags, hoping they hadn't been spotted. The car squealed to a halt, telling them that they had. They were up and running once more. Doors slammed behind them as the car's occupants gave chase. They ran around to the back of the showroom and across the street on the other side.

Up ahead was the church. Judy's family wasn't particularly religious, and she guessed Johnny wasn't either, so it surprised her when he bolted straight for it.

"Might be a safe spot to seek shelter," he panted as they ran towards its doors.

"I don't think these people respect the rule of sanctuary," gasped Judy.

"No, but old Pastor Mathews is a tough S.O.B. and might help us."

If he isn't out for young blood like the rest of the town, Judy thought.

The wide, double doors were unlocked, and, glancing back to make sure their pursuers hadn't seen in which direction they had gone, they heaved one open and slipped inside.

The lights were on but instead of finding a quiet, echoing room with perhaps Pastor Mathews snuffing out candles or whatever priests did before they clocked off, they were met with a full congregation, all turning their heads to look at them.

"Uh ...," said Johnny.

"More have heard the call," said a young woman's voice from the pulpit. "Do come in and join us!"

Judy's eyes widened in terror. It was Connie Lund, standing where Pastor Mathews stood every Sunday, for all the world as if she were preaching to a decidedly young flock. Mr. and Mrs. Lund were there, standing to the side, watching their daughter with proud smiles on their faces. There were some other adults too, mostly parents of kids Judy recognized from school, but the majority of the audience were kids. Some were teenagers, sitting in their usual cliques while some were little more than babies, sitting in the laps of their parents.

"Don't be shy!" said Connie. "We are all God's chosen ones. Step closer so we can see who you are!"

Judy and Johnny glanced at each other. They had no choice. If they turned and ran now, they would have an entire congregation after them. As they edged closer to the light, Judy saw a look of suspicion cross Connie's face as she recognized her.

"Judy ..." Connie said. "You had a change of heart, I see. And Johnny Packer too. How lovely!"

"Oh, Judy, isn't it wonderful!" another voice said. Susanne Crane crept out of the crowd to greet her. "I was so scared at first but once it was over, wasn't it just boss? I feel ten times braver than the mousy little girl I used to be! It was Connie herself who introduced me. Imagine that! Who introduced you?"

Judy was at a loss for words. This was all too horrible for her to cope with.

"I did," said Johnny, quickly. "My uncle Nick introduced me and I introduced Judy."

"And the rest of the Black Camelots?" Connie asked from the pulpit, the vestiges of suspicion still not quite gone from her face. "We were under the impression that you were subversives and Sheriff Benson had you marked for elimination."

"Most of them were," said Johnny. "I was converted early and tried to get the rest of them to turn but they wouldn't have it. So Sheriff Benson ... took care of them. I'm all that's left."

Judy saw his fists clench as he spoke and marveled at his ability to keep cool. She knew what it had cost his pride.

"Very good," said Connie and then she addressed her audience once more. "Our enemies are being vanquished, one by one, as we, the chosen few, gather here on the eve of our victory, ready to strike the killing blow! At first, they said that kids couldn't hear the call, but we are proof that we can! We may be few in number but that only increases our glory in fulfilling our task! God has chosen us brave few to be the tools of his avenging angel, his messenger from the heavens, and before this night is over, we will have wiped the slate clean for Ralston and ushered it into a new age!"

"Amen!" somebody cried and the word was picked up by all present. As they shouted it, they held aloft tools and weapons. Most were household items; scissors and kitchen knives. Others held more dangerous things like hammers and axes. A few had revolvers and hunting rifles.

"Let the purification begin!" cried Connie and the cry was taken up; "Purification! Purification! Purification!"

The crowd yelled out the word with such enthusiasm that Judy could almost see tears in their eyes. *They need this*, she thought. *They need to yell it loud enough to muffle the awfulness of what they're doing.* Even the alien's drug didn't numb their natural revulsion of murder, but they were compelled to do it nevertheless.

"Go now, children of the Messenger!" Connie went on, "Go out and do God's work! Seek out those who shut their eyes and cover their ears to the truth! You all have friends and family members who cower in their basements or hide behind their drapes, refusing to hear the word of the Lord. Go to them now and see that they stand in the Messenger's way no longer. Show them the final kindness for there is no place for them in the New World. Go now, Children of God!"

There were further cries of 'amen!' as the congregation, whipped into a fury, leapt up and began to move towards the doors as one unstoppable machine of destruction. Judy couldn't believe it. This was a juvenile death cult hell-bent on murder while their parents stood by proudly, urging them on. It made her sick to the stomach with fear and revulsion, but they had no choice but to move with the crowd and let themselves be carried out into the night.

First chance we get, we break away from this madness, Johnny signaled to Judy with his eyes. Three school busses had been commandeered and were parked out front. Karen Wood, Heather Marshall and Trudy Braddock – Connie's lieutenants - were dividing kids up and allocating them to the busses which they began piling into as if they were all heading off on a jolly field trip.

"Oh, Judy, come sit with me!" said Susanne, tugging on Judy's sleeve, pulling her in the direction of one of the busses. "Johnny too!"

"I ... ah," said Judy, "We really have to be somewhere."

"You should go with Susanne," said Connie, suddenly appearing behind them. "She's been very helpful in identifying subversives. She'll show you where they live. And with the strong Johnny Packer with you, you won't have to worry about much resistance."

Judy glanced at Johnny helplessly as they found themselves being pulled up the steps onto the bus. They found seats near the back; Johnny by the window and Judy and Susanne squeezed in next to him. Susanne was as giddy as a five-year-old and didn't seem to register that

she was part of a lynch mob setting out to murder inno-
cents.

With much whooping and cheering, the bus rumbled into action and rolled out of the parking lot with
Connie's father – retail estate baron Arthur Lund himself
– behind the wheel. There was an air of forced jubilation
that did its best to stifle the tense horror of what they
were setting out to do. Some of the kids at the front even
broke out in a hymn and the words of 'Blessed Assurance'
rolled through the bus.

Judy shivered. None of this had anything to do with
Jesus or God. The alien had no concept of God. These kids
were reacting to the drug that poisoned their minds the
only way they knew how; by rationalizing its terrible
commands, framing them in terms they understood.
They were on a mission from God now, not following the
orders of an alien creature whose only interest was in its
own survival.

As the bus headed through town, two teenagers suddenly bolted from cover and ran for their lives down the
street, their jackets clearly visible in the headlights; one
leather and one satin. Connie's dad slammed on the
brakes and everybody was thrown forward. He turned in
his seat.

"Say, I thought all of those gang punks were dead except for Johnny back there."

Heads turned to glare at Judy and Johnny.

"I wasn't there when Sheriff Benson attacked the
clubhouse," said Johnny. "I guess some of them escaped."

"Well get after them, then!"

The accordion doors slammed open and kids piled
out, brandishing their weapons and grinning manically.

"My god, Johnny, we have to do something!" Judy
whispered. "That was Tommy and Burt!"

"I know! I know! Just let me think!"

"Think while running!" She grabbed him by the arm and hauled him out of his seat.

They followed the gang of kids as they rounded the corner and bore down on Tommy and Burt who were visibly exhausted from being chased all evening. Their eager pursuers caught up to them and knocked them down. Tommy and Burt swung out with their fists, but they were surrounded and beaten.

"Stop!" yelled Johnny.

The crowd turned to stare at him. "Got a problem with this, Packer?" one of the kids from their grade asked, daring him to object. It was Vince Dodd from Judy's history class and he had a baseball bat. This gang of thugs would turn on them at the slightest sign that they had not been converted as they said they had.

"These punks are from my crew," said Johnny. "I wanna do the honors."

"Be my guest," said Vince, handing the bat to Johnny.

Johnny took it and walked behind Tommy and Burt. They were on their knees and were looking from him to Judy in bewilderment. Johnny held the bat over Tommy's head and Judy almost ran forward to stop him, but he looked up at her, threw her a wink, and she immediately understood.

With a savage swing, Johnny slammed the bat into Vince's belly, doubling him over with the blow. "Run!" he yelled to Judy and the boys.

The mob exploded in rage and went for Johnny. He swung at them again and again, fending them off with his newly acquired bat. Judy hauled Tommy and Burt to their feet, and they took the chance Johnny had given them to make their escape.

As they pounded down the sidewalk, Judy looked back and saw the mob nearly overwhelm Johnny who kept swinging at them. Eventually, when the bat was nearly ripped out of his hands, he turned and ran after Judy and the boys with the mob in hot pursuit.

It was the feeling of helplessness that was the worst. At least if he were combing the streets looking for the kids, Ray would feel as if he were doing something. But now, sitting by a radio and listening to Claire and the soldiers go deeper and deeper into the tunnels, it was more than he could bear.

Rose was asleep again and Ray had left her with Pastor Mathews. He envied her the ability to sleep through all of this. He wished he could do the same and wake up to find it all over or just a bad dream.

He left the front post, unable to stare into that black tunnel any longer and wandered through the camp. He lit a cigarette and listened to the conversations of the soldiers. As he passed the communications tent, he overheard some corporal yelling excitedly into a radio, the muffled squawks of whoever was on the other end equally excited.

"What's going on?" he asked as the corporal left the tent, hands on his hips, biting his bottom lip in frustration.

"Bad news for the town, that's what," the corporal said. "As if the police turning into murderous thugs wasn't enough, there are now gangs of residents roving the streets killing kids."

"Kids?" asked Ray in alarm.

"Yeah, the ones who haven't been converted. I guess the mobs know that they'll offer the most resistance to the alien and are doing away with them upfront. It seems to be organized. Our unit on Kellogg Avenue have reported school buses full of kids armed to the teeth passing up and down."

"My god," said Ray. "Something has to be done!"

"I'm on my way up to the colonel now," said the corporal.

Ray followed him up to the forward post. There had still been no news from the tunnels. Once the corporal had explained the situation in town, Colonel Baskin seemed less than interested.

"We're in the middle of a military operation here," he said. "I have no orders to declare martial law."

"Colonel, the people of this town are dying!" Ray exploded. "If you don't do something, who will? The police can't be counted on. It's a bloodbath out there and my kids might be in the middle of it! Please, Sir, I'm, begging you. You have thirty-odd men here sitting on their behinds. You have equipment to put up roadblocks. I'm not asking you to arrest people or do the police's job for them. I'm just asking you to save some lives. If the United States Army won't step in to protect civilian lives, then what is it really for?"

The colonel glared at him, clearly disliking having his job defined to him by a civilian but Ray could see that he had struck upon something.

"Very well," the colonel said. "I can send out the two squads I have left, set up a few roadblocks and try and disperse these mobs. It will have to do until morning. After that, I don't know."

"Thank you, Colonel!"

Within ten minutes, two trucks were being loaded up with soldiers and equipment. They had orders to head into town and set up roadblocks at all main intersections to halt traffic. Then, the two squads would move from street to street, seek out the roving mobs and disperse them, at gunpoint if necessary. Ray volunteered to go with one of the squads. He knew the town and could direct them if necessary. If Claire was going to be a pathfinder under the town, then he was going to be one on the streets above.

It felt good to be doing something at last and he kissed Rose's head and thanked Pastor Mathews for watching over her. Then he clambered up into the back of a truck and they were off.

The town was as silent as the grave. They encountered a mob just after they laid the first roadblock; a gang of twenty or so men and women striding towards the cluster of soldiers with the unshakable determination of natives marching against foreign invaders.

"Get back!" the staff sergeant yelled.

Rifles were raised and aimed at the mob. It halted, keen for blood but knowing that it would be futile to charge into the face of armed troops.

"Return to your homes!" the staff sergeant ordered them. "There is a curfew under effect! This town is now under martial law."

"You have no authority over us!" somebody in the mob called out. "This town is ours!

"Yeah, get out while you still can!" somebody else yelled.

"Hold your fire," the staff sergeant said to his men. "We've halted them, but God knows what this crazy drug will have them doing."

Sirens could be heard in the distance and before long, the blue lights of two radio cars could be seen coming down the street. Ray tensed. He still had no idea if Judy and Tommy were among the dead at Nick's garage and the very sight of the ones who might have murdered them made his gut churn with loathing.

His hatred increased as the cars parked up and Sheriff Benson got out. He smiled at the soldiers who gazed at him, unsure of what to do.

"That's far enough," said the staff sergeant. "Any further and we shoot!"

"Shoot?" said Sheriff Benson. "On the police? You boys really have lost your minds, haven't you? Who gave you permission to set up roadblocks in my town?"

"Permission of the United States Government," replied the staff sergeant. "This town is under martial law. Your reign of terror is over, Sheriff."

Sheriff Benson laughed at this. "No, boy, the reign of the United States Army, even the government is over. You think it ends with Ralston? Hell no, Ralston is just the beginning! The tentacles of our new leader are longer than you can possibly imagine. Soon it will be Stockton and Turlock, then all of California. State by state, this country will be absorbed into the new order until the United States is poised to usher the entire world into a future of peace. And anybody who stands in our way will be destroyed."

"That's enough out of you!" the staff sergeant said. "Move back. Tell your people to return to their homes."

Sheriff Benson grinned again and turned to the mob. "You heard the man with the gun. Their time will come but for now, go find other targets."

"But Sheriff ..." somebody in the crowd said.

"No arguments! I am still the sheriff! Get back from the roadblock!"

Ray and the soldiers watched in bewilderment as the mob reluctantly dispersed. The cops got back into their cars and backed up. The sheriff's car turned and accompanied the retreating mob down the street. The other car remained; its headlights pointed at the roadblock.

Suddenly, it peeled out, its tires spinning on the asphalt, powering it forward directly towards them.

"Look out!" Ray yelled.

The soldiers ran for cover as the car picked up speed. It showed no sign of braking or swerving and, as it smashed through the roadblock, it collided with the parked army truck and exploded in billowing cloud of flames.

"That cop was on a goddamn suicide mission!" said the staff sergeant as he picked himself up off the ground.

"These people are drones now," said Ray. "There is nothing on their minds but the protection of their master."

The mob had turned and, accompanied by Sheriff Benson's car, was running back to the smashed blockade, weapons in their hands.

"Open fire!" the staff sergeant yelled.

Rifles cracked and several civilians fell, leapt over by their comrades in their mad stampede. The sheriff's car swerved to a halt and Benson and the two remaining cops got out. They took up position behind it and began firing on the soldiers with their handguns.

Ray took cover behind the burning truck as the soldiers returned fire. A full-on street battle was in effect. The surviving members of the mob fell upon the soldiers and began attacking them with meat cleavers, clubs, gardening tools and kitchen knives. A soldier near to the truck was struck by one of the police's bullets and fell back, his rifle clattering from his hands.

Ray glanced at it. It was almost within reach, but bullets whizzed down the street. He lay flat on the ground and commando crawled over to the body of the soldier. Grasping the rifle with one hand, he rolled back behind the truck, wincing as a bullet nicked the asphalt a couple of feet from him.

Back under cover, he checked the rifle's magazine and then, hobbled over on his haunches to the other side of the truck. By peering around the corner, he could see the radio car farther down the street. The heads of two cops were visible over the roof of the car. One of them was Sheriff Benson, easily detected by his cowboy hat.

Ray lifted the rifle stock to his shoulder and took aim at Benson's head. *Now it's your turn to die, you bastard.* He squeezed the trigger and the rifle kicked into his shoulder. His shot went wide and dinged off the roof of the radio car.

Damn!

One of the cops noticed that somebody had taken a shot at them and began firing in Ray's general direction, but a handgun at long range was as good as useless and the bullets pinged off the side of the burning truck. Ray waited and tried to calm his nerves. He wouldn't get many shots at this. The fusillade of retaliatory fire ceased and he peeped out again. The cop was reloading.

He aimed the rifle again and fired. The bullet struck Sheriff Benson in the side of the head and knocked him back, blood spraying in an upwards arc from his shattered skull. Ray whooped with exhilaration.

One of the other cops was down and the remaining officer kept on firing at the soldiers who, having dispensed with the mob, were advancing on him. It was a courageous last stand, although clearly driven by the alien drug, and Ray watched grimly as he was finally riddled with bullets and fell back behind the patrol car.

Emerging from his cover, Ray saw that the mob had done some real damage on the squad. Three soldiers lay dead, their shirts torn and their faces bloody. The staff sergeant and his remaining troops were in poor shape with many wounds inflicted by improvised weapons. But the mob were all dead. At such close range the soldiers had little choice but to defend themselves with their combat knives. It was an ugly scene.

"You took out the sheriff," said the staff sergeant, approaching Ray. "Nice shot. You ever serve?"

"No but my father was the finest deer hunter in Virginia," Ray replied. "He didn't raise a city boy when it came to rifles."

"Will the fight go out of the mobs now the sheriff is dead?" asked a soldier who was having a nasty knife wound in his shoulder bound.

"No," Ray replied. "He wasn't their boss, just their co-ordinator. They'll be more disorganized now. More un-disciplined."

"That could work in our favor," said the staff sergeant.

"It might or it might not," said Ray. He looked around at the wreckage and the blood that ran in rivulets across the street. An alley led off from the street not far from their position. A car was parked in it, visible now from the flames of the burning radio car and truck. Ray walked over to it, recognizing its paintjob.

"I'll be goddamned," he said.

The car was a black '47 Chevy with flames down its sides. *Johnny Packer's car. But what is it doing here?* It meant that somebody had survived the massacre at Nick's garage, possibly Johnny himself. But how many others had survived?

It gave Ray hope. Despite himself, he let that hope fill his heart. *Someone had survived.* And that meant Tommy and Judy might be alive.

CHAPTER 22

There was a warm feeling in Claire's body as she gently bobbed about in the water. She could see nothing but was enveloped in a comforting feeling of safety and security. Water sloshed as it moved over her, and she had the curious idea that she was back in the womb.

As consciousness returned to her in dribs and drabs, the warm feeling dissipated and recent events shuffled into some sort of order in her mind. She sat up, a feeling of concern quickly evolving into terror in her gut. She was in the storm drains beneath the town. She was all alone in the darkness. The soldiers had deserted her. *The tentacle.*

Oh, God! The tentacle had got her!

She felt under her chin and there was a sore spot there with something hard in the middle, like a splinter. She pulled it out and threw it from her. She had been converted! It was an odd feeling, knowing that some alien drug was flowing through her veins, altering her thoughts and yet, she felt no different. She was still scared as hell and the only thought in her mind was that she had to get out of those lightless tunnels.

She moved forward through the water, having no clue in which direction she was going. Her feet bumped into something soft and heavy and she nearly fell headlong. She bent down and felt the object with her hands. It was a person. Dead.

Hiller! She remembered the unfortunate soldier with the flamethrower and how one of the tentacles had snapped his neck, instigating the full retreat through the tunnels. She felt around his person, her trembling fingers feeling the hard shapes of various pieces of equipment. She seized what felt like a 90-degree flashlight. She pulled it free from its strap and turned it on.

At last, she could see! She shone the flashlight up and down the tunnel. It was empty. She scanned the water for any sign of the map she had carried but that was long gone, trampled into the water and washed away. Still, she knew from which direction they had come and, if she went carefully, she was pretty sure she could retrace her steps.

She headed back to the tunnel that led from the main storm drain to the river and froze as she heard a lonely voice up ahead.

"Hello?" it called. "Sarge? Rodriquez? Henson? Can anyone hear me?"

"Hi there!" Claire called back.

"Who's that?" the voice cried out frantically.

"It's Claire Weldon!" She could see the distant beam of a flashlight heading down one of the tunnels on the other side of the main storm drain. Feet splashed towards her and a soldier emerged, his face pale in the beam of her own light. It was Greenbaum.

"Oh, thank God!" he said. "I thought I was all alone down here! Have you seen any of the others?"

"No," Claire said. "They left, I fell and ... must have passed out." She had almost told him that the tentacle had got her but something had made her lie. Something deep within her did not want to tell Greenbaum what had really happened. "Where did you all go?"

"We made tracks as fast as we could and headed deeper into the system, hoping to lose that thing and its damned tentacles. I got separated ... I don't know what happened, but I've been wandering about trying to find them. Say, do you still have that map?"

"No, I lost it when everybody stampeded."

"Then we're lost! We're stuck down here!"

"Calm yourself, Greenbaum," said Claire. "I know the way out. But the others, we should find them, if they're still alive."

“Sure.”

“You got a knife?”

“Yeah.” He drew his combat knife and handed it to her.

She took it and waded over to the concrete lip of the tunnel they were in and gouged an ‘X’ on it with the knife blade. “So we can mark our way,” she explained.

“Good thinking. Like Hansel and Gretel.”

“Come on,” she said. “Let’s move out.”

They headed deeper into the network of tunnels, marking each turn they took with Greenbaum’s knife. They called out the names of their comrades, straining their ears for any reply amid the echo of their own voices. Once, Claire thought she heard somebody whisper back ‘Claire!’ but it was so close and hushed that it couldn’t have been Sergeant Frost or one of his men.

“Which way now?” Greenbaum asked as the tunnel met another junction.

“Left is as good a choice as any,” said Claire, and she marked the side of the tunnel.

Greenbaum started off down it but Claire’s attention was suddenly drawn to movement at some distance down the tunnel leading right. She squinted into the darkness and saw a man standing there but he was not dressed in combat fatigues. He wore a waistcoat and grey pants. His hair was untidy and streaked with gray. The glowing end of his pipe illuminated a face she recognized down to its comb moustache. He hadn’t changed a bit.

“Father ...” she whispered.

“Claire,” he said. “My beautiful girl.”

No. It isn’t him. It’s the alien drug in my system. It’s making me see things that aren’t there.

“Hey, Dr. Weldon?” Greenbaum called back. “You coming?”

Claire squeezed her eyes shut and then opened them. Her father was still there. "I'm so very proud of you, Claire," he said.

She turned from him, her heart breaking as she did so. She wanted with every ounce of her being to run down that tunnel and give him a hug. But he wasn't really there! She forced herself to realize this. It was the drug, only the drug ...

She hurried after Greenbaum, her father's cries echoing after her; "Claire! Claire, wait! Come back!"

"You okay?" Greenbaum asked her, shining his flashlight in her face.

"Yes," she said. "Let's press on."

They had not gone much farther when they heard voices up ahead.

"That's the sarge!" Greenbaum explained. "Come on!"

They hurried onward, following the voices.

"Switch off your flashlight!" said Greenbaum.

Claire did so and they slowed their pace so that they crept along, barely disturbing the water. There was torchlight up ahead and the sounds of arguing. Claire didn't listen to what they were saying, it didn't matter, only that they could get close to them without giving themselves away.

She could make out Sergeant Frost and several others in the tunnel ahead, their outlines limned in the white light of the flashlights, completely unaware that they were being sneaked up on.

It was only then that Claire wondered why they were creeping up on their comrades. For some reason, she had got the idea into her head that they were the enemy and Greenbaum had too, because he had now gone down on one knee and was aiming his rifle down the length of the tunnel at his comrades.

He's been converted too! And now he means to murder Sergeant Frost and the others!

She made to stop him but some involuntary response in her froze her limbs. She wanted to rip the gun from his hands. She wanted to call out to Sergeant Frost and the others to take cover but neither her muscles nor her vocal chords obeyed her. Instead she was forced to stand idly by as Greenbaum opened fire.

Orange blasts of light lit up the tunnel as his bullets found their marks. Men screamed and fell while others flung themselves against the wall of the tunnel and re-turned fire.

Suddenly Claire had the use of her muscles once more, but only to throw herself down into the water to avoid being hit. Greenbaum continued to fire, pumping round after round at the remaining soldiers.

Claire covered her ears and screamed at the awful-ness of the situation. She was now an accomplice of the very thing she had set out to destroy. She was compelled to let Greenbaum murder his comrades because some-thing within her told her it was the right thing to do yet she hated it and hated being a part of it even more. Was this how it had been for the others; this awful guilt and self-loathing for doing what they had no choice but to do?

Yet there was a small flicker of resistance within her. Everything that had happened in the last few months had given her an objective view of the alien. To a person of science, it was something fascinating, something to be studied and learnt from. She had never felt the same fear and revulsion for it that other residents of Ralston had felt. But now that fear and revulsion landed on her like a ton of bricks. This thing threatened the very essence of humanity. She may be a woman of science, but what good was science if there was no society left to learn from it?

With a sudden motion that, for some reason, made her sick to her gut, she drew the pistol at her belt, pinged the safety off and pointed it at Greenbaum's skull. Her finger depressed the trigger and, again, there was that same involuntary freezing of the muscles. Her very finger seemed to be made of stone, refusing to bend to her will.

Greenbaum continued firing. *They are all dying,* Claire thought. *I Have to do something. Come on, Clare, you can do it! Don't let this bastard win!*

With a force of effort that felt like she had climbed a mountain in a split second, she pulled the trigger. The gun went off and Greenbaum's brains splattered against the curved wall. He slumped forward over his rifle which hissed as its hot barrel went under the water.

Claire gasped and retched. She felt poisoned. It was as if she had committed the gravest sin and she both hated and loved herself for it. She had done it! She had defied the alien and its mind-altering drug. If she could do it once, she could do it again ...

"What the hell is going on down there?" she heard Sergeant Frost yell. "That you, Dr. Weldon?"

"Yes," she called back. "Don't shoot!"

"That Greenbaum with you?"

"Yes. I think a tentacle got him. I saw him creep into this tunnel and open fire on you." She was lying again without even thinking about it. "So I ..."

"Put a bullet in his head," said Sergeant Frost, looking down at Greenbaum's floating corpse. "Thank you. We thought we'd lost you."

"Greenbaum, Man," said one of the soldiers and Claire realized it was Rodriquez. "Why'd he do it?"

"That's what the tentacle does," said Frost. "It plays with your mind and makes you do things you wouldn't ordinarily do."

"That's why we must destroy it," said Claire and she had to fight to hold her composure against a sudden churning in her gut that nearly made her throw up. *The drug is fighting me.*

"The only thing we're doing is getting the hell out of here," said Frost.

"We're not going on?" asked Claire.

"There's only four of us left! That thing took apart my whole squad! Ain't no way we can take it on now. We must pull out and return in larger numbers. You got that map, Dr. Weldon?"

"No. I lost it. But I can lead you out. I know the way."

"All right, we leave the dead where they are. We need to move fast. We'll recover their bodies when we come back. Dr. Weldon, if you please."

Claire turned and led them back to the main storm drain, silently noticing the crosses she had cut with Greenbaum's knife. When they reached the wider tunnel, she shone her flashlight down its length and said; "Hiller's corpse is over there. The tunnel that leads to the river is straight ahead."

She led them over to it and the soldiers gladly clambered up into it. "Man, will I be glad to breath fresh air again," one of them said.

"Yeah," Rodriguez replied. "I'm starting to forget what the outside world looks like."

Claire hung back and watched their backs vanish into the darkness ahead. They hadn't noticed that she was no longer with them and she wanted to keep it that way. Without too much splashing, she made her way back to the tunnel from which they had come. She couldn't remain with them. Not now she had been converted. How long until she turned her gun on them like Greenbaum had done?

Soon she was back with the corpses of the men Greenbaum had slain. She began ransacking them for weapons and equipment, ignoring the nausea and dizziness her actions were causing her. She had to fight it! She had to ignore the pain and fight her own body long enough so she could destroy the alien and end this once and for all.

She slung the strap of a machine gun over her shoulder and took a couple of extra flashlights. The batteries in hers were starting to fade. In one pouch she found explosives and fuses and set about wiring them together, making a bomb that could take out an apartment block.

"What are you doing, Claire?" said a voice behind her.

She spun, shining her flashlight in its direction. It was her father again.

"Don't do that, Claire. If you do, we can't be together."

"You're dead," she told him.

"I'm right here, Claire. Now, come give your old man a hug and things will be just like they were."

"You're just in my mind," said Claire as she wired the fuse to her bomb. "Just in my mind ..."

"Isn't everything? Ask all the others who have benefitted from this being's presence. Do they look unhappy to you? They have everything they desire. And so can you."

"But it's not real!" Claire shouted.

"To them it is. It makes no difference. And who are you to take that from them? Who are you to decide what is real and what isn't? I can be with you, always, Claire. You'll never miss me again. And I'm the very best of me, the good stuff you remember, not the sordid things you have come to learn about me. I am exactly what you lost."

"What I lost never existed!" said Claire. She quickly drew her gun and shot her father.

The bullet hit him in the chest. The betrayed look on his face as he fell backwards into the water brought tears to her eyes. She turned away from him and completed her bomb, placing it gently in a pouch at her belt.

As she prepared to set out, a figure rose from the water in the tail of her eye. It was her father, she knew it, but not the one she fondly remembered. This was a figure from her darkest nightmares; skin blackened and crispy, hair all burned away.

"Claire!" it hissed through a lipless mouth. "Look at me, Claire!"

She refused to look. Instead, she marched on, ignoring the splashes of the thing's feet in the water as it followed her.

"Look at me!"

She went deeper and deeper into the network and the burnt thing followed her every step of the way. She had no idea where she was going, she only hoped it was in the vague direction of the recharge basin.

"You are such a disappointment, Claire!" said the thing behind her. "Meteorites? A lifetime studying those worthless bits of junk hurtling around the heavens. I was a genius! To think how far the apple has fallen ..."

"Shh!" Claire snapped. The beam of her flashlight had caught some movement up ahead.

She hurried on and entered another tunnel. There, slithering on its way somewhere, was a tentacle. It knew she was there, there could be no doubt as to that, but it seemed to ignore her. *It must be able to detect those who have been converted.* On and on it stretched, its translucent skin undulating, its thick muscle getting thinner and thinner as it stretched across incredible distances.

All I have to do is follow it to its source, she thought.

Another convulsion shook her body and she doubled over in agony. Sweat started out on her brow.

"Everything all right, my child?" the thing who wasn't her father whispered into her ear. "Give it up! The pain will stop and we can sort all this mess inside your head out. That's what you want, isn't it? Admit it!"

"No!" said Claire through gritted teeth. "You can't tell me anything that I don't already know because you are just in my head!"

She forced herself on, following the tentacle around corners where it grew thicker and thicker. *Must be getting close now.*

Other tentacles crept out of adjacent tunnels and inspected her with mild curiosity. They let her pass. *It thinks I'm harmless. But it doesn't know I'm coming to destroy it. Good.*

Sweat burned all over her body as what felt like the worst illness she had ever experienced intensified with every step. She gasped in the fetid air, not knowing if it was getting warmer of if she was just feverish. Voices called to her from various tunnels; voices she recognized. Some were of the soldiers Greenbaum had killed. "You stood by and let him do it!" they hissed. "Murderess! Bitch!" Other voices were ones she knew from Ralston; people who had died, committed suicide or been murdered. They accused her of bringing this doom to Ralston. "If you had reported this when you knew about that meteorite then none of this would have happened!" said one. "This is your fault! Our blood is on your hands!"

She could hear movement in those tunnels; things splashed about, accompanying the voices. *Tentacles or the dead walking?* It didn't matter, she told herself. Neither could hurt her.

The tunnel she was in opened into a wide cylinder and she knew she had found the recharge basin. The tentacle dropped away into the darkness at her feet and, by shining her flashlight down into the depths of the well, she finally saw it.

It was an enormous, gelatinous lump that sat in the shallow water of the well, looking up at her with one, milky eye the size of a tractor tire. Tentacles fanned out from its grotesque body, entering the various inlets that let storm water into the well. The creature was truly hideous, yet Claire felt a strange affinity for it, even love which she put down to the drug in her system. She also felt a strange form of pity for it. It had let her wander right up to it, carrying a bomb with which she intended to blow it to pieces. Why?

The drug only worked one way. Every hallucination – good and bad – was in the recipient's mind, products of their own creation. She thought of Andy's crab that carried an urchin on its back and the crocodile who let birds pick its teeth clean. What did the crocodile know of the bird's mind?

"You let me get close because you think I'm one of your minions, don't you?" she told it.

The milky eye gazed back. It was pathetic, she decided. An alien in a world it didn't understand, doing only what its nature dictated. All this creature was doing was surviving, as its species had survived for perhaps millions of years in some far-flung corner of the universe.

"Well," she said. "It's over now. I've got you and, by God, I'm going to destroy you."

Knowing that the creature couldn't understand her, she spoke mainly for her own benefit, to convince herself to go through with her plan and fight the compulsion to walk away and leave the thing alone.

She fumbled in the pouch at her belt for her homemade bomb. She could see the creature eying it as she lifted it out. *It knows I'm doing something*, she thought. *But it doesn't know what.* In her pocket she had a cigarette lighter she had taken from one of the corpses. Her hand began to shake as she struggled to light it.

It's not the creature stopping me. It's just my mind.

A voice called to her from the blackness that surrounded the well. It was her father's. "Don't do it, Claire! If you light that fuse then you will never see me again. I will be lost forever! I beg you, don't do it!"

"You were wrong about me," she said. She didn't know if she was speaking to the alien, the vision of her father or her own subconscious. Perhaps all three. "You thought you understood us through our grief. You thought you could heal our misery by giving us clay puppets molded to fill the holes in our lives. But there is one thing you did not understand; not all puzzles have a piece to fit them. You felt my grief and you mistook it. You thought I grieved for my father. I loved him, sure, but I came to terms with losing him long ago. What I wanted, what I desperately needed to fill the hole in my soul was answers. And you don't have those. You have no power over me because you can't give me what I really want; the truth."

Maybe one day she would learn the truth of what had caused her father's death, but that day was not today. And, for the first time in six years, she felt okay with that.

She ignored every impulse in her body and lit the fuse.

The creature seemed to understand at last that she meant it harm and a panic set in. It retracted its tentacles which slithered back through the tunnels and dropped into the well to support itself. It started to rise, pushing itself up out of the water. The great eye rose up towards Claire and below it, she could see its mouth; a horrible black beak that opened and shut in futile terror.

She dropped the bomb. It landed in the water with a splash. The alien saw it and desperately reached underneath itself with its tentacles in an effort to remove it. Claire turned and ran.

The creature wasn't going to let her get away. Although it didn't realize that its fate was already sealed, it sent out its tentacles in rapid streams to seize her and destroy her.

On and on she fled, splashing through the tunnels, desperately trying to remember the way she had come. A

tentacle thumped into her back and knocked her forward. She rolled onto her back in the water and brought
up her gun. The tentacle hovered above her, sucker unfurled, poised to strike.

She squeezed the trigger and pumped several rounds
into it. Blood and mucus spattered the tunnel, raining
down on her face. Then, she was up and running again,
trying to outrun the fuse she had tied to the explosives.

More tentacles snaked out of tunnels to the left and
right. Again and again she fired at them, riddling them
with bullets. One swung wildly at her, its length catching
her in the middle and lifting her off her feet. She landed
in the water, the machine gun strap slipping over her
head and the weapon flying from her hands.

The wind knocked from her, she drew her pistol and
fired again and again at the tentacles as they made to
punch down on her and hold her head underwater until
the life was choked from her.

A massive explosion rocked the underground network. The tunnels shuddered and the water rippled as if
in the midst of a storm. The tentacles spasmed and then
fell slack, one of them landing across Claire, winding her
for a second time.

Trapped beneath its weight, there was nothing she
could do as the tidal wave of water, muck and ooze came
rushing down the tunnels and over her. She tried not to
think that she was drowning in the blood and entrails of
the creature that were being pushed down the tunnels by
the force of the explosion and concentrated on freeing
herself and escaping.

Pushing with all her might, she was able to lift the
tentacle enough to wriggle out from under it and then
she was swimming upwards, fighting for air.

She broke the surface, coughing and spluttering. She
was alive! And the creature was dead at last. She pulled
another flashlight from her belt and switched it on. All

around was gore and chunks of unidentifiable matter. The smell nearly made her gag and she yearned for the fresh air. Turning to face the tunnel ahead, she moved forward, looking for her marks that would take her back to the main storm drain and then to the outside world.

CHAPTER 23

They had run a few blocks now and were beginning to tire. Tommy and Burt were already exhausted and could barely keep pace with Judy who kept urging them on while constantly looking back to check on Johnny's progress. He was mere feet in front of the mob which bayed for their blood. They couldn't keep this up. Sooner or later, one of them would stumble again and then it would all be over.

A car suddenly roared out of nowhere, riding up onto the curb beside them. At first, Tommy thought it was yet more homicidal maniacs eager to kill them but he realized it was a hot rod. In fact, he recognized it from the club. The passenger door swung open and two greasers peered out.

"Johnny?" one of them called.

"Get those doors open and get Burt and the others in!" Johnny yelled, still pelting down the street.

One of the greasers got out and flung the back door open. Judy and Burt squeezed in. Tommy followed them, turning to watch Johnny spin on his heel and lay one of his pursuers flat with a crack to the chin. The rest of the mob slowed up and encircled Johnny.

"What are you waitin' for?" Johnny yelled to the driver of the hot rod. "Peel out!"

Wheels spun and Johnny took one last swing at the mob before diving into the car, landing on the laps of the three in the back seats. The car roared down the street, leaving the mob in a cloud of exhaust fumes.

"Where the hell did you two come from?" Johnny said to the two greasers up front while he squirmed about for space. "I thought the whole club was wiped out."

"Nearly all of us were," the driver replied. "The cops really did a number on us, gats and everything. Then the gas pumps went up which was kind of our fault, but we took that as an opportunity to scoot while the cops were running for cover. But what about you, Johnny? We heard you got suckered by the alien."

"Yeah? Who told you that?"

"Never mind. When we saw that mob chasing you, we figured you were still one of the good guys so we decided to pull off an emergency extraction."

"How many of you made it out?"

"Not many. Us two, Eddie, Glenn and John Dixon. Plus some of the girls."

Johnny sucked his teeth in frustration. "Four club members. And the rest all dead ..."

"Hey, we're still alive," said Burt. "That makes us six."

"Seven," said Johnny, throwing a weak smile at Tommy. "Hell of a time to join the club, Kid. We're at rock bottom. But we'll come back up. I'll drag us back up and we'll take back this town."

The two in the front said nothing as they pulled into the parking lot of the bowling alley on Rockwood Avenue.

"We going bowling?" Burt asked.

"You can knock down some pins if you like," said the driver. "This is where we've been hiding out. It's pretty swell. We help ourselves to cokes from the bar and we've even smashed open the cigarette machine. Place is ours now."

"As long as the doors are secure, it's as good a place as any," said Johnny as they got out and headed for the entrance.

The greaser who had been driving hammered on the double doors which had been secured from the inside by a length of chain. A face appeared in the glass, frightened and suspicious.

"Let us in, Eddie!" the driver demanded.

"How do I know you haven't been converted?" Eddie answered.

"Are you kidding? It's us! Open the door!"

"No! You might try and kill us all!"

"Whoa, he's right," said the second greaser who had been riding shotgun in the car. "We never got no system in place to make sure."

"System?"

"Yeah, like a password or something."

"What good's a password? Even if we did get converted, we'd still know the password, Dummy!"

Eddie seemed to be conferring with somebody inside the bowling alley. He turned back to the door and pulled the chain away.

"About time," the driver said.

As soon as they were admitted into the red-carpeted lobby, they could hear that a small party was in progress. The lamps above the score tables up ahead shone through a haze of cigarette smoke and the silhouettes of what remained of the Black Camelots and their girls could be seen horsing around, drinking cokes and eating peanuts. A jukebox played Elvis Presley's 'All Shook Up' and was occasionally drowned by the clatter of a bowling ball smashing into skittles.

As they approached the score tables, eyes turned to glare at them, and at Johnny in particular, with uncertain fear.

"Say, what's the big idea?" the one called Glenn demanded. "Why'd you bring Johnny here?"

"Are you crazy?" shrieked one of the girls. "He'll kill us all!"

"Easy," said the greaser who had driven them there. "We thought the same, but the mob was chasing Johnny, Man! He and the other three were runnin' for their lives!"

"So you brought them back here, no questions asked?" said Glenn. "Don't you think it might be a trick?"

"What are you talking about?" Johnny demanded. "I ain't one of the converted!"

"Yeah, well you would say that, wouldn't you, old buddy," said Glenn, pulling a switchblade from his pocket. "But we got a witness who says you got suckered."

"Oh yeah? And who might that be?"

"Me," said a voice from the shadows.

Over by the bar, a figure sat hunched, the glowing end of his cigarette going up and down in the dark. A girl sat behind him, her slim hand on his shoulder. Tommy heard Judy gasp in shock. Johnny could only stare, speechless. It was Mack and June.

"What the hell are you two doin' here?" Johnny asked them.

"Leading the Camelots," said Mack, blowing out a cloud of smoke. "After your desertion."

"Desertion?"

"Sure. Archie the junkie led us out to that old house. You and Marie got suckered. June and I barely escaped with our lives."

Johnny snorted. "I reckon that alien really scrambled your brains because it didn't play out like that." He looked at the other members of the club. "He's the one that got suckered, not me!"

"Nice trick," said Mack. "You thought you could weasel your way in here with that line and then wipe us out, right?"

"No!"

The gang looked from Johnny to Mack, unsure whom to believe. Mack stood up, flicked his cigarette across the room. "They've all been suckered, fellas. We gotta take care of them now before it's too late."

The gang tensed itself for a fight. Weapons appeared from jacket pockets; knives, chains and knucks. Johnny put up his hands. "He's lying! You guys gotta believe me!"

"It's true," said Tommy. "None of us have been suck-ered."

"Yeah!" added Burt. "We're clean!"

"Nothing you say can prove that," said Mack. "But I know the truth. And my club believes me."

"*Your* club?" Johnny said, his voice like a knife edge.

"Sure," said Mack with a grin. "They won't follow someone who's been suckered."

"All right then," said Johnny. "But you know the rules. You don't take the club from me without fighting for it." He glanced at the others. "That's the way, right? He has to challenge me! And you don't know who to believe, so why not let a good old fight sort it out."

Mack smirked. "Sure. Why not? Glenn, give him your knife."

"Knives?" asked Johnny.

"This is for keeps like nothing else has been before," said Mack. "These guys won't suffer the loser to live, knowing that he's been suckered. Why, you chicken?"

"No, I ain't chicken," Johnny replied, accepting the knife from Glenn. "As you say, this is for keeps."

Judy grabbed his arm as he shrugged off his jacket. "Johnny, no! This won't prove anything!"

He shook himself free of her and shoved his bundled-up jacket into her arms. "It'll prove who leads the Camelots."

Mack handed his own jacket to June who kissed him for luck. He drew his own switchblade and they stood in their white tee-shirts, facing off, framed against the lights of the bowling lanes. Mack swiped at Johnny who stepped back but not quickly enough to avoid the knife blade slitting his tee open and scoring a line of blood across his belly.

"You're finished, Johnny," Mack sneered. "You were finished even before all this started. This club needs a leader that ain't chicken. One who ain't so high and mighty that they'll turn down good money 'cause they think they're too good for it."

"What do you mean?"

"Hop's the future, man. Everyone agrees with me. And they're fed up with you cutting us out of the racket."

"It was you," said Johnny. "You're the Jungle Duke's dealer in Ralston."

Mack grinned. "More than that. I'm their pick to lead their new chapter here in Ralston. Once you got bumped off, I'd take over the club and we'd all change jackets for ones with tiger patches. But things worked out differently." He shrugged. "Just as good. There was always going to be some squares who would remain loyal to you so I guess the cops did my job for me."

Johnny lunged at Mack who sidestepped and cut at him again, this time nicking his arm. Judy clasped her hand over her mouth. Tommy and Burt began to cheer Johnny on while the rest of the gang could only watch helplessly, not knowing whom to support.

Blood streaming from his wounds, Johnny ducked and sidestepped a flurry of vicious attacks from Mack. They were out in the bowling lanes now, the polished wood slippery with blood beneath their boots. Johnny stumbled as he stepped down into one of the gutters and fell against the ball rack. His knife fell from his hand and went skittering across the lane.

Mack came in for the kill, knife held low in a gutting grip. Johnny seized one of the balls from the rack and hurled it at him. It bounced and rolled before knocking Mack's legs out from under him. He fell heavily and landed on the divider between the lanes.

Johnny hauled himself to his feet and grabbed another ball from the rack. He advanced, ball held high, poised to smash it down on Mack's head.

There was a slam in the dark recesses of the building and Tommy realized that it was the lobby door.

Something powerful slammed into it again, breaking the chain. Soldiers spilled in from the lobby, rifles aimed at them, yelling for them all to get down.

The teenagers froze, not knowing what to do. Were these guys converts? Or had martial law finally been declared, and soldiers were going around town rounding up anyone they thought was a convert? Either way it spelled bad news for them.

Mack was the first to be up and running. Johnny looked down and saw that his prey had escaped. He cast the bowling ball aside and yelled to the others; "C'mon! Let's beat it!"

They ran across the lanes, ignoring the yells of the soldiers behind them.

There was a rear exit that led to the parking lot out back and they made for it. Mack had already pulled the chain away and the doors were just swinging shut in the wake of his passing. They slammed into them, squeezing through and out into the moonlit parking lot.

As they ran across the asphalt, Mack shot out of the dark and knocked Johnny to the ground. They grappled and rolled, each trying to get their hands around the other's throat.

"We don't have time for this!" Judy yelled. "Those soldiers are coming!"

But it was no use. Johnny might have wanted to get away but Mack was as one crazed. He was desperate to kill Johnny and nothing else mattered to him. His fingers worked their way around Johnny's neck and he began to squeeze, pressing down with his greater weight.

Johnny began to gasp for air, his face turning red and the veins standing out on his forehead. Suddenly they were bathed in the light of an approaching car.

"Get outta the way!" Tommy yelled and they all fell out of the path of the oncoming vehicle. It was black, it was fast and it had flames painted on its side. Tommy recognized it as Johnny's Chevy just as it bore down on the two grappling boys.

Mack looked up, his enraged face pale in the bright headlights, frozen like a deer on the road. The car swerved to the left, but only slightly and the corner of the fender caught Mack in the belly, lifting him off Johnny and carrying him for several yards. The car slammed on its brakes and Mack sailed through the air, landing on the asphalt with a nasty crack. He rolled once, twice, and then lay still.

Coughing, Johnny sat up. The others crowded around him. He seemed to be unscathed by the passing of the car. They all watched as the driver's door opened and a man got out.

"Dad?" exclaimed Tommy and Judy in unison.

Their dad gave a low whistle and looked at the car he had just stepped out of. "Do you know, I think that car might be growing on me?"

"Dad!" Tommy cried again and he and Judy ran forward to give their old man a hug.

"Are you kids okay?" he asked them.

"Yeah," said Tommy. "You just saved Johnny's life."

Their dad looked down at Johnny with concern. "I saw them laying into each other and figured one of them had been converted. Did I hit the right one?"

"Yeah," said Johnny. "Thanks."

"Are there any others?"

"Just her over there," said Tommy. June had run over to Mack's motionless form on the asphalt and was weeping over him. He looked to be dead.

The soldiers had exited the bowling alley and were hurrying over to them.

"It's all right, Boys!" Ray said. "I think these kids are ok. Take the weeping girl into custody, she's a convert but the others seem to be fine."

"Dad, how come you're with the army?" Tommy asked. "And why were you driving Johnny's car?"

"Long story. I convinced these boys to try and protect this town's kids from the converted. It's a massacre out there. We saw a couple of hot rods parked outside the bowling alley and I prayed to God that you were inside, converted or not. While the soldiers busted their way in through the front entrance, I went around the back to see if there was another way in. That's when I saw you kids. It's been a hell of a night, but the army seems to be getting things under control now. You had all better come back with us. There are still bands of converted roaming the streets but they won't be a problem for long."

"How come?" Judy asked.

"Your mother she ..., well, she's gone into the storm drains with a bunch of soldiers to destroy that thing once and for all."

"What?" Judy exclaimed.

"I know. I've been worried sick about all of you but at least you two are safe and sound. Come on, let's head back to base and see if there's any news."

When they got to the forward post at the entrance to the storm drains, they found that Rose had awoken and was overjoyed to see her family returning for her.

"Rose!" said Judy, scooping her up in her arms.

"Thanks, Pastor," said Ray.

"I see you rounded up most of your flock," said Pastor Mathews with a smile.

"Just my wife now. Has there been any news?"

"Sergeant Frost and three of his men came out of the storm drains not long ago," said Pastor Mathews. "There was some sort of trouble. One of the soldiers was converted and opened fire on the others but Frost is adamant your wife was unharmed. She was with them as they were exiting the tunnels but vanished en route."

"Vanished?"

"Got separated somehow. There was an almighty explosion a short while ago," said Pastor Mathews. "After Sergeant Frost and his men returned. I'm surprised you didn't hear it."

"Jesus, an explosion! That means Claire must have tried to complete the mission on her own!"

"It would seem so. Colonel Baskin is up by the tunnel entrance."

Ray left the pastor and went up to the forward post. Tommy and Judy hurried after him, Judy carrying Rose in her arms.

"Colonel, Sheriff Benson is dead along with most of his department," Ray told him. "Your boys are continuing search and rescue operations across town."

"Very good," said the colonel.

"What's been going on here?"

"We lost contact with the squad and feared the worst but Sergeant Frost and some of his men made it out. They are in my tent awaiting debriefing. It seems that one of them turned ..."

"Colonel, my wife!"

"We have no idea where she is. Frost said she was with them and then she wandered off. There was a detonation of some kind not twenty minutes ago. We can only hope to God that whatever it was, it took the alien out."

"Can you not send in more troops?"

"We don't know what the hell is going on in there. For now, we wait."

Ray bit his thumbnail and turned to Tommy and Judy. "Your mom's gonna be okay," he said. "I just know it."

Tommy and Judy said nothing. Neither of them shared his optimism although they dared to hope.

"There!" a soldier cried, peering through his binoculars at the tunnel entrance.

They all leaned forward and could make out a lone figure appearing from the darkness and moving shakily towards them. Rifles were raised and trained on the figure.

"Don't shoot!" Ray yelled. "That's my wife!"

Judy and Tommy exchanged a look of relief. It really was Mom.

"Your wife might be a convert," said Colonel Baskin.

Ray walked out in front of the rifles and approached Claire. She threw her arms around him and the two embraced for a long time.

"Keep your guns on her," said the colonel. "It could be a trick. Watch for any sign of hostility."

Tommy swore and he and Judy stepped out to join their parents' embrace. It was a strange sort of reunion, with twenty rifles trained on them and their mom dressed in combat fatigues covered in some sort of gooey slime, but they were a family reunited at last. It was a long time before they let go and headed into camp.

The debriefing took the best part of an hour. The whole family sat in the colonel's tent and sipped coffee as they listened to Claire recount what had happened in the tunnels. Soldiers still held a close watch over her, ready to open fire at the slightest sign that she had been converted. Colonel Baskin was still displeased at the loss of most of his squad, but he seemed satisfied that the creature was dead.

"It's going to be a hell of a clean-up operation," he said. "Even if the monster is dead, its converts will still be operational, at least for a while. They will need to be kept secured until we are sure the drug is no longer in its system. That includes you, Dr. Weldon."

"Colonel," said Ray, setting his coffee cup down and rising from his seat. "This family has done more than its share in saving Ralston tonight. You are welcome to have your concerns about my wife's state of mind, but you will not be putting her in some pen to be held at gunpoint until you think she's safe to be released. Now, we are all very tired and I am going to take my wife and kids to a motel out of town where we can all have hot showers and a long sleep."

The colonel said nothing as the Weldon family filed out of the tent and headed over towards their car. The sun was beginning to rise over the fields to the east and the sky was flecked with pink. There was a deathly stillness over the town, like it was in mourning. They got into the car and set off towards the highway heading south.

"Will we ever return to Ralston?" Judy asked as they looked out of the windows at the smashed store fronts, burnt out cars and dead bodies that littered the streets.

"I suppose so," said their dad. "But not just yet. Right now I want to be as far away from it as possible. Let's leave them to their grief for a while."

"It's a double grief in a way," said their mom. "They have lost many loved ones tonight but there are many in this town who must come to terms with a different kind of grief. The grief of crushed dreams and broken hearts."

"You OK, Mom?" Tommy asked.

"Sure, Honey," she replied. "I'm exhausted and I have a strange compulsion to go near water but that's just the alien drug wearing off. I'm still fighting it."

"Will it wear off completely?" Judy asked.

"Time will tell but, yes, probably. It will be a hard fight for many. I was one of the lucky ones because I was so happy before. Maybe that's why I was able to overcome the drug in the end. It wasn't able to offer me much. Others were not so lucky. As the euphoric delusions begin to leave them, all the disappointments and failures and humiliations of their old lives will suddenly become real again. They'll have to come to terms with their old lives once more, however hard they were." She sighed deeply.

"I suppose they must learn to be human again. That's the price we have paid tonight."

"Is it worth it?" asked Judy.

Claire smiled. "I think so."

THE END
A P. J. THORNDYKE PRODUCTION